# I Miss You, I Miss You!

# I Miss You, I Miss You!

## PETER POHL AND KINNA GIETH

### TRANSLATED BY ROGER GREENWALD

R & S Books

STOCKHOLM    NEW YORK    LONDON    ADELAIDE    TORONTO

AB Rabén & Sjögren Bokförlag Stockholm

Translation copyright © 1999 by Roger Greenwald
All rights reserved
Originally published in Sweden by AB Rabén & Sjögren Bokförlag under the title
Jag saknar dig, jag saknar dig!
Copyright © 1992 by Peter Pohl and Katarina Gieth

Printed in the United States of America
Designed by Abby Kagan
Special thanks to Jenna Kaufman
First edition, 1999
Library of Congress Cataloging-in-Publication Data
Pohl, Peter.
[Jag saknar dig, jag saknar dig! English]
I miss you, I miss you! / Peter Pohl and Kinna Gieth; translated by Roger
Greenwald. — 1st ed.
p. cm.
Summary: Thirteen-year-old Tina Dubois and her identical twin sister, Cilla, are
extremely close and yet different personalities, and when Cilla is suddenly killed, Tina
and her family struggle to come to terms with the loss.
ISBN 9129639352
[1. Twins—Fiction. 2. Sisters—Fiction. 3. Death—Fiction.] I. Gieth, Kinna.
II. Greenwald, Roger. III. Title.
PZ7.P75173Iae 1999
[Fic]—dc21 97-25424

Excerpt from "Gracias a la vida" by Violeta Parra, taken from Colección a viva voz,
edited by Mario Benedetti (Buenos Aires: Espasa Calpe, 1996). Copyright © 1996
by Violeta Parra.
Grateful acknowledgment is made for permission to reprint the following: "Mid-Term
Break" by Seamus Heaney. First published in the United States of America in Seamus
Heaney, Selected Poems 1966–1987. Copyright © 1990 by Seamus Heaney. Reprinted
by permission of Farrar, Straus and Giroux.
"I Saw You Dead" and "Dearest, You Whom I Buried on Wednesday" by Marie Louise
Ramnefalk. First published in Sweden in Någon har jag sett (I Have Seen Someone).
Copyright © 1979 by Marie Louise Ramnefalk. Used by permission of the author.

"My Beloved Sister, there's one thing you must know!"
    I felt a pain run through my heart just then.
    "No," I said, "there's nothing I want to know."
    "Yes, there's one thing you must know," continued Lalla-lee.
    At that the flowers stopped singing and the trees stopped playing, and I could no longer hear the brook's melody.

—Astrid Lindgren, *My Very Own Sister*

# I Miss You,
# I Miss You!

*1*

Now it's April and two girls named Cilla and Tina are home at Rosengården, Rose Manor. They are identical twins and will turn fourteen this summer. But Cilla won't be there—soon she's going to be killed in a traffic accident. That's the most horrible thing that's ever happened to me, and I'm telling it right away because this isn't meant to be an exciting story with a clever ending that has to be kept secret until the last page. This is about Tina, who was left behind and had to try to stand up straight and keep her balance in life without Cilla. And the one who's telling this story is me, Tina, but I know I can't manage to talk about "me," so I'll say "her" instead.

Actually, they aren't named Cilla and Tina, but Cilibelle and Martinelle. Those are the names they were given when they were born in France almost fourteen years ago, names that may be okay when you live in France but just won't work here in Sweden. The girls came here when they were two years old. Pappa Albert (who was pronounced Ahl-BEAR back then but can now be pronounced the way he's spelled without getting offended) took the twins with him and left France when their mother died of cancer. That's something they don't remember, so describing it isn't painful. They have a photo of their mom, and they know that the beautiful face in the picture is her, their mother, but she herself has faded from their memory—there's nothing left of her voice, not even the musical laughter that Albert says she so happily spread around her, no memory of how she caressed her girls, picked them up, kissed them, held their hands when they walked. Nothing more than a face in a picture.

Albert Dubois chose to move to Sweden because his mother's family came from here. But more important, it seemed just right for his work. He would have moved sooner or later anyway. Now it was sooner. He worked, and still works, with computers— developing hardware, he says, when someone asks. He doesn't give any details, because the industry has a lot of secrets. Albert suspects all foreigners of being thieves and spies out to swipe his ideas or beat him to the punch with new products. All the same, it didn't take him more than a year to decide he should trust people and fate enough to take the leap and propose to Monika. She worked, and still works, at the same company— though in software, Albert likes to point out, with a knowing smile at the joke; it's the kind of joke that people in the computer world understand.

Monika said Yes! to the proposal, and that's how Cilibelle and Martinelle got a mother again, and a nine-year-old brother,

Jonny, in the bargain. Jonny was the main reason the family soon gave up speaking French at home. He was the one who decided that the girls just couldn't have those dumb names if they were going to live among regular people. He called his new sisters Cilla and Tina, and soon no one remembered any other names for them, or had any reason to try.

Right after Monika and Albert got married, they spotted an ad saying that Rosengården was for sale. The price seemed awfully high, but once they'd seen the place, all their reservations disappeared. With a mortgage and some help from Monika's generous brother, Jan-Olof, as well as lots of initiative, they succeeded in pulling together what they needed. One lovely day in May they moved into Rosengården. It was in the country, as the ad said, but not out of the way; it was only six miles to town and just over half a mile to the beach and the harbor, where there was a berth for the sailboat that came with the house. Yes, everything was just as fine as the ad had promised. Rosengården itself consisted of a pretty house and a fabulous garden, where the scent of roses sweetened the days for almost all of spring and summer. It was clear at once how they would spend their free time: partly in sailing, of course, but both Monika and Albert liked gardening, so they felt like they'd landed in paradise.

That's what visitors usually say too: You're living in paradise! And it's true; not only Rosengården but also the countryside all around it has the sort of restful beauty that lifts your thoughts to images of paradise.

Hell lies close by, as you'd expect. After a five-hundred-yard curve, the friendly little gravel drive from the house swings up to a crowded and badly maintained section of the main road. It's one of those heavily trafficked roads that you find here and there throughout the country. The locals have nicknamed it Death Road. For several miles in either direction, the signs warn you:

DANGEROUS ROADWAY. SLOW DOWN!
SAVE YOUR LIFE! DON'T TAILGATE!
POOR VISIBILITY. NO PASSING!

And so on. But appeals like these are of no more help on this road than they are anywhere else. Here the drivers go as fast as they like, until they come to a standstill because, for no reason they can figure out, someone has skidded off the road and taken one of our bike-riding neighbors with him into the concrete barrier. The truckers who drive big semis press their huge cabs up against the trunks of the cars whose drivers dare to keep the speed limit, until the speed increases—no, until the accident happens. Here happy, smiling people risk passing, in complete confidence that they'll make it, that they're in full control, but the crash that follows shows that yet another person was mistaken. Seriously injured families are forever being rushed to the hospital, though just a minute ago they were headed for a weekend at their summer cottages.

And here is where, ten years after the move to Rosengården, Cilla will be struck down and killed and will become a Death Road statistic. If Monika and Albert had known this, surely they wouldn't have moved here. The question is, where could they have lived instead? The traffic has increased so much everywhere—or rather, the drivers' sense of morality and responsibility is now so diminished—that there's no place where people are safe anymore. No one who sets off for school can be sure of getting there. And if she gets there, she can't count on coming home alive when the school day is over. If it went all right yesterday, and the day before, and every day for six school years before that, it still may not work today. Everyone has to learn to live with that uncertainty. Nobody can grow up now believing that life is something you have a natural right to and will of course enjoy.

It gets quiet on the road for a while after an accident happens. Then everything goes on as before. Countless drivers didn't see what happened. They drive any way they want to, until something happens to *them*. If someone on the car radio talks about consideration and responsibility, they laugh at such old-fashioned nonsense. If only they could laugh themselves to death, every last one! Then maybe it would finally be peaceful on the roads.

■ ■ ■

The twins who moved into Rosengården were one hundred percent exactly alike, impossible to tell apart. Yet in time you could tell them apart anyway, because one of them ended up with Pappa most of the time, and the other with Mamma, until you knew who was who from where they were sitting. It was Tina who became Albert's girl and Cilla who became Monika's. And both became Jonny's little sisters; he took on the important job of raising them. Of course, no one had asked him to do that, least of all the girls, and as the years passed they showed less and less interest in being raised by their brother and joined forces more and more often to put him in his place.

Maybe it sounds like this must have been an extra-nice, harmonious family. But it's not like that, no, they yell and fight and tease each other, just like any other family. Being Pappa's daughter isn't always all that much fun. Why are you always so nasty to Tina? Monika sometimes asks accusingly.

So she'll turn out to be a better person, is Albert's defense. I'm sure I won't be a *better person* because you're horrid to me, sobs Tina. A better artist maybe, she hopes behind her tears. You become a better artist if you have a tragic childhood, but not a better person.

Besides their parents there are also relatives to try to get along with. The worst one is probably Justine, Albert's mother and therefore their grandmother, whom the twins aren't too terribly fond of. Every summer they're forced to spend two weeks with her in Brou, a boring dump in France. She has loads of ideas about how everything should be done, how girls ought to behave, how a woman must wait on her lord and master, yes, how in general the man-lord-father is life's exalted ruler. She is capable of spewing out stuff like that in her awful broken Swedish even on Christmas Eve. Every Christmas she visits them for the whole holiday, until Twelfth Night, and they get an earful.

She adores her son, of course, and finds it totally incredible that he and Jonny should have to help out in the kitchen. But since they do, well, naturally everything they come up with is an out-and-out miracle. The waffles on the eve of Twelfth Night, for example. Oh, Joney, Joney! What a chef! So-o-o marvelously delicious!

Sure, they were delicious. But Tina turned red and declared twice in a loud voice: Actually, Jonny wasn't the only one who made them. Actually, *I* made half of them.

Maybe Justine didn't hear that, but Albert looked at his furious daughter and told her gruffly to be quiet.

That's how it is! thought Cilla afterwards. His damned ma-maah puts crazy ideas in his head. A guy like *that* has to be our father.

On Twelfth Night, Cilla and Tina helped to make waffles.

Forget the night before! Waffles are so good, and Justine is going home tomorrow.

Should I help you? Jonny asked.

Each girl gave part of the answer. Cilla: The gentleman can go read today's paper! Tina: A man needs to rest; the woman must do everything.

To hell with you! Jonny sputtered.

But when it was time to eat, he showed up, of course. As for Justine, she said precisely nothing until Albert asked her how she liked the waffles. Then she opened her mouth for an unenthusiastic *Pas mal!*

That means "Not bad." If it's said with a little oomph, it's praise, but said like that, it can only be translated as "Passable." Contrary to what Justine thinks, Cilla and Tina speak French really well, because Albert managed to get them enrolled in home-language classes. But you don't need to understand the language when the tone of voice is so clear. Tina jumped up from the table and screamed that she wouldn't claim they were the best waffles in the world, but she'd be god*damned* if they weren't better than Jonny's yucky dishrags yesterday—

That's enough! roared Albert and backed it up with his fist—*thunk*—on the table.

Tina had already left the dinner table, and Cilla was hesitating: follow her or stay put?

She stayed put. It was interesting to study Justine's expressions as she sat there trying to keep up appearances. She very much wanted to say that these girls were badly brought up, but she could hardly say that, since it would have meant criticizing Albert.

The emotional storm had begun to quiet down when Jonny came in with the family's guest book. He'd gotten it as a Christmas present from Justine. Tina's comment afterwards, when the girls were alone, was that she had no doubt given it to him just so she'd be able to write something memorable in it. It was only proper that Grandma should write some fine words in it now, Jonny said. Tomorrow might be too hectic.

Justine turned to him, *flattered*, and spouting ooh!s and ah!s, but then she suddenly decided it was "only right" that each of the girls make a drawing first, as a frontispiece for the book. After all, you paint so *belle*, so *belle*, yes?

Now *there's* a really *great* idea! was Cilla's reaction. Sketch in the guest book, like a goddamned stranger!

Don't be so damned . . . , Jonny implored.

Albert cleared the table, to Justine's twittering admiration, while muttering about the likes of such pigheaded . . . *caractère boudeur!*

Jonny wandered upstairs to Tina and asked if she wouldn't honor the guest book with the first entry, a drawing from the depths of her great artistic talent. But the waffles were not forgotten, or forgiven either, and Jonny's request sounded suspiciously villainous, so Tina screamed *Piss off!* and slammed the door.

Jonny now went to Cilla and whispered that surely she wouldn't be so cruel as to let some dumb poem by Justine be the first entry in the guest book, a book that would be lying there on display in their home for who knew how far into the future.

Don't blow in my ear! snarled Cilla. You can go hang that book up in the can, in case we run out of paper!

Then she went upstairs to the room she shared with Tina and slammed the poor, well-used door just as emphatically as Tina had. And we're supposed to love these idiots! she sighed and flopped down on her bed.

Tina was looking at her face in the mirror. Shit! she said.

*Shit, shit, shit! Can you believe how awful this is? This whole damned Christmas has been awful.*

*Justine*, was Cilla's explanation. *Grand-mère!*

But that couldn't be the whole explanation. Justine had been there for many other Christmases, and those seemed happy and radiant in the girls' memories. As far back as they could remember, on Christmas Eve they had played music, sung songs, and performed skits with Jonny for the family, which included Justine almost every Christmas, and always Monika's brother, Jan-Olof, and then his fiancée, later his wife, Marika, and little by little their children, a growing flock of cousins, all of them fond of the traditional Christmas celebrations at Rosengården. When the twins were five, they stood with their guitars and accompanied Simon and Garfunkel in an acclaimed lip-synch concert. That Christmas all the French relatives were there and shared in the festivities.

After that, Jonny gradually made his sisters more aware of the value of their performances. No matter how badly you play the violin, every note you play yourself is worth more than a whole record by professionals, he declared when Tina was eight. There's no art to playing a record by Gunilla von Bahr, he said when Cilla was doubtful about playing the flute on Christmas Eve. But what you play yourself—that's art.

He was probably right, but even now, after many changes in taste, the girls still had a place in their hearts for Simon and Garfunkel's music. When they heard it, they saw themselves as five-year-olds lip-synching to it. A cherished memory like that can never be erased, no matter how life may change your opinions and tastes.

Jonny even succeeded in getting the girls to sing for their audience. Not by claiming that their voice teacher was wrong when she complained that they sang off-key, but by daring to sing himself without inhibition. Anyone could tell that his voice wasn't his strong point, but he had the courage to sing, so the girls did, too.

This Christmas, though, everything was awful, just everything. The twins were thirteen; that was awful to begin with. It's an unbearable age, according to the older generation, and that's a generation that doesn't keep its opinions to itself. This particular opinion is guaranteed to kill both the spirit and the joy of thirteen-year-olds when they try, at least at first, to be nice. So even their trying was seen as unbearable.

Christmas might have gone all right anyway, if Jonny hadn't decided he didn't want to be part of the show. This was something new, and it was definitely bad. All that remained of their Christmas tradition was a halfhearted musical recital: Les Sœurs Dubois performed a Christmas melody on flute and violin. Pretty shitty, with Justine sitting there thinking badly of them no matter what they did.

Afterwards they nearly wept from misery. Danced alone in their room to "Puerto Rico Salsa," a Latin American beat on the radio, hot stuff if you're in the mood, yet the dance can be melancholy for two girls who feel that something's been lost. They didn't know what, but something was gone and the entertainment was painful. Everything's going to vanish, sister, my dearest sister, everything!

No, not you, not me. We'll always have each other.

Yes, always! And no one can take away our memories.

■ ■ ■

So much for Christmas Eve. It was awful. Every day after it was awful, Twelfth Night has been awful, and it's all Justine's fault, says Cilla.

Then Albert opens the door and walks in. He gives Tina, who's nearest, a resounding box on the ear. After that he screams at the girls that they're disgusting, ungrateful, and surly and ruin everything. By God, he'll—

Then he leaves them, goes down to Jonny, and says without making any sense: You sure don't have it easy! You always come through for those two, and all you get for your trouble is a hard time.

The girls stare at each other through their tears. I think I'm going to die! one of them moans. Who comes through for who, really? the other one wonders.

Yes, Tina just keeps crying and crying, but in the living room Albert is already chatting and laughing with his mamma, carrying on a completely normal conversation in French.

They're *sick*, for Chrissake! complains Cilla.

The worst part is that Monika keeps out of it and pretends that nothing is happening or that what's happening is perfectly all right. It's too much to bear. Cilla locks herself in the bathroom, takes the nail scissors, and cuts a gash in her lower lip. It hurts, so she can't go very deep, but it bleeds a lot and she looks dreadful. She comes out and totters down the stairs.

There's a delicious moment when Justine lets out a cry, Albert shoots up from the easy chair, and Monika comes rushing in from the kitchen. Then they see that it's not so serious.

*Mon Dieu*, how *theatrical* they have to be! Albert sighs and sits down again.

Monika cleans Cilla up and helps her to bed. What good was that? she asks.

None of her business. But to Tina, Cilla explains that she wanted to commit suicide but not die.

What about me, then! says Tina. I'm the one who should commit suicide, if anyone should. A goddamned fascist for a dad, who comes in and whacks me right off the bat. And Olle Brick hasn't called or written once in the whole Christmas break. This whole damned Christmas has been awful! I love him and he doesn't give a shit. I want to die! No, I don't want to die. You have to suffer, that's good, that makes you a better artist. Yes, I want to suffer! Let's suffer, Cilla! Someday we'll show the world.

I've figured out how to commit suicide without dying, Cilla tells Tina. Suppose you die from three sleeping pills—

Three probably isn't enough, Tina remarks. Four.

Sure, okay. So you take two in the morning at school. And then you go to class and get really sick and faint. You've also written a letter that slips out when you collapse: *Farewell, all of you who don't understand me. It's best this way.* Aha, suicide! they say. But feel this: there's a weak pulse. She can still be saved! And then hopefully Fredde Lindgren tries mouth-to-mouth—

I'd rather have Olle Brick, says Tina.

Yes, of course Olle, he's a Scout. Cool, huh! I'll sell you the idea for nothing.

We can do it together, Tina muses. Then everyone will realize how horrid things are for us at home. *Farewell, everyone who doesn't understand me and everyone who hits me . . .* Olle for me and Fredde for you.

But what if it's Maja Sjövall who tries mouth-to-mouth, Cilla says. She's always trying to show off, and she's totally brain-dead. Yuck! Maybe I don't go for that idea after all.

Maja Sjövall's perfect for you! Tina says. Oh, hell, it's impossible to live here. I'm going to run away. To Australia. Or I'll move to Lotta's.

Then I'll move too, declares Cilla. To Sandra's.

But inside, Cilla is beside herself because of Tina's jab: *Maja*

But Tina says— Cilla started over again.

She doesn't know any more about it than you do, Monika consoled her. Tina's just teasing, she's probably a little jealous because Fredde's been hanging out with you for so long, while her guys just keep coming and going.

We haven't been hanging out together, Cilla said defensively. Boys are so immature, so shallow, it's horrible!

Even so, you seem to get along fine with Fredde, Monika said.

Cilla shrugged. You can't talk about every single thing with your mamma. There's no point explaining that you have to pretend to be a little thrilled when someone like Fredde comes over and puts on airs, no matter what you think of him. Otherwise you'd end up with nobody at all, and then Tina would really have something to talk about. You *are* a lez, admit it!

But it's irritating the way boys lack maturity and depth. They have no interests that make any sense. With girls you can talk about important things. You can delve into things. Not with all of them, but with some. With boys it's completely impossible. They're coated in a shell of crap and you have no way of getting through. If a girl wants anything to do with them, she has to be pretty and sexy. What she thinks about and dreams about doesn't count.

*Sjövall's perfect for you!* She makes remarks like that a little too often. *Are you a lez, or what?*

You're thirteen years old and only moderately interested in boys. So are you a lesbian? Tina is immoderately, hugely interested; she's crazy about boys and constantly in love. It lasts a week, maybe two, then come tears and sorrow, a broken heart, and presto! another one. There was a program on TV about being homosexual. Cilla didn't know what to think. It was a problem, but it wasn't a problem—that was the message. It was other people who made it a problem. Tina and her teasing . . .

Cilla thinks Sandra is cute in that haircut that shows off her neck, and Sussy is so pretty you lose your breath when you look at her. *So are you gay?* she asks her diary. She's also written that she dared to talk with Mamma about it. This is how it feels, and they said on that TV program, and Tina says, but I also like Fredde Lindgren a little bit, and . . .

Monika was really helpful this time. She didn't brush it aside, but explained that at this age feelings and love and friendship are all jumbled together and go in every direction, so you don't need to worry. Look around and you'll see that the girls hold each other around the waist and the boys hang all over each other. Sussy really is very pretty, so there's nothing wrong with thinking so. And it's true that you can lose your breath when something really lovely appears before you, whether it's a girl or a boy or a view or a painting . . . That catch in your breath shows that you're sensitive to *beauty*, and that's something you should never be ashamed of.

Beauty? Cilla pondered. Sandra is so alive, so pretty when she gets excited. Her eyes . . . look like there's a fire inside her.

You're pretty too, when you get excited, Monika said. On fire—exactly. Enthusiasm—desiring something—that makes people beautiful.

*2*

Strange that so many peo-
ple think it's interesting in some special way to be twins, especially if you're identical twins and so similar that it's impossible
to tell you apart. But "interesting" probably isn't the right word.
Between twins there are strong bonds, which don't have very
much to do with their identical appearance. It's more a question
of being so close to each other that sometimes one is a part of
the other. Love is usually described that way—and if that's the
right definition, then life has given Cilla and Tina the gift of
being touched early by love. That's how it is, and that's why "interesting" isn't the right word.

Interesting—that's what someone thinks who isn't prepared
and suddenly sees two identical editions of what's usually
unique: a human being. But you get used to it; all of Cilla's and
Tina's friends have gotten used to it. When the girls started ju-
nior high in town, after their relatively idyllic six years at the

elementary school near home, there was a new period of adjustment to work through. Just being two means you're odd, contrary to what mathematics has to say about it.

The girls certainly behaved differently from each other, but it took time to discover that when you didn't know who was who. Cilla tended to wear baggy clothes, often a suit jacket or a man's sport coat. Tina wore more typical girl's clothes. Whatever deeper significance that surface difference might have had, it meant that some students considered Cilla a little strange, while Tina had an easier time blending into her surroundings, since those surroundings preferred what's called normality.

To be considered a little strange can mean that you're treated with a certain respect by some people, while others use it as a pretext for being nasty. Did you buy those clothes secondhand? Cilla would hear. She could put up with such comments, but she could not put up with three boys from the eighth grade circling around her, saying: I hate her! —I hate her more! —I hate her most! —No, I do! —No, I do! . . .

That was too much. Too much for Cilla and too much for Tina, who at the time happened to have a crush on one of the three. A sudden end to love, and Tina came to her sister's defense. Only three against one? You fucking wimps, why don't you get a few more guys to help you—but you'd better tell 'em to watch out, 'cause now there are two of us!

Now they really were alike! Rage in their eyes, curses flowing . . . The boys tried to blink away their double vision but soon lost steam. Respect for the twins gradually grew. You didn't pick on them. You and I are one and the same, my darling sister!


Naturally, Cilla and Tina themselves were the first ones to get used to their likeness. They were very small when they realized that they were each other's mirror images. They would face each other. Tina laughed; immediately Cilla laughed back. Cilla raised her hand, and in a flash Tina raised her mirror-hand. Soon they'd developed a whole routine of movements that they would perform exactly alike. Jonny set up a frame between them, so it really looked like one girl in front of a mirror. As they grew up they went further, learned to read each other's signals. If Tina put a new movement in among the old ones, Cilla put it in at the same time. Tina was equally alert in mirroring Cilla's sudden improvisations. If you saw the girls carrying on like that, you could only believe that the routine was carefully rehearsed. Not even the twins themselves quite understood how it was possible for one to know what the other would do next.

But the mirror game no longer amuses them. They revive their little stunt only during warm-ups at their drama club. Now they're very eager to emphasize their differences. You're you and I'm me—that particular difference is just as big as between any two people: the difference between what's me and what's not-me. There's no such thing as almost-me. Well, maybe if I'm sick, if I have a fever, I can feel like almost-me. But no one else, no one else, not even my identical twin, is almost-me. You're a part of me sometimes, and I'm a part of you. Then we have something in common, but I'm not almost you and you're not almost me.


*I hate being a twin!* is a sentence that appears several times in both Cilla's and Tina's diaries. When they're in that mood, one girl feels like killing the other because she's so damned alike. *To always have a living copy of yourself right next to you—I can't stand it.* They're both individuals and would like to be seen as such, instead of forever hearing that it's impossible to tell them apart.

From time to time they also can't stand that they have no privacy. You can't hide your diary properly when you share your room and your whole life, when you write sitting across from each other. They read each other's entries on the sly, but each one gets furious when her own diary is examined by her sister. The cover of Tina's diary is pasted over with labels warning off the curious and ordering people not to open it. Cilla's diary is equipped with a small lock, which couldn't keep anyone out. So the most important thoughts have to be disguised. Who *you* is in Cilla's poems is something Tina will just have to guess at.

But Cilla is a shade craftier than Tina suspects. She has a second diary, one that Tina never even thinks of looking for when she's been led up the garden path by the flimsily locked and less carefully hidden diary. In unobserved moments, Cilla confides her true secrets to the other diary. *Am I a lesbian?* Tina doesn't suspect, and I can't let her find out, how much anxiety she causes me with those taunts she doesn't mean anything by—I promise, Cilla, I didn't mean anything by them!

But there are times when things are different. Times when they can show each other what they've written and talk about absolutely anything, when each one knows that the other is listening and will remember and will never betray a confidence. Times when they discover that they are after all different enough so they can always give each other something new amid all that is familiar. Each finds security in the other. Cilla's security isn't the same kind as Tina's, Tina's is different from Cilla's. The girls are indistinguishably alike on the outside, but inside they are distinct in many important ways.

■

The indistinguishable likeness arises because identical twins have exactly the same genetic makeup, as everyone probably knows. Everything that determines how a person looks is the same from the moment of conception. Dudde, the family's good-natured golden retriever, looks in confusion from one sister to the other when Albert tells him to go over to Tina. The years pass and he never learns who's who. Yet everyone knows that dogs have a sense of smell that enables them to distinguish Master's scent among twenty guys who we think look the same, for example when Master is out practicing with his pals in their soccer club's red track suits. But the fact is that genes also determine the scent that a dog follows, and identical twins have exactly the same scent "fingerprint." It's impossible to change that fingerprint for Dudde by using different perfumes or soaps. The girls have tried, but he can't distinguish between them no matter what they do.

Dudde is plain stupid, a hopeless case, is what they thought at first, but gradually they learned that that's just how it is with dogs and identical twins. One of them can leave and he doesn't notice. Cilla said exactly that: I could die, and Dudde wouldn't care!

He would if I died at the same time, Tina said.

They looked at each other and knew: If you die, I can't go on living.


But for people the indistinguishable likeness resides above all in appearance. The girls can stand next to each other in front of the big mirror they have in their room and search for differences without finding any. But they don't need a mirror for that, you might think. They could stand facing each other, like they did when they were little, and they'd still find out just how they both looked at that moment. How do they look, then?

*Height:* five-foot-two—a little too short, they both think.

*Complexion:* rosy—but then, what healthy girl of thirteen doesn't have a rosy complexion? Yet it seems natural to point it out in Cilla and Tina's case, probably because their French blood gives them a slightly higher color than is usual in Scandinavians.

*Hair:* deep brown and a little curly; they'll get it cut for the summer.

*Eyes:* blue, clear blue. Here in Sweden people think that all Frenchwomen have brown eyes. That's why no one thinks about the girls' French origins, not even those who would make an issue of it.

Their *smile,* which shows even, white teeth, adorns their faces. So it's good that it doesn't take much to get Cilla and Tina to smile and laugh; yes, especially Tina breaks easily into a happy face. And it's neat, when you're standing face-to-face and examining your sister, to be able to say: You're pretty! Of course you wouldn't dare to say that to your image in the mirror. Well, to be sure, it's not very often they say it to each other, either. Teasing is easier: I sure am glad I don't have that pimple on my nose.

Their *body* is well-developed, a little too much so, they both think. You're a little too fat! they sometimes say, when they're in that mood. It didn't help matters that their breasts had begun to develop early. But on the other hand, the girls clearly became more interesting to boys the moment their breasts could no longer be hidden.

And boys—they're a major interest, at least for Tina. An obsession, you might say. Yes, let's leave the mirror and take a look at the girls' interests.

In the summer a mild interest in sailing comes to life. The family packs itself into Rosengården's sailboat and takes off for a few weeks. A fine time. Monika and Albert are relaxed and contented; they kid around instead of nagging the way they often do the rest of the year. The camera gets used a lot. So in the fall they have visual evidence that they're a family that gets along just fine. Sometimes it can help to have such a reminder, when people are slamming doors and banging on walls at home.

Music is another interest. Cilla plays the flute, and Tina the violin. Now and then they trade instruments, but they soon trade back again. It's best that way. In their room there's always some tape or record playing. They know the lyrics by heart and sing along enthusiastically. If you ask either of them to sing solo, it's No way, I can't sing. That verdict comes from Majvor, their music teacher in elementary school. She issued it sometime in the second grade when the girls raised their joyous voices to the rafters. Now please, take it easy. After all, you can't sing! Something died at that moment. Two children lost a part of their fearlessness. Thanks, Majvor! That comment was never forgotten. The girls study flute and violin with Einar Roxén, a teacher from the conservatory who is also a music teacher at their school. He encourages them and persists in declaring that they *can*.

They both read a great deal and write their own poems and stories. To save time, one of them often reads aloud while the other does their math homework, with a Bob Dylan tape playing in the background. No wonder you never learn any math! says Albert.

He very much wants the girls to get interested in the world of computers. If you've got any brains, that's what you have to go in for, he says. But the girls never respond with much enthusiasm. For Christmas each of them got her own kit full of circuit boards and micro-gizmos, which she could assemble into an eternal clock if only she would make the small effort necessary to figure out how the whole thing worked. It's guaranteed to keep going as long as you live, Albert explained. For your entire life you'd be able to check the time, set the alarm differently for each day of the week, find out the date of Easter and the day your birthday would fall on, and so forth and so on. Tina couldn't manage to decipher the dense instruction booklet, but Cilla had an attack of patience and patched her clock together. Now it hangs on the wall and displays her time down to the second, both digitally and with hands. For a lifetime, as the guarantee says. But Albert peeked behind the clock face and said ironically that he guessed Cilla didn't believe in eternal life.

Finally, the great interest, the one that gives their lives direction: the theater. The girls are members of a drama club, Studio Three, where the drama teacher, Synnöve, insists on letting the students work on the scripts and the direction and all sorts of things besides acting. They tease her by saying that she really isn't needed at all, but they know very well that without Synnöve the club would soon fall apart. The twins receive a lot of praise for their efforts, and sometimes it seems as if they live only for the theater. They dream of fame and honors in that field. They're planning on gradually specializing. Tina's going to write film scripts and plays and direct Cilla in the roles in which she'll enchant the audience. *Cilibelle Dubois dans un film de Mar-*

*tinelle Dubois*—won't that look great! When Cilla gets an Oscar for her fantastic acting, she'll hand it over to Tina in front of the cameras and the audience. They've already rehearsed that scene several times. How they fling their arms around each other and weep with joy!

The purpose of their aspiring toward the stars isn't exactly what you might imagine. Some years ago Cilla inserted in her secret papers a sheet that described that purpose:

*When I grow up, if I do, I'm going to be famous—on film. In one film I'll play a nun, in another a hard-boiled cop who gets into a shoot-out on every corner. It'll be the bad guys who get wiped out, crooks and speculators and people like that. They're going to come to the film shoots and get blown away for real. Then I'm going to be in a Steven Spielberg film—if I get the part. I'm going to give all my money to people with AIDS, to the poor people of the world, especially in Colombia, and to others who need money, if my money stretches that far, of course. After that I'd like to be treated like a normal person. Because the way I see it, all famous people are treated like gods, and that's wrong. And then I'll become President and make sure that everyone's treated the same: rich and poor, colored and uncolored, punks and presidents (including myself), healthy people and crazies.*

*My children will be named Jim or Jimmy, Nicole, Anastasia, Alexander, just to give a few examples. My husband will be nice but not a wimp. And he'll tell all about interesting things that he knows. And also he won't be out on the town every night. I'll be as nice to my children as to their friends, and they'll go to a French school.*

*I'm going to live in Paris or New York, and I'm not going to* drink beer. No, because beer tastes like sewage. To put it po-litely. But wine now and then, the kind that tastes like fruit juice. But only at parties and at extra-special dinners.

If I divorce my husband, my children must not be harmed by it.

*3*

ertainly it's very important
to cultivate your interests, but like all other kids, the twins also
try to excel at school. Cilla manages that task very well, but
Tina neglects her schoolwork a bit, since her first priority is to
attend to her jumbled love life. Boys are, as mentioned before,
a major interest, and this spring term has been a pain. Olle
Brick evaporated during the Christmas break; that was sad, but
just one part of a whole Christmas that turned out to be awful
in every way. So Tina had no trouble forgetting him when she
got back to school and noticed that Benke was looking at her
in a way that could only mean one thing. She looked back, and
then he looked away and blushed. Tina blushed too, because
now she had a crush on Benke, she knew it.

She discovered that she didn't know anything about Benke,
so she wrote a note to Gitta, who'd gone out with him for a
whole eight weeks in the fall:

*Tell me* <u>*everything*</u> *about B. T.*
*I'm head over heels, totally sunk!!!!*
                              *T--a*
*P.S. Don't say a word to anyone! T.*

The note came back crossed out. On the back Gitta had written:

*The party in question is a NERD!!!*
                              *G.*
*P.S. Now I've warned you . . .*

Tina wasn't satisfied with that. Get with it! she said at recess. It's serious this time.

Okay! Gitta said. Here come all the pluses for Benke, and there won't be many. Number 1: He's cute.

I can see that myself! Tina pointed out. His eyelashes—mmm!

Number 2: He's nice. Number 3: When you're seeing him, he calls every day. That's it.

But there'll be lots of minuses, Gitta promised. Number 1: He's an egotist, and thinks he's super-cool.

He *is* super-cool! insisted Tina.

Number 2: He's cold and has no feelings.

He probably just doesn't dare to show them to *you*, Tina suggested.

Number 3: He leaves you after a day or a week. After that, you mean zero to him. Then he comes back. Then he leaves you. In the end it's just zero, zero, zero.

You told a different story in the fall, Tina reminded her.

I know better now, claimed Gitta. Number 4: He has shitty taste in clothes and music. Check out that jacket! And the songs you have to listen to on his out-of-this-world CD-stereo-hi-fi-sixteen-thousand-channel-megawatt . . . Like, I mean: Never!

What songs, exactly? wondered Tina, who was sure she'd like Benke's music.

Number—what am I up to?—6: He cares more about his pals—the guys, you know—than about you, even when you're together, I swear. If you want to go out with him, his idea is to go over to the garage with Sigge and tinker with some old engines. Number 7: He thinks of himself as grown up, but what he is is deadly boring. Reads books like *Mammals of the World* and *Labyrinths of Power*.

Sounds great, Tina said. That means he'll have something to talk about.

The guy I go out with shouldn't be talking about power and mammals, Gitta declared. He should look at me and tell me I'm his main squeeze. That's enough. But all that damned literature turns his monkey skull inside out. And from there I get to minus number 8: His talk's so damn refined.

Sounds like *you* could use a little culture, objected Tina.

Number 9: He has no rear end.

He's great! was how Tina thanked Gitta for her information. Can't you ask him if I've got a chance with him?

Me! Gitta shrieked. You think I'm going to talk to *him*! Please!

Never!

But I'm dying, this is serious, can't you see that!

I can ask Sigge to ask, Gitta offered. You can't go out with Benke without Sigge hearing all about it anyway.

I'm dying! moaned Tina.

But Gitta took two days to approach Sigge and Sigge took two days to ask Benke and Benke waited three days before answering Sigge and Sigge took it easy for a whole day before he brought the answer to Gitta and Gitta was annoyed at Tina for not paying any attention to her warnings, so she waited an extra day too. If you calculate carefully, you discover that for nine days Tina went around suffering and wanting to die and declaring to Cilla that to be more miserable than this was a human impossibility.

No, eight days, because on the ninth Tina began to have a problem who was called Kennet Axberg and was in class 9-A. A Kennet in ninth grade has a much more exalted ring to it than a Benke in seventh, so Tina didn't hear what Gitta said that Sigge had said about what Benke had answered. Now Kennet was the point, Kennet, whose looks were perfect—you could say that without exaggeration. He had the finest eyes you could wish for, and he used these divine lights to *looook* at Tina. One look like that and she was totally crazy about him and sure that he was crazy about her, too. But who *isn't* crazy about him? she asked her sister, after entertaining her with a detailed description of Kennet.

Better ask if there's anyone you don't go nuts over, Cilla suggested in a sour tone.

You don't understand that this is serious! You just don't get things like this! I'm crazy, out of my mind, in love, hooked. I could do just about anything with him. He's so incredibly adorable!

Kennet didn't give her much more than glances to weave her dreams on. But what glances! They just had to mean something.

When your heart is overflowing, you have to talk to someone. Since Cilla didn't grasp how serious this was, Tina told Maja Sjövall about her feelings for Kennet Axberg.

Oh, Kennet! Maja agreed. If anyone's cute, it's Kennet.

The winter sports break had just begun, and Tina sat in the

snack bar at the public swimming pool scanning the water, since there was a chance that Kennet would come there to exercise. She devoted the whole break to this: waiting and anticipating. But Kennet never came. He must have been getting his exercise by doing some other sport, somewhere else.

Tina had Maja Sjövall to talk to, because Maja was sitting there in the snack bar too, hoping for approximately the same thing, though her dream was named Kristian and was in 8-B. Kristian was adorable, with the curliest hair Tina had ever seen on a boy, but he couldn't compare to Kennet, of course. Maja didn't express an opinion on that point; she just said she could certainly understand how a girl could fall for Kennet.

Cilla declared herself totally unable to understand the vigil at the swimming pool. For Maja Sjövall to sit there is one thing, that's okay, 'cause she's brain-dead. But you . . . !

This criticism had no effect. Maja and Tina sat there getting each other worked up, so that when school started again, Tina was so afraid of meeting Kennet that she got sick and stayed home for two days. Then she couldn't get out of it anymore, she had to go to school, but she sneaked around and hoped she wouldn't run into him and hoped she would and hoped she wouldn't, but that somehow . . . and a few days passed like that. Once in a while she caught a glimpse of Kennet, who didn't show the slightest sign of suffering in the same way she was. It was so damned unfair!

Meanwhile Maja Sjövall must have been gossiping, because suddenly her best friend, Anna-Karin, confided that she too was totally sick over Kennet but that unfortunately—unfortunately she knew—yes, knew for sure, that he was more interested in Tina. Wasn't he adorable!

Watch out for Anna-Karin! warned Cilla. You know she's as false as a fifteen-cent piece.

But two are stronger than one. Together Tina and Anna-Karin ventured down into the school lounge, where they knew they would find Kennet. Now she was going to bring matters to a head, Tina decided, and began staring at Kennet. It didn't take long for him to notice, and instead of looking away and getting embarrassed, as some other boys would have done, he looked back, so they sat there looking into each other's eyes across the lounge without feeling awkward. Tina felt in every fiber of her body that they understood each other perfectly, and jeezus how gorgeous he is!

This solemn ritual ended when Kennet's buddies said it was time to go to math. He left without taking his eyes off her, so the door cut them off, and Tina collapsed on the table, moaning.

But Anna-Karin betrayed her, it turned out, just as Cilla had predicted. She was the one Kennet asked out to a movie, and afterwards there was pizza and a stroll in the night, and a bit more, if you really want to know . . . she related.

Kennet was a fink and a hypocrite, no matter how perfect his looks. Tina felt emptiness and despair, but she was forced to maintain her composure as long as Anna-Karin was watching her reaction. Later she couldn't even manage to cry over the disaster, just told Cilla in a monotone that everything was over, life isn't worth living, are you happy now, huh?

But Cilla wasn't happy, she just thought Tina was being too childish about her boys. That things kept fouling up for Sis wasn't anything to be happy about. I've written a poem, she said, and read it aloud to Tina:

> *When someone looks at you*
> *and you look back,*

*just for a second or less,*
*I get mad.*

*When you talk to someone else*
*I get jealous.*

*When you hug me*
*I know you are mine.*

Tina nodded. Thanks! she said. That's exactly it! I'm the one who suffers, but you write about it.

Cilla laughed a somewhat sad laugh and let Tina go on thinking what she thought. Cilla's poem was in fact aimed at someone. But Tina didn't find that out, no, Tina didn't even suspect it.

■ ■ ■

Before the emptiness had become too overwhelming, Tina got a call from Micke Englund, who was nice and had always been good to talk to. He told her that he had a crush on Lotta, Tina's best friend, but didn't dare to meet her alone, and he was wondering if Tina might like to go out with Tobbe, Micke's pal, so that all together they could . . . well . . . you know what I mean?

But Tina had her doubts. She didn't even know Tobbe, though she'd heard from Lena that he was really good-looking. But then, obviously she wasn't seeing anyone at all just now, so in the end she said yes.

A day or two passed. Then Micke called again and said Tobbe had thought backwards and forwards about Tina and decided that he'd like to get to know her before they went out together. Considering how Micke had put things in his last call, this was downright insulting, so Tina canceled their plan, abruptly and immediately.

Later the same evening Micke called again. He was in despair, he was even crazier about Lotta now, had to meet her, but just didn't dare to do it alone. He'd had a good long talk with Tobbe, a save-my-life talk, and Tobbe had come to his senses and wanted to go out with Tina.

Piss off! said Tina, who was still insulted. I'd like to get to know him before anyone starts talking about us going out together.

Micke was desperate: Okay, then, I'll come over to your place with him. You'll get to know each other in no time. As soon as you set eyes on him, you'll like him well enough.

No one was going to try coming out to Rosengården to strut his stuff like some goddamned suitor, Tina decided. Besides, by this time she knew what Tobbe looked like, and it was just as Lena had said: he was really good-looking. But you shouldn't make it too easy for boys. This getting to know each other could be arranged at school.

So it was arranged, and there was nothing major wrong with Tobbe, so now Micke could ask Tina to ask Lotta if she would go out with him, after which they could all celebrate by going for pizza, Micke's treat.

Lotta had already noticed that something was up. She said yes right away, and so they ended up at Micke's eagerly longed-for pizza outing, where he sat there laughing foolishly and staring at Lotta's sweet face the whole time and let Tina and Tobbe take care of the conversation. And they talked, so the evening wouldn't be embarrassingly silent, but Tina had a feeling that it would never work out between Lotta and Micke; he was way too lovesick over her.

A drag, because Tobbe was really great. Talked easily and just cool enough, and played with Tina's ear the whole evening, so she could feel a tingling all the way down to the backs of her knees. When he said goodbye, he gave her a quick kiss on the same ear. And all of this Cilla got to hear about late at night, when Tina couldn't sleep.

Micke called the next day, thanked Tina for her help, and said that Lotta was even nicer than he'd imagined. And Tobbe is totally hooked on you, he confided. He'll call you this weekend.

Yeah, right! Guess if he called on the weekend! The phone just sat there silently; Tina got more and more nervous as she waited.

Are you unhappily in love again? asked Albert, but there was absolutely no need to answer that. Maybe you're not the right type of girl for the boys you get stuck on, he suggested.

Do you have to torture me! Tina screamed. You're a sadist, for Chrissake.

Maybe they can't take your moods, Albert went on teasing, but Tina rushed up to her bed, shoving aside Dudde, who'd parked himself in the wrong spot.

This is my bed, she snarled at the dog, but he stayed beside the bed, so she had him to hug while she soaked her pillow with tears.

Suddenly Cilla was sitting there and reading to her:

> Everyone smiles at me
>    and the world is full of life and joy,
> but inside me there's nothing.
>
> Everyone's laughing, they all seem happy
> but inside me it's dark.

*A life without you!*
    *I can't manage that.*

*Don't you see me?*
*I see you.*

*I'm completely empty,*
*except for one red flower that starts growing*
*when I see you.*

Cilla! wailed Tina. I love you!
Cilla stroked Tina's hair: I love you, Tina.
I'm so unhappy! Tina declared, as if Cilla didn't know. Tobbe is the most gorgeous boy I've met.
Cilla didn't say anything for a while, but then she spoke her mind: What you need is to be *really* in love sometime. So you forget about yourself.
Tina wanted to protest but couldn't find the strength. In spite of all logic, it felt like Cilla was somehow right.

■   ■   ■

The week passed, and it was always Micke who promised that Tobbe would get in touch, Micke who said that Tobbe would call, that he hadn't called because something had come up. Tina just felt more and more despair. And she couldn't talk to Lotta, either—Lotta, who until this horrible spring Tina had always been able to talk to about absolutely everything, Tina's best friend, and now she was completely hooked on Micke and didn't notice at all that Tina was bursting with longing to tell her about her broken heart.
So when the phone rang at home, there was no way it could be Lotta—strictly speaking, it could only be misery—and Tina

switched to answering, Hello, this is Cilla . . . No, Tina's out just now—an old trick the girls always used when they couldn't face talking with whoever was calling.

In the end she couldn't get herself to answer at all. Cilla took over. Blah-blah-blah, Tina could hear.

Just a sec! said Cilla. Hang on and I'll get Tina.

Now Tina couldn't get out of it. She took the receiver and whispered, Hello?

You sound like you're about to cry, said Micke's voice, not Tobbe's voice, no, not Tobbe's.

I'm crying already, Tina said, and started laughing because she could hear how silly she sounded. Don't you dare say one more time that Tobbe's going to call soon, don't talk about Tobbe, I hate Tobbe!

Give yourself a break, Micke said in a friendly way. You shouldn't cry over him. I won't talk about him, but he's a decent guy, I swear.

You're nice, Tina said into the receiver. But I can't be consoled anymore. I'm dying! You're invited to my funeral.

Should I tell him you want to end it? Micke asked. Then maybe he'll get a move on.

In a way I really do want to end it, but I know I'd regret it later. The fact is I'm depressed as hell, I can't take this. I thought Tobbe cared about me, but he's just like all the others. They want to go out with me, but none of them cares about me for real.

I care about you, Micke reminded her. Although of course I'm seeing Lotta now. And that's thanks to you. I'm fantastically happy! I just wanted to tell you.

Thanks! Tina said, then hung up and cried, cried, cried. Tobbe, Tobbe! And Lotta! I've lost my best friend! I traded her away for Tobbe! And then he doesn't give a shit about me!

■ ■ ■

An unhappy, miserable Easter came and went, and who knows how this sad story would have ended if Tina hadn't found out that Tobbe was spreading ugly rumors about her. Giving his fantasies free play, he embroidered all sorts of detailed stories about what it was like to be with her. At that point her sorrow changed to anger. The Wednesday after the Easter break Tina stood up right in front of him in the lounge and yelled so everyone could hear it—and did they ever hear!—that if he didn't stop lying and spreading bullshit rumors about her, she would tell the whole world that he was an impotent pig—and go straight to hell!

Tobbe was disgraced, and Tina had gone at it with such force that she got sick again! She was lying in bed with a fever of 102 when Jonny's friend Martin woke her by putting his hand on her forehead. When she opened her eyes, he said: I can tell from your blue eyes that you're very sick.

In a flash she was in love with Martin. She'd already seen so much of him and heard so much about him from Jonny that he didn't need any testing period. He had his own car, didn't just borrow his dad's. And his eyes were as green as the sea near the shore, Tina now saw.

He teased her a little, saying she should get up: Sweet Tina, we need the pleasure of looking at your fine face!

Or was it *cute* face he said? Tina was so happy that she lost track of the words, she almost fainted. She couldn't breathe. Couldn't breathe and couldn't answer.

When Martin left the room, Cilla said, What's with him, all of a sudden?

God, what good hands he had! Tina sighed. And his eyes!

Would you please remember that he's seven years older than you! Cilla chided her.

Tina was just about to snap back, Then you'll have to admit he can't be too childish, won't you— when Martin knocked and came back into the room laughing, pointed first at Tina, then at Cilla, and said: I've just got to tell you that I've met a girl! Isn't that fantastic!

I don't know, said Tina.

Aren't you happy for me? asked Martin, stopping and looking at her. Then he looked at Cilla: Isn't she happy?

Should Tina be happy about *that*? Funny idea, the girls thought, and looked at each other questioningly when Martin had bounded out through the door.

Could he mean me, wondered Tina.

Remember that he's seven years older than you! she heard again.

But Tina had a standard reply to that kind of remark: You won't understand this sort of thing until you reach my age, my little friend.

Tina was born a full fifteen minutes before Cilla. Cilla has to hear about those fifteen minutes fairly often. It's annoying that she can never catch up. Sometimes she retaliates and says something about senile old Aunt Tina. But not this time. This time she let Tina have the last word.

# 4

*P*erhaps you're beginning to wonder: What has Cilla been up to this spring while Tina was bouncing like a ping-pong ball from one infatuation to the next? It may sound strange, but most of the time you saw Cilla and Tina together. It looked like they were doing the same things, but that was only true on the surface.

If they were both sitting around the lounge talking, this is how it could look: there are Cilla and Tina, talking. But look a little closer. Who's Tina talking to and who's Cilla talking to? Is the conversation going in all directions, everyone speaking with everyone? No, if that's what you think, then you looked too quickly.

Sure, it looks like they're both discussing something important with Sandra and Mag. And certainly Cilla is talking to Sandra. Sandra is Cilla's best friend; they can talk for real, about their deepest concerns, even when something else is going on right next to them. And Tina seems to be talking to Mag in the same way, but in fact is watching Tom, over there in the other corner. She twists and turns and directs her laugh so he'll hear it. Now and then she notices that he's looking in her direction. Then she gives Mag a dazzling smile and comments on something Sandra has just said. Cilla looks puzzled, because Tina's comments often don't make sense. But then she catches a glimpse of Tom behind Tina and understands why the conversation is so disjointed.

Similarly, it can appear that the girls go to the same concerts, movies, and dance clubs. They hum the same songs afterwards, so in that sense it's true. But while Tina has checked out the guys playing the music, Cilla's been inspired by their songs to write a poem in English on one of their themes:

> It's time to open our eyes
> and see what's going on,
> see what we have done to the world.
> The world we soon, some of us, are going to leave
> and some of us are going to take over.

■ ■ ■

The ninth-graders arranged a dance to give Ola and Bahir a real tryout. The duo was going on tour in the summer to try to make it nationally, so it was only right for everybody at home to spar for the guys and encourage them to go all out. The dance turned into an enormous bash, since Ola and Bahir had sound equipment worth a couple of thousand dollars to help them deliver their fireworks. Tina thought that if there was any justice in the world, a hunk of a singer like Ola just had to end up on TV before the year was out.

Cilla had gotten something else from the music. After the

show, she went and asked Bahir if he and Ola would consider writing music for the play she was working on.

Play? asked Bahir.

Our underdeveloped-countries thing, Cilla explained. Our class is going to put on a play about how an underdeveloped country gets robbed of its resources. If there's any money left over, it'll go to development projects. So we can't pay you anything, but if you think you guys could do it anyway, maybe?

How come your class is studying underdeveloped countries? Bahir wanted to know. I mean, in seventh grade?

Joint effort between Swedish and social studies, Cilla explained. That produced Project U. A few of us in the class are in Studio Three. You know, the drama club. So we got the others involved too.

But Cilla didn't tell him that she was the driving force behind the project, that she was the one whose hard work inspired the others to give great performances. She'd gained the knowledge she needed from Studio Three, knew how a script should be written and sweated to write it that way. Being in the club had also taught her perseverance, and she needed that when she started struggling with directing the play. Yes, she struggled and slaved, she infected even the most sluggish students with her enthusiasm and fire, she radiated an irresistible power. If she suggested to some classmates that they go out into the town and survey people about their views on underdeveloped countries, they went and did it.

Tina, too, followed Cilla's instructions. One day the twins were going to be famous actresses, celebrities who wrote their own scripts and had the world at their feet. Then their friends would remember this term. Even back then! they would say. Even then they were brilliant!

Ola and Bahir came and watched a rehearsal. The boys in the

class were impressed by the visit from on high, and the girls quivered. Cilla didn't quiver; she explained that the play wasn't finished, but maybe they could get a rough idea.

Tina didn't dare to go onstage as long as the super-sexy Ola was watching.

Are you thinking of carrying on like this when we're celebrities too? Cilla asked. You can't go into a panic every time a gorgeous guy comes around and looks at you!

She went onstage and played Tina's part. Ola and Bahir didn't notice, and the other actors were too absorbed in their acting to think about it. But I'm telling you, I did it just this once! Cilla declared to Tina. *Jamais plus, j'en jure!*

Bahir had a discussion with Ola. Cilla waited for the outcome.

It's probably going to be a good play, Bahir said. There's a lot to it.

I hope so, Cilla said.

But to be honest, Bahir said, I can't imagine why it needs any music.

Really? Cilla wilted a bit. I kind of thought that your sound fit the atmosphere I wanted . . . somehow.

Bahir pondered. Yeah, maybe, he granted. I think I know what you mean. There's a certain likeness.

I thought there was, Cilla repeated.

Don't you think the match is too good, sort of? Bahir asked.

Yes, he was really asking, not just dismissing Cilla's words and making only his own count. How so? she asked.

Same message on two channels, Bahir explained. Two spreads on one sandwich, he elaborated. Like screwing twins, he let slip before it hit him that maybe this particular comparison wasn't suitable just now. If they match too well, then one can, like, knock out the other. I don't want to write music that you guys are gonna knock out with your play. And I don't want to knock out your play, either, with the "perfect" music for it.

Maybe you're right, Cilla nodded. Could be. I didn't think of that.

Yeah, that's the kind of thing that doesn't occur to people, Bahir nodded in a friendly way. But if you do music, then you learn pretty fast to think about things like that. Thanks anyway for asking us. It's an honor just to be asked.

But isn't it odd that the match can *be* that perfect? wondered Cilla. I mean, what we're doing here is words and stuff. And then your music—there's some kind of connection. Isn't that odd?

It's pure magic, Bahir agreed. There's so much out there. Like, that's why you keep working at stuff.

Cilla nodded. So, no music for the play, then.

■ ■ ■

A week later yet another tremor rippled through the girls in the seventh grade. Without warning, Bahir came to a rehearsal. He was looking for Cilla, no one else needed to tremble, and Cilla seemed quite calm: Hi, what's up? Wasn't there at least one quivering string inside Cilla nonetheless?

He gave her a cassette tape. Hey, kid! he said and stretched out his hand so two fingertips touched her Bob Marley necklace. He smiled faintly and took off.

Cilla smiled too. She didn't know what to think. This is how things could look when a guy was trying to hook up with a girl. Had he made a mistake and thought she was Tina, perhaps? But Bahir was so much older than she was. That was more or less what he got across with his "kid," after all.

On the cassette box she read: *Ola and Bahir play Cilla*. So far so good, he hadn't meant Tina. Though it sounded odd: "play Cilla."

There was a little note inserted between the cassette and the label card. It was in the same handwriting:

> *It's even more magical*
> *that a person*
> *can be certain music.*
> *This is Cilla!*
>     *Bahir*

At home Cilla listened to the music that was supposed to be her in magical ways. Yes, there was something magical there, even though she didn't see her own image when the flowing sound painted pictures all around her. The notes created a dancing pattern she could see. If there was a face, then it resembled Bahir's more than her own, she thought. But mainly it emerged as a smile on top of that pattern. A warm and melancholy smile on which she could lie down and slowly, rocking like a cradle, glide out into space.

What's this? asked Tina.

I asked Bahir to write music for Project U, Cilla explained quickly.

If they go at it like that, nobody'll listen to the play, Tina said, and turned over the cassette box so she could read the title. *Ola and Bahir play Cilla*.

She gave her sister an inquiring look. The antenna that Tina had in her twinned being was telling her that something here wasn't the way Cilla wanted her to think it was. That title was a coded message, the music was another part of the code, and

Cilla's explanation yet another. But Cilla was careful to look away at that moment. The room was full of the smiling pattern, but Tina didn't see it; she couldn't find the key to the code.

Whatever you do, save this cassette, she advised. If they're a hit on their tour, it'll be worth a fortune.

Cilla nodded.

And of course she saved the cassette. Saved it, played it, and in a short time learned to listen in a way that was completely new to her. Bob Marley's music, John Lennon's, Bob Dylan's— that and all the other important music she had, and all the lyrics she'd thought she knew so well—began to grow around her and take on new meanings. From one day to the next, she couldn't recognize the thoughts she'd just had. It wasn't a simple matter anymore of just liking this music, it went further and deeper. Over and over she became part of the music and vanished from space and time. Pure magic, Bahir had said. He was right, but that was no explanation.

■ ■ ■

Meanwhile life was supposed to go on as if nothing was different. The new energy field she felt around her repulsed her friends—no, rather, pushed them slowly away. She saw them coming to school, all bubbly and skin-deep, and couldn't get herself to take part in their gossip. Unfortunately, she didn't manage to hide her contempt; they soon felt the chill coming off her. To them her behavior could only mean one thing. What did she have to be stuck-up about? They responded in their own way, of course. When she wasn't surrounded by complete silence, someone was whispering, she noticed. She happened to read Maja's datebook, where *Party at Vivvi's* was entered for Friday. Neither she nor Tina had heard anything about a party at

Vivvi's. How shitty, Cilla said, but Tina took a different attitude and went to Vivvi and asked if there had been some mistake. Have we done something? Are you guys freezing us out for some reason?

Nah, Vivvi said nervously. You can come if you want to, Tina. But Cilla . . . I don't know . . .

Um, I see, Tina said, and tried to understand.

I don't give a shit, Cilla said when Tina told her.

It was true yet not true. She thought they should be able to tell her what was wrong to her face, instead of whispering and gossiping. But she certainly had no intention of forcing herself on them if they turned their backs on her. Let Vivvi have her party and play her sappy music! Petty—they were so petty! She didn't give a damn about them, but it hurt just the same. You go ahead, she said to Tina.

The hell I will! Tina protested. She knew without a doubt whose side she would be on if it came to a feud. But she wanted to know what the feud was about. Before she managed to find out, though, she lost her bearings by falling in love again.

The new situation was not good for the play. Too many students stayed away from rehearsals. Cilla couldn't bring herself to explain to the deserters that the play dealt with something much bigger and more important than what they thought of her. The point was to throw light on the exploitation going on in the underdeveloped countries. This was a large issue, but her classmates had more important things to attend to, it seemed.

Bahir came to one of the last rehearsals. He saw immediately that something had gone wrong. Did you lose heart because of me? he asked.

Not at all! Cilla assured him. I haven't lost heart. It's the others—they've . . .

Bahir saw her look away. They've what? he wanted to know, but he got no answer. Hey, kid! he whispered and touched her lightly with his electric fingertips. Don't cry. You're too good for them.

For the first time in her life, Cilla felt that she wanted what Tina was always raving about: to lean against a boy's chest and just forget everything else.

> There's a flower in a meadow,
> miles and miles away.
> It's in the middle of the meadow,
> all around the grass is high
> and the breeze is slowly blowing.
> Children run around it,
> laughing and playing.
> I want that flower from you.

But Bahir had disappeared before she even discovered what she wanted. So she decided to grin and bear the hurt, called Tina, and went home. On the bus she said nothing, said nothing and more nothing, while Tina chattered on about her own affairs. This was during the happy phase of Tina's Kennet period. She and Cilla sat beside each other on the bus, close to each other, it might appear. But in fact there were several hundred miles between them just then, though only Cilla felt the distance. Tina filled the gap with Kennet, Kennet, Kennet.

Cilla looked out into the darkness beyond the window—no, looked at the bus reflected in the glass and mentally put a poem up between the specks of light rushing by outside:

*I want to be a tear,*
*be born from your eye*
*travel down your cheek*
*die on your lips.*


Albert saw her looking dejected. Is it your turn now to be unhappy in love? he asked sarcastically.

Cilla answered with a hiss.

Strange, Albert said. You're all set: you're thirteen years old
and have everything a person could wish for. Yet we have to
look at your sour faces all the time. Is that what you call counting your blessings? And being grateful to your parents, who
smooth the way for you? We let you fill the house with your impossible music until we can hardly hear ourselves think. And
then you can't be bothered to wear expressions we can stand to
look at!

Then stop staring at me! Cilla hissed. Nobody asked you to.

And what an agreeable tone, I must say! Oh well, I know
that's how you have to act to be "in" these days. *A Dieu ne
plaise!*

He turned his back and walked away. Cilla cast a black look
after him. If that man doesn't let up, she confided in Tina, then
sooner or later I'm going to commit patricide, *j'en jure!*

He can't help himself, Tina pointed out. An immigrant,
poor guy!

Alienation, Cilla nodded. Culture shock.

And with such a god-awful mom besides, Tina continued.
What a childhood he must have had!

And he has to take that out on us, of course. It'll come to
murder, that's my last word.

Suicide is better, was Tina's view. Then he has to be sorry for the rest of his life.

Not a snowball's chance in hell that he'll feel sorry for anything, Cilla was sure. It'll just make him happy if his whiny daughters disappear. I wouldn't give him the pleasure. No, a slow death under extreme torture is what *his* sentence should be!

*5*

The play was put on ice, for the time being—or so they said, but Cilla didn't have much faith in resurrection. Synnöve tried to encourage Cilla to keep going, but of course didn't quite understand where the rub was. Cilla's classmates were ostracizing her, but the girls didn't show their "school" selves to Synnöve when they came to Studio Three, so she didn't notice anything. As for Cilla, she convinced herself that she didn't care. The girls only talked about stupid things, after all. Read a book, airhead! she would think when she saw them comparing their new hairdos. Almost all the girls in seventh grade changed their hairdos this spring. Cilla and Tina were waiting until the summer, so they wouldn't be like all the others.

The ones who preened the least turned out just fine, Cilla thought. Sandra and Sussy, for example, weren't at all affected. Sandra had an incredibly lovely neck that Cilla could see a lot of now, since most of the time Sandra was turning her back. That Sandra in particular—until now her best friend—should turn away hurt Cilla very much. Beautiful Sussy's enmity hurt her in a different way. She and Cilla had been so gentle and good together. Now Cilla got the cold shoulder. For a long time Sandra had looked Cilla in the eyes and answered when Cilla said a few words to her. But in the end she went along with the others.

Cilla wrote a poem, wrote it as always in such a way that Tina wouldn't suspect who it was addressed to:

> *Imagine—if you would just see*
> *imagine—if you would just turn around and see . . .*
> *see how much I love you.*
> *Imagine . . . and turn to me!*

And Tina made Cilla's poems her own in her fashion, reading into them her own romantic troubles. She didn't have much time to spare for pondering Cilla's problem. Otherwise Tina might have discovered that the sister who was right beside her was lonely, lonelier than Cilla herself could understand. Understand? Endure was what she had to do. There would be a turning point, she believed. She would break through their coldness and rejection; she would turn them toward her again. Not by force, but by the power of patience. Of love, in spite of everything.

> *I see a rose in the asphalt.*
> *Right in the middle of the road.*
> *All around it there are cracks.*
> *I see that it's growing.*
> *It looks a little odd,*

*so red and soft*
*against the hard black asphalt.*
*It is beautiful.*

■　■　■

This might interest you! Synnöve said, and handed out flyers to the members of the drama club.

Cilla read. Literature and Drama Camp this summer. Read, write, do drama exercises, meet an author and a director, have discussions. Secondary-school students from the whole county are welcome. What do you think? she asked Tina.

When is it?

The beginning of August.

You think there'll be any cute guys coming?

How the hell should I know!

They considered it together. Cilla was the one who was most interested. Tina was a bit cool in the beginning but not hard to persuade. Drama exercises in a different group from the usual one, discussions of literature—well, why not! They looked over the list of required and recommended reading. The required books were included in the price of the course.

Nothing by Jackie Collins, Tina pointed out. Nothing by Sidney Sheldon.

They don't need to include *them* in a course, Cilla said. Everyone's read them anyway.

Each participant was to bring along a book that he/she liked and give a report on it.

Tell them about *Tracy's Revenge*, said Cilla. You described that so well for me that I didn't need to read it.

*Tracy's Revenge*? Tina pondered. I've forgotten that one.

Hope I don't get that scatterbrained when I reach your advanced age, Cilla sighed.

Notice of who had been accepted would be sent at the end of April.

We're applying, Cilla decided. Albert can afford it. The thing is, if we take off to this camp, we get out of going to Justine's this year.

Albert didn't object at all to begin with. But then he realized that the camp conflicted with the trip to France. The trip couldn't be rescheduled. Vacations here and vacations there—there were no other times to choose from.

Cilla and Tina knew how to play their cards. They put on worried faces when Albert mentioned that they might not get to visit Justine at all this year. Of course they wanted to visit Grandma, they nodded, and fed Albert a cue by pointing out that the worst part of it all was that Justine would be terribly offended if Albert and Monika came on their own.

Of course she won't! Albert defended his mother.

She'll have such a bo-o-o-ring time without us, Cilla said.

Nah—I'm sure she'll survive that, Albert replied.

Sure enough, from there it was a short step to Albert's announcement that he'd come up with the idea that he and Monika should travel to France without the girls.

Maybe Jonny could . . . ? Tina suggested delicately.

But Jonny had to devote himself all summer to an important job he'd landed at a drafting firm, where he would be on probation. It was entirely out of the question for him to go to France. The only difficulty in connection with Jonny, according to Monika, was that if he couldn't get a ride to his job with Albert, then he would have to drive with Martin. Could they really go off to France with peace of mind, knowing that back at home Jonny was racing up and down Death Road with a buddy who drove like a car thief?

You're exaggerating! Jonny said. He drives with a little zip, but he doesn't take any risks.

A little zip! Monika repeated. Does he have to skid into the drive here so the gravel sprays straight across the flower beds? One fine day Dudde will be lying there sunning himself and won't manage to get out of the way. A poor innocent dog!

Even that much is called taking risks, Albert added.

Then don't go to France! Jonny roared. If you think I can't take care of myself. I'm nineteen! Martin is twenty. Do you know that a person's legally an adult at eighteen?

So we'll be applying to the camp, then, Cilla concluded.


At the end of April they received notice that they'd been accepted. The program and list of participants were enclosed; the books would be sent as soon as the fee was received.

They read through the list of participants. There were young people from the whole county—impressive. They didn't know anyone.

Only five boys, Tina sighed. Twenty-seven girls, and most of them from eighth grade. What've I gotten myself into!


Martin looked in on them, as he was in the habit of doing when he'd talked to Jonny for a while. There was no longer any doubt: he was interested in Tina. Now he wanted to take her along to the Nonviolent Generation rally. He'd drive her there and back.

Jonny had tipped Tina off, so she was ready, wearing party clothes. Even so, she blushed.

In the most proper fashion imaginable, Martin added when

the blush appeared. I was thinking that Cilla should come too.

At that Cilla blushed as well. I can't, she said. I have to finish writing my essay.

But strangely enough, she, too, was already dressed up. When they were in these clothes, you really couldn't tell the girls apart. God, how pretty you are! Martin exclaimed. Two roses at Rosengården!

Of course Cilla went along. I'll take care of my essay over the weekend, she sighed—without sounding particularly unhappy about it.

Jonny attached himself to the outing.

Don't kill my children on the road! Monika implored, only half in jest—no, only a quarter—no, not even that much; not at all in jest, actually.

Martin raised his right hand: I swear I won't do more than forty miles an hour on the main roads.

And that you won't try to pass? Monika added.

Only tractors, Martin said.

There were no tractors to pass; there was no passing at all. Martin skidded impressively on the gravel lane, but once he was up on Death Road he kept his promise.

It wasn't easy to park in town, because "everyone" had come to the NVG rally, which featured a torchlight parade, speeches, songs, music, solemn promises . . . Lofty words from the open stage, ringing responses from the sea of people out in the square. And also, naturally, an echo: drunks and the rest of the bar crowd, who hung out on the neighboring side streets and bellowed at them.

Ola and Bahir came onstage and played their song "All through the World." At least a thousand young people raised cigarette lighters toward the sky and joined in on the refrain.

No music teachers were there to dampen their enthusiasm by telling them they couldn't sing.

Ladies and gentlemen! Ola shouted into the microphone. Here comes our song "Peace." Let us know if you think we should play it on our tour.

As soon as they'd played the first few bars, Cilla recognized one of the songs on her cassette. It wasn't called "Peace" there, but that didn't matter. She scanned the faces all around her and tried to make out what people thought of it.

Suddenly Bahir roared into his microphone: *Are you here?*

*Yeees!* Cilla shrieked, and so did a thousand other voices. Yet she was sure that Bahir caught her eye and then played just for her, played her, played Cilla so the walls around the square shook and Cilla shook deep in her being.

Christ they're good! sighed Tina on the way home, without breathing a single syllable about Ola, since Martin was listening. Did you recognize that song, by the way—"Peace"?

Guess!

Have you two heard it before? asked Martin, surprised. It's brand-new.

They gave me a demo tape, Cilla explained.

Martin whistled, impressed. What a gift! he said.

He returned to Rosengården with all of Monika's "children" intact. Jonny went inside, but Cilla and Tina hung back so they could say goodbye to Martin. Thanks for a lovely evening, little angel! he said, and kissed Tina lightly, so lightly, on the forehead.

Thank *you*! she said, as her eyes closed from giddiness.

Thanks for the lovely evening, little angel! he said again, and kissed Cilla the same way.

Cilla didn't blink; her clear, observant blue eyes laughingly met his green ones, pierced him, no, filled him with their light as she gibed: Don't you know who's who?

Yes, *now* I know! he exulted, then jumped in his car and tore away from Rosengården so that yet again the gravel went flying into the flower beds. Tomorrow Monika and Albert, muttering curses, would pick the stones out one by one until it was time to go down to the Walpurgis Night bonfire.

I'm jealous! Tina moaned. If you swipe Martin I'll never forgive you!

But Cilla couldn't take seriously the infatuation of a guy seven years older than them, no matter which sister he had a crush on. I won't swipe Martin, she promised calmly. He's yours, *j'en jure!*

And who's yours, then? Tina asked in a peeved tone. Is it Sussy, maybe?

God*dammit!* Cilla burst out. I hate you and your damned innuendos.

Lez! Tina jeered. That's no *innuendo*, is it. Lez, lez . . .

*You* don't seem to get on very well with any of your *boys!* Cilla lashed out.

So what! Admit it's me they like. Everyone can see there's something wrong with you.

And the evening was a success? asked Albert, when he saw their angry faces. Brother Jonny nice, and the cavalier duly attentive? Everyone on good terms and happy?

He got no answer. They tossed their heads, glared in opposite directions, and swept by him.

## 6

*W*ake up! Albert urged them. It was early, early, the second of May, an intensely sunny day, already stifling, even in the morning. I have to go to the airport now. I want you to wake up Monika in a nice way together with Jonny, before you go off to school. Try not to quarrel with her, for just this one day. And not with each other or Jonny, either. I'll be back home this evening, *gens de revue!*

The girls were wide-awake from pure anger. Who the hell was planning on quarreling! We never quarrel! He's got a screw loose—who are the ones who quarrel in this house, really!

They padded down to the kitchen, where Jonny was waiting for them with the coffee tray ready.

Oh, Joney, Joney! Cilla rolled her eyes to the ceiling. What a chef!

Tina giggled and Jonny laughed good-naturedly. They arranged their presents on the tray and carried it in to Monika, entered her room singing. She was truly surprised and impressed.

There was time to sit and talk for a while. Just think, in one week we'll have lived here for ten years! Monika sighed. To me it feels like we moved in yesterday.

Yesterday! Tina objected. From her perspective, the beginning of those ten years was lost in a distant haze. But Monika was turning forty-three today, so of course she had a very different perspective.

We should have an anniversary party, Jonny suggested.

And we were newly married . . . , Monika continued.

A garden party, Jonny went on. A Rose Garden Party.

Albert carried me over the threshold . . .

I never promised you a rose garden, Cilla said into the air.

Monika returned to the present, looked a bit questioningly at Cilla. I think they've been a very fine ten years, she said in a defensive tone.

The time! shouted Tina. Duty calls.

The girls hurried out to the kitchen and wolfed down some breakfast. Then they got their things together, but Tina couldn't find the key to her school locker. Who the hell has swiped my key!

No one swipes your things, Monika declared from her bed. You do a great job of losing track of them on your own.

If you gave a damn about straightening up this place more than once in a while . . . Tina shot back, and with that the quarrel was on, the quarrel that Albert had asked them to avoid in honor of this day. But there was no time for it to develop and no time either for the key to turn up, because the girls had to get going if they didn't want to miss the bus.

They'd gotten halfway up the drive when they heard Monika shout. She came running out in her nightgown, waving the key. Tina grabbed it, still angry and unforgiving. But Cilla turned around, Tina's understudy stepping in as Friendliness, and made her smile outshine the glow of the morning sun, tossing Monika a bright *Thanks, Mamma!*

They could see how that thank-you warmed Monika as she turned back to the house and they hurried on their way.

It's her birthday, after all, Cilla explained, as if Tina had asked her something.

Yes, you're certainly the best daughter she has, Tina said, as if Cilla had said something else entirely.

Their conversations often go this way. They think one thing and say another, but nonetheless hear the thoughts that the words were supposed to hide. Now Cilla takes Tina's arm: You're the best sister I have!

They almost have to stop walking, because Tina needs to catch her breath, she's so moved by this sudden reversal. Thanks—and likewise! she says. Though I don't deserve it, Cilla. I feel so touchy these days.

To me, you deserve everything! Cilla says.


But help! There's the bus, already at the bus stop. They pick up their pace.

Hell! Cilla pants behind Tina. School's such a load of fun— and here we are, *running* to get there!

He won't drive away without us! Tina calls over her shoulder just as they run up onto Death Road.

Sure—not if he sees us! Cilla calls back.

Tina bolts across the road. A couple of steps into the far lane, then she hears a *crump* behind her—describe that sound, if you can and dare to—tires screeching on the asphalt and a rustle as if from scared birds breaking cover. Tina turns around, turns around immediately, turns around in that instant when she hears the *crump*, the screech, the rustle, but my God, how did Cilla end up over there? She can't be lying there! Where are her legs? Is it snowing? No, it's paper that's floating down, the essay Cilla finished over the weekend, falling incomprehensibly from the clear blue sky, and there's a stench of burnt rubber, Cilla, for God's sake, have you gotten off the bus in the middle of the road! and in the car over there Martin is sitting and staring, staring, the black skid marks on the asphalt end near him, end at the tires on his car, his own car.

Turn off that radio! someone shouts at him from the bus, but he doesn't react, just stares and stares, inane music gushing out over the scene.

Now another car stops, someone leaps out of it and takes hold of Tina: What's your name? Where do you live? Who is she?

Does he get an answer? He has a phone in his car, calls for an ambulance, but the bus driver has already done that. The car driver guides Tina into the back seat of his car. Someone's already sitting there, an older man who puts his arm around Tina: There, there, we'll drive you home. Is it down this road here?

She was just hit, Tina says. She was just hit, not run over. She was just hit, that's not so serious, is it? Promise!

When the car turns off Death Road, she sees that someone is giving Cilla artificial respiration. So it's not so serious, right? She was just hit, Tina repeats, and doesn't take her eyes off the scene—she's waiting for Cilla to get up and wave to her to come back, take the bus . . . we have to go to school.

Are we on the right road? asks the man whose arm is around Tina. We have to take you home, little girl. Tina, wasn't your name Tina? They'll take good care of your sister, you'll see.

Up the hill here! Tina only needs to give them directions

once. The rest of the time it's as if the driver senses which way to go.

They swing in at Rosengården. What a paradise you live in! the driver says. To think that something like this should happen here!

Monika and Jonny have interrupted their peaceful breakfast and come out onto the front steps. What is it? asks Monika. Then she sees Tina. O my God, what's wrong?

An accident out on the road, the driver explains. Maybe you'd better come back there with us.

Is it Cilla! Monika cries, but she already knows.

Jeezus, don't take her there! Tina begs the arm that's holding her. She knows how Monika will react—scream like crazy, cry, get hysterical—and Tina can't be part of that, she needs Monika's protection now, needs to draw comfort and strength from her and not be the one who takes care of Monika. But they push their way into the car, fill the car with their anxiety, their questions. Cilla was just hit, Tina explains, just hit, not run over, so it can't be serious, can it? We're twins after all, and here I am, I'm alive and I'm strong.

And as the car takes them back to Death Road, Tina starts singing a song, the first one that comes to mind: *I believe the children are our future* . . .


It's a hundred years since Tina heard the wrenching sound behind her, but the scene on Death Road is mysteriously unchanged when they get there. Someone is still trying to breathe life into Cilla, who is still lying there playing her horrible lifeless role. And Monika rushes over to her and screams, screams, just as Tina knew she would scream—yes, Tina knew though she's never heard a drowning person's scream, knew anyway, and now she hears that scream, now Monika is screaming like that, now she's drowning, now she's screaming away any faith or hope Tina has that Cilla has come around or will soon, she's screaming for help for her drowning soul, while Tina sits paralyzed, silent, praying: Merciful God . . . no, not a prayer to that distant, distant god, instead she implores her sister, prays without faith, without hope: Get up, Cilla! Get up and stop putting us on!

An ambulance and a police car arrive and change the scene. Cilla disappears, Monika goes with her in the ambulance, why are they taking Cilla away? Why are they leaving me alone with strangers? What are the police measuring?

Jonny is at Martin's car, helping out by giving the answers that Martin himself can't give: who he is and where he comes from. But Jonny can't explain how the accident happened. He comes back to Tina, who's still being kept in the car by the older man. Was Martin driving too fast, or how else . . . ?

She's just been hit. It's not serious, right? Tina says again and again and again. With her wide-open eyes she sees everything: she sees clearly a film that's being projected at the same time as it's being filmed in slow sequences, painted in the purest colors, but the things people say to her and the questions they ask don't register at all, not right now, though somewhere her tape recorder is on and recording the sounds that go with the images. She will play back that tape a million times as she reels through the film. A million times. But not now, not now.

We'll drive you and your brother to the hospital, the driver says.

Jonny jumps into the car. Please Tina! he begs her, but she's babbling nonstop.

Some distance away there's a man, a guy, an old bastard, scanning the accident site with binoculars. Stop the car! Tina screams, suddenly wild with fury. Stop, I have to kill that bastard! What the fuck does he think . . . stop, goddammit!

There, there! The arms give her a gentle shake. The car has already passed the man. Tina rages for another little while, then switches to singing. She sings everything that occurs to her, sings, keeps singing till the car turns in at the entrance to the hospital.

Where do we go from here? the driver wonders, but Tina doesn't want to go anywhere, doesn't want to go in through any doors, wants to wait here with Jonny until Cilla comes out with Monika so they can leave this place, why on earth should we be here?

Okay, we'll wait here, Jonny says. Thanks so very much for all your help, he tells the men in the car.

The driver and the old man understand there's nothing more for them to do. They nod to Jonny and Tina. Well, then! Hope things turn out all right! the driver says, then quickly falls silent again and bites his lower lip.

Tina and Jonny are alone outside the entrance, alone among people who hurry past, on their way in or out, concentrating on their own worries.

Hi! says a voice—no, it says, Hi?

Who is she? Slowly Tina puts a name to the face: Anna-Karin, someone from her class, surely, from the school that's far, far away, someone called Anna-Karin, who's just had her follow-up appointment—my arm, you know . . .

My arm, you know, my arm, you know . . . no, Tina doesn't know. Cilla is in there, she says, and points to the doors behind Anna-Karin. My sister, you know, we're twins.

I know, Anna-Karin says, and laughs at Tina for trying to put her on.

I don't know if she's dead, or . . .

Anna-Karin gets confused, directs a quick questioning look at Jonny, but he doesn't meet her eyes, doesn't answer the question she doesn't ask, doesn't open his mouth, just clenches his jaws, has his arm around Tina's shoulders, doesn't even know that Anna-Karin is there, and then she isn't anymore, she's gone already, she's left, but has she understood? No, but some time later she will understand that she was the first one in the school to find out, that she could have gone there carrying the message: Cilla is in the hospital, Tina said that . . . But she missed her chance to be the Teller; by and by she will understand this. And because Anna-Karin is a certain type of person, that missed chance will grieve her more than anything else.

# 7

ina stands near the hospital entrance and talks, talks, talks. Jonny holds her, lets her talk, but says nothing himself. And what she's saying? Well, what can she be saying when her only clear thought is: *Now, Tina! It's now* I have to keep my self-control, I can't let anyone see how scared I am, keep the mask up, Tina, I'm scared, of course I am, but I'm strong, I can control myself, yes I can, I can.

Out of the main entrance comes Arne Mellerud, a doctor at the hospital and a good friend of Albert's. He walks up to them: Come along now, Tina. Your mamma needs you.

She's dead, isn't she? Tina asks. Say it: she's dead.

But he doesn't answer her, makes a gesture that forces them to follow him into the cool dimness. She chatters: Just say it, tell me. She's dead, isn't she?

A nurse takes over. She doesn't answer either, no one tells

Tina anything, so her certainty grows together with her determination not to show her fear, not to show, either, that it is gradually changing into despair, not to show how the despair in its turn is growing apace with her certainty that the impossible has struck, has happened, has become reality. *If you die, I can't go on living!*

Tina and Jonny find themselves in a room where Monika is already sitting. Monika is finally silent; she is composed, one might say. She hugs Tina, who feels something like calm setting in, something like it, but definitely not calm. Cilla's dead, isn't she, Mamma?

She can feel the answer when Monika puts her hand over her neck.

Then they sit there, Tina, Monika, and Jonny. They're waiting for time to start again, for someone to come in and apologize for the interruption, the mistake: it was another girl who was run over on Death Road, a stranger that no one will miss. Here's Cilla, the whole thing was a mistake.

But no one comes. Well, many people come and with new words and messages tear down the tiny hope that Tina is trying to build up. She lifts stones up onto the wall, watches them fall down, lifts new stones, they get heavier, heavier, the wall collapses, she can no longer hide behind it, even though she's so small, small, small, can't manage to lift any more stones. Cilla, come help me! We'll always help each other, yes we will. We'll always be together.

She smiled at me so beautifully this morning, Monika says to no one. Thank God the last thing I had from her was a smile!

In the silence after that, Tina remembers that she herself had quarreled with Monika then, that morning Monika is talking about. What if it had been me who . . . I'll never quarrel again, never, no more quarreling!


I have to call school! says Tina suddenly. I have to explain why we're not coming.

They don't stop her, they don't say yes or no, why should they? Maybe they don't even hear her. You can call from here, a man says. Since it's been decided that all nurses should be called "Sisters," he is Sister Björn, according to the nameplate on his uniform pocket. He directs her to a telephone.

Tina stands there with the receiver in her hand and wonders where she should call, what to say to whom. School—of course! The number? She leafs through the phone book at random. It's incomprehensible, incomprehensible, just full of names and numbers. Sister Björn helps her. He dials the number too. Do you want to speak to them yourself? he asks.

Of course Tina wants to speak to them herself. Hi, it's me, she says, when Gunn-Britt answers—Gunn-Britt, the secretary.

Uh-huh, and who's "me"? asks Gunn-Britt's friendly voice.

Tina remembers her name and which class she's in. We're not coming today, Cilla and I.

Okay—aren't you feeling well?

Sure, I'm fine, Tina answers automatically. Though Cilla . . .

Yes? Gunn-Britt asks patiently, prepared for almost any reason for an absence from school, just not the right one.

Cilla is dead, I think. So we can't come today.

But sweet child! Gunn-Britt gasps. How horrible, you poor little thing! Where are you? Is anyone taking care of you?

Mamma's here. I'm not in any danger, Tina reassures her. Cilla will probably be all right. She was just hit; it's worse to get run over, isn't it?

I don't really know, Gunn-Britt says, bewildered. But go to your mamma now. I'll let them know that you and Cilla . . . that you're not coming.

Thanks for your help, Tina says in a monotone, but politely.

She goes through the wrong door and wanders around in the corridors for a while until Sister Björn finds her and sends her in the right direction. A woman has come into the room, a chaplain's aide named Gunilla. Monika is talking to her a mile a minute.

Tina hears Monika relate once more how Cilla smiled so brightly and said, Thanks, Mamma! Again she feels the chill from the thought that goes flying past her: *If it had been me . . .*


Gunn-Britt must have understood more than Tina told her. What else can explain that after a short while Lotta turns up? She doesn't see Monika, Jonny, or the chaplain's aide, sees only Tina, rushes over to her, throws her arms around her and weeps. Tina doesn't cry, she has to control herself and be strong, but in some mysterious way it's good that Lotta's crying, it's good to have her hugs, good that nothing needs to be said. *Lotta is my best friend!*

It's impossible to remain in the room, the air is so dense with sorrow. Tina and Lotta walk slowly toward their school. The sun is in their eyes. The traffic rumbles by. Every doorway and window, every street corner, every opening between buildings carries a message from Cilla. It was here that we . . . It was over there that you . . .

Cilla walks alongside them and laughs cheerfully at the memories. We really put some life into this dump!

She's so close now, so close; she's in the sunlight that enfolds them, and Tina feels now that life is wonderful, is enormous, is powerful, is worth having. She laughs, laughs from her great happiness at having all this, laughs loudly and shrilly and can't stop, not until Lotta screams and slaps her hard in the face. *Smack* on one cheek, *smack* on the other. Then Tina quiets down. *Lotta is my best friend!*


The class is playing rounders when they get there. Tina and Lotta stand at the far corner of the playing field and watch. Sandra comes running in their direction and manages to make it safely to a "sanctuary." How's Cilla? she asks.

It's Tina who answers, since Lotta can't get out a single word. Sandra sinks to the ground, crying. Never before has Tina seen cheerful Sandra cry, though they know each other well.

The game peters out. Some of the students come over and ask Sandra what's happened. They see Tina standing there, but they ask Sandra what's happened.

Ask me! says Tina, when Sandra doesn't answer.

They ask her. Tina reports without feeling, as if some distant stranger has passed away.

Nah, you must be kidding! says Lena, accustomed to Tina's exaggerations.

At that the self-control cracks a little and lets Tina's tears out through the shell. Cilla is DEAD, for Chrissake! she screams at Lena. Do you think a person can joke about absolutely everything!

Lena stretches out her hand, dismayed and ashamed, but Tina is already out of reach. She's crying in Lotta's arms, Lotta's crying too, Sandra is crying where she sits, the tears are contagious, all the girls are crying. Now it's become the truth for all of them: Cilla is dead.

The boys stand off to one side. They're not happy either, but of course a man isn't supposed to cry. Finally, Fredde Lindgren steps up to Tina, draws her close, holds her tight, and says in her ear: Steady, Tina! I don't think Cilla wants it to be like this.

Tina gets a grip on herself, calms down remarkably fast. Fredde's right, he's a good guy, he knows what Cilla wants. Control's the thing. Strong—exactly. Death—so what! Keep laughing every day, you'll chase your cares away.


Tina, Lotta, and Sandra return to the hospital, Lotta because she doesn't want to desert Tina, Sandra because Cilla is so fond of her.

Jonny has left, but Albert has arrived. He received the message, broke off his trip, and came straight back. Now he takes Tina into his arms. Big, strong Pappa—Tina realizes that she's been afraid of this meeting the whole time, afraid of discovering that there is something that he can't fix either, that even Albert is powerless, and that this may make him small and afraid.

Everything's okay, Tina says inside Albert's arms, consoling the heavily thumping heart inside his jacket. Everything's okay. Cilla is with John Lennon now. She's with him and all the others she admired so much who died. They're sitting together now and Cilla is singing their songs. They're applauding because she knows them so well. That's what's happening, Pappa, that's what's going on.

Albert hugs her, mumbles in a shaky voice: Of course that's what's going on.


Arne Mellerud comes into the room. He makes his follow-me gesture. It is time to say goodbye. He says, We've made things ready in a room over here.

Tina says she doesn't want to. She's never seen a dead person at all, let alone her own mirror image in death, and she's afraid that Cilla will be mutilated, will give her a horrifying last image to remember.

Monika decides otherwise. Naturally we're going to say goodbye to Cilla.

We have to, Albert agrees.

We have to, we have to. And there lies Cilla in her deep, deep sleep. It's impossible to grasp that, lying right here, she is so far away that you can't reach her, can never reach her again.

Tina weeps and weeps. She promises: Cilla! On your gravestone it's going to say, *The Gifted Actress Cilla*, because for me you're the greatest actor who's ever lived.

Maybe it's a foolish promise, maybe it's dumb to let Monika and Albert hear these words, maybe it's good—in any case, Monika cries too, leaning against Albert, and the things she says aren't terribly sensible either. If only we had something other than words to talk with; if only people had another kind of language!

Maybe we do? Albert says nothing.


Monika and Albert want to stay with Cilla a while longer, but Tina can't take any more now. She goes looking for Lotta and Sandra but runs into Martin. He's had some shots, he tells her, and he's been answering questions all day. How's . . . your sister?

Tina recognizes the form of the question from way back: it means that the person asking doesn't know which of the twins he's talking to. So he asks how the other one is doing. Tina wants to be a hundred miles away, but she's been asked the question and has to be the one to tell Martin what he's done today. Couldn't someone else have been given this assignment?

Cilla? Tina answers in a faint voice. Yes, she . . . she's happy now.

I can't remember very clearly, Martin explains. But there was a hell of a smack. So she's okay, anyway?

She's HAPPY, Tina repeats so emphatically that Martin begins to suspect something. She watches the sea green of his eyes sink toward the darkness of the depths.

She's happy now? he repeats too. You can't mean that . . .

Yes, Tina nods. She's dead.

Couldn't someone else have been given this assignment? She sees all the injected tranquillity rush out of Martin. She sees him turn pale faster than she ever thought possible. She sees him stagger, then sit down on a chair that happens to be there.

No, no, no! She doesn't have the strength to stay there and pile his stones on top of her own. She runs off, finds Lotta and Sandra, leaves the hospital—away, away, she never wants to go there again, never as long as clocks go forward, never as long as time and life can't be turned back.


Somehow they end up at Sandra's place. Sit there drinking juice and listening to music. As time passes, others arrive. Finally almost all the girls in their class are there. They talk in hushed tones, cry suddenly, stop crying and go into the bathroom to make themselves presentable. When you're wearing mascara, you can't just cry to your heart's content.

Tina tells the story, how it happened, what happened. She tells it, time after time she tells it, there is always someone who has just arrived and hasn't heard it, or someone who's heard it but wants to hear it again—will it be the same story, or will Tina change it little by little?

But Tina has a tape that's running, and nothing on it can be changed. Between her recitations she talks frantically and cheerfully, comforts her friends, and sings along with the music that keeps playing and playing.

You're acting so *normal*, Tina, says Maja Sjövall suddenly. No one could tell from looking at you that Cilla has died.

Tina is startled, stops talking and looks at Maja. Has Cilla died?

Everyone has grasped it—everyone but Tina.

■   ■   ■

After a while she has to go home. Albert picks her up and drives her, down Death Road toward home. At the turnoff she realizes that in the future she will have to come here almost every day, will have to walk on the stains that have long since been worn away, will have to pass twice a day the place where Cilla died.

Almost every day, but not again today. They come home, home to an inescapable void. And the heat won't let up—Tina is sure she's going to suffocate. She can't find a place in the house where she can settle down, instead roams around the garden for a while, finds Jonny just sitting there. She lies down on the lawn next to him. He stretches out too. They look up into the sky, where not a single cloud blocks the view to eternity. *Give me a sign, Cilla!*

A few words pass between them now and then. Jonny reaches out with his hand and touches her hair. Tina reaches out and feels her hand touch his rib cage.

You're my brother.

You're my sister.

It's a magic incantation they have, a vestige from childhood, when they sometimes needed to calm themselves with a simple thought.

And because the sun slowly changes its position, they experience the strange fact that the earth they live on is still rotating on its axis, just as it did yesterday and the day before and all the other days when nothing at all happened. Can one small human being really believe in a meaning behind all this indifference?

In the evening a lot of people come to Rosengården to offer their condolences. There are Monika's relatives, who'd been planning on coming anyway because of her birthday, and there are neighbors. They all have somber faces, hug Monika, hug Tina, but are more hesitant when it comes to Albert and Jonny. Some of them try to say a few comforting words, but each attempt only proves that language lacks the words a deeply grieving person needs to hear.

Just the words *I'm sorry for your loss!* and an outstretched hand are so formal that receiving them makes you a stranger in your own heart. Tina stands there with that outstretched hand in hers and doesn't know what to do or say, only that some sort of answer is expected of her. *Think nothing of it!* can't be right, yet it's on the tip of her tongue, because it's exactly as chilly as the visitor's words.

The visits don't last long. Albert has secluded himself somewhere; the guests steal away as quietly as they came. Only Monika's brother, Jan-Olof, remains. Monika sits down and reads aloud to Tina, a fairy tale—like when the girls were little, but this one is very different from the ones she used to read back then.

There was once a very, very old soul that had lived many, many human life spans on the earth and now was almost done with its existence as a soul too; yes, soon it would fuse with and become a part of the Great Spirit that fills Eternity.

Just now the old soul felt a bit lonely sitting in the void between its last human life and the imminent Fusion. Its best friends had left; the old soul could see them down there on the earth, could see how each of them filled its human with enthusiasm, curiosity, wonder, and thoughts of all kinds.

I want to go there, said the old soul. I still have a good deal of joy left. I want to go there and give it to them.

But there's so little time until your Fusion, warned the Watchman. Of course you can give them joy, but if you are with them such a short time, you will also cause them enormous sorrow when you leave them.

I know, said the old soul. But I want to anyway. I will give them so much joy that it will help them through their sorrow later.

Then let it be as you wish, said the Watchman, and sent the old, old soul on its way.

And a human couple on Earth had a baby then that they had wanted for a long time. It was the loveliest child, one who filled them with joy from the day she was born, the unclouded joy that humans feel when their souls meet and with great delight recognize each other from Eternity.

But don't you have only a very short time remaining? whispered the mamma's soul to the old soul in the little girl.

And even though the mamma couldn't hear their conversation, the whispers aroused a foreboding in her, a whiff of the knowledge that we don't really own anything on this earth, not each other, not even ourselves. In the end everything will be taken from us, all our burdens, all the loved ones around us, finally even our lives and our bodies.

But the girl-child grew, and her joy made her mamma forget such thoughts. And her pappa was with them, and he, too, was filled with joy. Yes, the old, old soul got to live out its last time exactly as it had wished.

But time was short, even by human standards, and the day came when the Fusion was to happen. The old, old soul received the summons—that it must present itself without delay for the ceremony—and it had to obey.

To the humans it seemed as if the girl suffered a sudden death. Their sorrow was tremendous, just as the Watchman had predicted. But since all their memories of their child were of joy and only joy, they could endure their sorrow, just as the old, old soul had predicted.

And therefore, instead of having the old, old souls sit out their last little drop of time in the void, it became the custom in Eternity to send them out to give their last great joy to humans who need it. The sorrow afterwards, the inevitable sorrow—yes, the joy has given humans the strength to bear that and gradually turn it into something good.

■ ■ ■

Who's going to sleep with Tina tonight? Who's going to lie in Cilla's terrifyingly empty bed? Tina stands in the doorway for the first time today and doesn't dare to enter her room.

Jonny! she suddenly exclaims. Look!

Jonny rushes over, afraid that Tina is seeing Cilla's ghost.

But Tina points at the wall, at the clock, at Cilla's eternal clock with the lifetime guarantee, at the hands that have stopped at 7:35, at the digits that say 07:35:14, fourteen seconds after the scheduled departure of the bus that morning.

Jesus! Jonny wails. It can't be true!

But it is true. It's the nature of reality that it contains both its everyday trivialities and the special symbol-world of the fairy tales. And because the everyday is gray and ordinary, is precisely what its name says it is, we too easily draw the conclusion that when the fairy tales are verified, their truth is not real. But that is wrong. In reality, too, a mirror can crack, a picture can fall down from its hook, and a clock can stop because its owner has died.

Yes, the clock has stopped, and if Cilla had been alive now, Albert would have gone to great trouble to get his money back under the guarantee. Now he can't do that, doesn't feel like it, either: he's shut up in a room, turning over his questions. Jan-Olof's the one whose arms Monika can cry in tonight; she can look to her brother for comfort. Just as Tina finally goes into Jonny's room and sleeps next to him.

She has a good dream about Cilla. They're out biking, they swim in the sea, everything is bright and beautiful, as bright and beautiful as the best times life has offered, so bright and beautiful that she doesn't want to leave Cilla afterwards, there in the dreamworld.

But morning comes and Tina has to wake up, has to, has to. She hears Monika crying. Life will never be the same now, she knows this as she wakes up. But it has to be lived nonetheless. In time, perhaps, with joy again.

*8*

*N*ever again, never, never again! *Jamais plus!* Well, one more time—Tina will get to see Cilla one more time. It's just before the memorial service in church; Cilla is lying in the viewing room in the small building adjoining the church. Outside, it's as hot as summer and bright, so green and alive that it's hard to believe that death is so close. But it is there; inside the building its presence can be felt. It is dim and cool there, where Cilla is lying so small and childlike in her white nightgown. Next to her is the stuffed rabbit she got from Albert a long time ago, and on the other side she has the well-worn cat that Monika gave her. Around her neck she has her Bob Marley necklace, of course; why shouldn't she be wearing it?

At first Tina's glance locks onto Cilla's hands, hands that are lying there bruised and broken, as crooked as an old, old person's. But her face is clear, soft, free of pimples and of any traces of the accident. Her lips are a little blue, but otherwise she's so lovely, yes, Cilla is lovely, she is very lovely in death. And her quiet little smile confirms what so many people have said to Tina in the last few days: Cilla is happy now.

No doubt this is meant as a comfort, but Tina's the one who isn't happy, and these words aren't what she most needs to hear.

Tina stands there thinking of a poem that someone has just given her. A poem called "Mid-Term Break" has found its way here, all the way from the 1960s in Ireland, where Seamus Heaney wrote it so that Tina would find it and be moved.

*I sat all morning in the college sick bay*
*Counting bells knelling classes to a close.*
*At two o'clock our neighbours drove me home.*

*In the porch I met my father crying—*
*He had always taken funerals in his stride—*
*And Big Jim Evans saying it was a hard blow.*

*The baby cooed and laughed and rocked the pram*
*When I came in, and I was embarrassed*
*By old men standing up to shake my hand*

*And tell me they were 'sorry for my trouble'.*
*Whispers informed strangers I was the eldest,*
*Away at school, as my mother held my hand*

*In hers and coughed out angry tearless sighs.*
*At ten o'clock the ambulance arrived*
*With the corpse, stanched and bandaged by the nurses.*

*Next morning I went up into the room. Snowdrops*
*And candles soothed the bedside; I saw him*
*For the first time in six weeks. Paler now,*

*Wearing a poppy bruise on his left temple,*
*He lay in the four-foot box as in his cot.*
*No gaudy scars, the bumper knocked him clear.*

*A four-foot box, a foot for every year.*

The last line! It tugs at me, I keep reading it, only that line! I
hate it, I love it!

■ ■ ■

It's only been eight days, but they've been as long as years. Tina
went to school the day after the accident, but that was a mistake, she soon realized. Her friends wore odd expressions and
didn't know what to say or how to look when she turned up. It
was as if grief surrounded her like a bad odor. People stood there
and talked and made an effort not to let on that they smelled
it, but they failed, their efforts were obvious. Most often they
moved a little to one side as soon as they saw her; they didn't
even bother to pretend.

One reason to go to school was that there was to be a minute
of silence in the morning. And after a brief memorial address by
the principal, that minute of silence descended over the school.
If it's true that the collective power of the intense thoughts of
many people can budge death's logic and reality's truth, if it's
true that the fervent will of those people can have any effect on
how Destiny steers its steps, if it's true, if it's true, then Cilla, un-
scathed and full of life, should have come strolling across the

schoolyard as the end of that minute approached. But she didn't come, so it isn't true.


Synnöve came hurrying into the school just as Tina was sitting in the lunchroom, trying to get down the rubbery lasagna. The hell with the lasagna! Tina rushed out, into Synnöve's arms. At last Tina relaxed her tough self-control. There they stood outside the lunchroom and sobbed, the two of them, Cilla's twin sister and her drama teacher. And it was good to cry like that, it was the best thing all day.

The rest was emptiness, time that passed, the need to put one foot in front of the other in order to get anywhere. When Tina came home, she understood why she had gone to school. The silence at home was even worse. Cilla's absence inhabited every corner. Jonny stayed away completely, but Monika and Albert kept tramping around—who knows what they were up to. Only Dudde behaved normally: met her with a swish of his tail and the usual bark. But then his unconcern became as frightening as the others' grief.

The only vital person at home was Jan-Olof. He'd known Monika all his life and was her comfort now, when Albert fell short. Jan-Olof stood one step outside the family, just that little step that enabled him not to drown in a grief of his own. He hugged Tina so her stiffness softened a little, hugged her and whispered, Poor little lamb! in her ear. Poor little, little lamb!

And it was infinitely beautiful to be just that little, little in his arms.

You're strong, Tina! he said. You're going to make it through this.

And it was beautiful to hear that, too, beautiful to hear it said in a way that made her believe it, since most of the time she herself doubted that she would be able to manage much longer.

On Sunday morning Albert was poking around in a flower bed when Tina went out into the garden, trying to escape the silence of the house. He looked up when she came out, their glances happened to meet, locked on each other; they couldn't tear them away at once.

Hi! How's my girl, Albert said.

Tina smiled faintly and nodded. He dropped his small spade and stepped onto the lawn, close to her.

Could a person hug you a little? he asked.

Tina fell toward him, that was answer enough. There they stood in the middle of the bird-warbling morning and wept quietly, quietly. The same tears from the same grief.

That Albert could cry! And that he was doing it, too! This was the greatest comfort Tina could have just then, because at that moment she also learned—the insight flowed through her—that the ability to lock your feelings inside was not evidence of strength. The strong person is the one who dares to show his feelings, show his joy, show his sorrow. To be a man and cry in his daughter's hair. To be a girl-child and cry against her pappa's chest. To be a defenseless person and dare to meet another person unarmed.

If I was weak and lonely before that meeting, I left it stronger, not lonely anymore; when I went off on my own I had my pappa with me, even though he stayed behind and kept me with him as he resumed working in the flower bed.

■  ■  ■

Carina, the school psychologist, undertook to help the class, undertook to help Tina, or wanted to, but Tina was suspicious and avoided her. Carina has a reputation for not being able to keep what she hears to herself, so who can trust her? Quite a few students claim that she's full of stupid techniques and ready-made solutions for those who seek help.

Just come and talk to me if you feel you need to! she said, but Tina didn't have the least intention of taking her up on the offer.

Whatever the truth might have been about Carina, she did succeed in discovering, through her conversations with the students, that something wasn't right. She conveyed her discovery to Tina: There are a lot of guilt feelings here.

Tina didn't understand the words, Tina wasn't listening, Tina wasn't there.

Carina expressed herself more clearly, came closer, tried to be intimate: It almost seems like the class was ganging up on Cilla. Do you know anything about that?

Ganging up?

Yes. Gave her the cold shoulder, and things like that.

I would have noticed that, Tina said.

Yes, that's why I'm asking you.

But Tina didn't know about anyone ganging up on Cilla. She brushed aside Carina's question and forgot it. Until Sussy came to her and said: That Project U, you know. We're planning to follow through on it. To put the play on the way Cilla wanted it. To do it in memory of Cilla.

Aha, Tina said, and managed to press her lips together so the rest of her thought didn't come tumbling out of her: I suppose *now* the time is right, hm?

She had almost forgotten Project U, almost forgotten what

she'd been working on this winter, almost forgotten that Cilla had suddenly grown weary of struggling with her recalcitrant classmates.

Maybe it'll be okay, she said.

That was on Monday, five days after Cilla's death. We're starting rehearsals right away, Sussy explained. We're planning to put the play on at the end of May. Mag's pappa is gonna give it some publicity in the paper and on the radio.

Maybe it'll be okay, Tina repeated. Though I can't take on Cilla's job, if that's what you were thinking.

I'm sure you could.

Nope, I'm telling you I can't manage that. I'll act my own part, of course, that's all right, but I can't do Cilla's job.

It'll work out, Sussy said curtly.

Carina's right, somehow, Tina thought. There's something hostile about Sussy. Strange I haven't noticed it before!


Yes, she wound up with a great deal to ponder. In addition to all her other torments, Tina began to suspect that she'd lived right next to Cilla this winter and spring without really seeing her. What had happened: when and why did the rehearsals stop? What was that party at Vivvi's all about? We didn't go, but what was really going on? Tina searched her memory, but in every direction her view was obscured by something that had interested her more at the time. Faces got in the way: Benke, Kennet, Tobbe . . . What the hell was I doing!

She's asked herself this almost constantly since Monday; she asked it just now as she was saying goodbye to her contentedly smiling sister in the cold viewing room; and she is still asking it in the church as she sits enclosed in her thoughts at the memorial service.

Memorial service . . . yes, certainly everything's solemn here, certainly the memory of Cilla is hovering in this space. Everyone is here, everyone, everyone—to think we know so many people, Cilla! All the people are here, you're the only one missing—no, you're lying in the coffin—no, not you, your body is lying there, your spirit's abandoned garment.

Organ music, singing, and long speeches . . . there's so much to sing and say to Cilla. Someone suggested that Tina play the violin, with Einar Roxén, the music teacher, taking Cilla's part on the flute. Tina refused, she couldn't even stand the thought of it. Now two music teachers play instead, Roxén and Evy Andersson. Better this way: Tina has a hard enough time managing the simple task of sitting in the pew and listening. A third person comes up and sings unaccompanied, alone and standing erect: Lennon and McCartney's "Yesterday." As if Cilla herself had chosen the program.

Who did choose the program? Maybe the minister, maybe the music teachers, maybe Monika and Albert—by asking around, nodding or shaking their heads. Bahir offered to perform a piece he'd written specially for the service. Albert didn't like the idea; Bahir's music belonged to the general racket that didn't mean a thing to him.

If you care the least little bit about what Cilla herself wants, then you'll let Bahir play, Tina said, upset by Albert's veto.

Albert heard her and believed her—and now Ola and Bahir are firing off vibrating electronic tones the likes of which have never been heard beneath this vaulted ceiling. *Memorial Cilla*, a musical devotion in despair's most modern idiom. No matter how little Albert may think he understands of young people's music, he nonetheless finds some meaning in these cascading notes; and as he sits beside Tina now, he certainly does not regret that he allowed her to persuade him.

Now and then the congregation also gets to sing. Who selected these pieces? Lying hymns about God's goodness and glory. Where was that good God on the second of May, at 7:35 in the morning?

One other person is missing from the memorial service, one who cannot believe in the nonsense about God's good reasons for everything that happens. Martin isn't here.

On Monday Jonny told Tina that Martin had taken his car up to the Cliffs and driven it over the edge. At first Tina thought she was being told of his suicide, that yet another horror had struck close to her, but soon it became clear that he had rolled the car over the edge while staying behind to watch its final journey: the drop through the air, so much better portrayed in hundreds of action films, the crash into the water, the sinking to the bottom. Afterwards he went home and cut his driver's license into tiny, tiny pieces. Never again, never, never again.

So, he's alive after all. Alive, but not very well. No one has accused him of anything, but since the accident he hasn't dared to come to Rosengården, and he doesn't dare to come to the memorial service either. Somewhere or other he's brooding, can't look people in the eye. His parents watch him closely, anxious about what he might do.

The memorial service is exactly what its name says and nothing more. Cilla is evoked time after time and finally delivered into the Lord's hands. The burial will take place later, with a much simpler ceremony. They've already chosen a plot, but it will be a little while before Cilla can move there.

Monika wanted them to bury Cilla at home in the garden, but Tina protested in shock. Albert didn't think it was a very good idea either. One of the church's employees showed them a spot, at the extreme end of the churchyard, that looked out over the smiling paradise of this region. They liked it.

Yes, the soil is really good here, the man commented.

He didn't notice their astonishment. He didn't hear them discussing later whether they should have Cilla buried somewhere else, someplace where there weren't any people like him. But it was probably no use searching for that place. Presumably there were people like him everywhere.

*9*

*E*mptiness, loneliness, silence! How would Tina ever have gotten through the month of May if she hadn't been able to immerse herself in the play they were working on? No one could imagine how, least of all Tina. In memory of Cilla, Sussy had said. But she might just as well have said, In support of Tina.

Of course it was hard when they started, before anyone wanted to put on Cilla's director's hat. Sometimes they turned to Tina with their questions, but she couldn't cope with that, couldn't cope. Without any formal decision, it fell to Sandra to take Cilla's place and explain how she wanted things done. This was fitting, everyone felt it was fitting. After all, Sandra was the one Cilla had liked best, the one who'd put up with Cilla's oddness for the longest time that winter, the one who'd never really gone along with freezing her out. Now Sandra's interpretations made Cilla's purposes clear; the class forgot, or forgave, that she had been a pain. "In Memory of Cilla" became "For the Rehabilitation of Cilla," though no one put this into words.

There were some students who didn't need very much direction now. Fredde Lindgren, for example, was guided by the memory of how Cilla would send her sharp blue gaze deep into his being and explain that he, better than anyone else, could play the loathsome estate owner, because he himself was the exact opposite. A cruel person can never portray cruelty convincingly, Cilla told Fredde. To do that, you have to have goodness and warmth.

Sandra, of course, didn't know anything about such directions, because Cilla had given them only to the boys and had spoken softly. Intensely, so her words were unforgettable. Fredde truly was acting in memory of Cilla.

But Sandra, too, knew what she was doing. And whatever she didn't know to begin with she soon learned. Tina watched Sandra flying from one task to the next. Her lively, glistening face, her arresting glances as she gave directions. How beautiful her enthusiasm makes her!

In the wings there is someone watching Tina as she works on her role. How her face awakens from its stiffness, how her gaze focuses inward toward her core, how her body calls out its wordless language. How beautiful her enthusiasm makes her!

Sandra didn't dare to give Tina directions. The twins' identical likeness made it feel like directing Cilla, so Sandra got flustered every time she tried. Tina would have to interpret her role on her own. And Tina felt that right now this was all she had to live for, so she was happy to do the interpreting; she entered her role and was liberated from her reality for several hours a day for the rest of the month.

■

On Ascension Day and the following Friday, Saturday, and Sunday, they performed *Let U = Unexploited* on the main stage at Town Hall. At first they'd thought of using the stage at school, but Mag's pappa swung into action with all the promotional machinery at his disposal, and soon it was clear that the school's small auditorium wouldn't be big enough. Town Hall had 1,024 seats, and there were people standing along the walls as well. More than four thousand people paid for seats; close to five thousand in total attended the play during its four performances.

The play was a success. The review in the local newspaper was a rave. *Astonishingly professional performances by a group of junior-high-school students*, it said. Sandra's acting and directing were called highly promising. Tina earned praise for her intense style of acting. Fredde's repulsive estate owner raised the temperature in the theater by several degrees, the reviewer thought.

After such praise in the Friday paper, the cast was on cloud nine and fired off the three remaining performances with a wild energy that took the audience's breath away. After the Sunday performance, Sandra came onstage alone. Small and gleaming in the narrow cone of light from the spotlight, she stood there holding all the flowers she'd been given and told the audience that the class had put on this play to honor the memory of Cecilia Dubois, who had been the original force behind it but had died in a traffic accident almost a month earlier, before the play was finished. And we will now follow her wishes and contribute all the proceeds to projects in underdeveloped countries.

Most of those present knew this already, but Sandra's improvised speech clearly gripped the audience nonetheless, and no one stopped to think that Cilla's real name was Cilibelle. Sandra's lonely little figure seemed to fill the whole stage for a time; then applause broke out again, and after that it was all over.

■ ■ ■

Yes, it was all over, but it had a lasting effect: the class had been changed by the intense work. They regarded one another with respect and warmth; all envy and egotism were gone. You've mastered something, I've mastered something, together we can do anything.

All the teachers had seen the play and read the review, and now they retroactively forgave the students for their flagging attention and poorly done homework during May. Forgave, yes, but now we have to make a really big effort in the days that are left and see what we can do to catch up.


Catch up? Big effort! When that sort of reality resumes for Tina, she discovers how weak she still is in her enormous loneliness, discovers that her intense work on the play was a form of escape. She had laughed for a moment now and then; and for long stretches she was able to do something like forget. But now she's back almost at square one, even though it's June according to her daybook—an ordinary calendar, that is. Tina hasn't touched her diary, where time stopped on May 2nd. Now she has sat down for the first time since Cilla's death to try to compose herself enough to write in her diary. The last time she wrote a few words there it was March.

*So much has happened,* she begins, but is immediately at a loss and raises her eyes to the mirror. Sees Cilla, there behind the looking glass, simultaneously raise her head from her diary and meet her glance. So much has happened. Should I really write about the accident, Cilla? A person keeps a diary to remember, but I know for sure I'll never forget that, no matter what.

Write a few words anyway, Cilla answers.

*So much has happened. About a month ago Cilla was hit by a car and died. To be precise: on my mamma's birthday, the second of May.*

She asks the mirror for advice again. It's okay, Cilla nods. Don't ask me about everything! It's your diary, after all.

My diary? Watch this.

*So the rest of this book is for you, Cilla! Did you hear that? You can read my diary. How does that feel?*

Cilla laughs. By all means. I do what I want to, of course, but it's nice to have permission; then I won't have to feel ashamed.

I've composed a poem, Tina says, and changes books—because poems have to be written in a special, separate book, which Cilla gave her. *To Tina from Cilla, on our 13th birthday,* it says on the first page. On the cover Cilla drew a peace dove, and on the inside front cover she wrote:

> *The deepest feelings*
> > *hide furthest inside you*
> *among the unspoken words.*

How many unspoken words I have for you, murmurs Tina. We talked about so much, but maybe the deepest feelings never get said—yes, it's just like you've written. But I've composed a poem. It's time for you to read it.

Gladly! Cilla says, and she, too, rummages through some papers in front of her.

Tina writes out a fair copy of the poem in a slow, beautiful hand:

*She's gone.*
*Will never come back*
*ever again.*
*Gone forever.*

*She's dead.*
*I can't, I won't*
*believe it.*
*It's impossible.*

*She was here*
*a second ago,*
*laughing, talking,*
*so happy and alive.*

*Then she took a step,*
*just a single step*
*and life will never be*
*the same again.*

*My whole life*
*she's been with me,*
*we've never*
*been apart.*

*Now*
*and for the rest of my life*
*I have to manage*
*without her.*

*But her memory is alive*
*in my heart.*

*Here she has her own place*
*and can stay forever.*

Congrats on having gotten it at last, Cilla sighs, when Tina has finished. I will always be with you, *j'en jure*. Closer than ever before. Don't forget that! And lighten up, Tina!

Tina is back to her diary:

*Everyone's so terribly sad, Cilla. Especially me—so damned*
*sad. I miss you, I miss you, I miss you!*

She looks up and meets Cilla's eyes, as sorrowful and blue as her own. And Monika is sad, she tells Cilla. Albert is sad, Jonny is never home, it's so sad here—you just can't imagine what you've done to us. How the hell could you!

Write, says Cilla. Don't talk; write.

*Cilla, you're not mad at me, are you? I've been silly so often,*
*but . . . Please, don't be mad.*
*I care about you so very much.*

Now she has to say it aloud nonetheless: I care about you so very much.

Cilla says the same thing at the same time: I care about you so very much.

To think that I could never say that to you while you were alive!

Oh yes you did—it got said now and then, Cilla objects.

Did it really? All I remember is being touchy all the time. But I didn't mean anything by it, I swear.

I know, Cilla says. I know! I care about you so very much. I love you, Tina!


Suddenly Tina is telling Cilla about the whole play, telling her how great it turned out, telling her what Sandra accomplished, telling it all in a voice that little by little grows steady and strong. She gets up and acts out small scenes in front of the mirror. Cilla pays close attention the whole time, repeats and imitates, laughs along with Tina at the punch lines.

And the party afterwards, on Sunday, you shoulda been there! God what fun we had! Fredde Lindgren had a fit and chased me up the stairs! Then we improvised a pop concert and in the middle of it all Synnöve shows up and says we should guess how much the proceeds came to. She helped us with money and stuff like that, nothing else. Nobody could guess, of course. Come on! she says, Don't they teach you math in school anymore? Town Hall didn't charge a rental fee, everyone volunteered, you know the costumes didn't cost us anything, there were a thousand seats and four nights—so? Guess what it came to, Cilla!

Tina stops and points a finger at her sister. You haven't gotten one bit better at math, have you?

Cilla shakes her head and laughs.

Okay! In that case you get it as an exercise! I'm not gonna tell you.

She flops down again and writes in cheerful, curving letters:

*It looks like Fredde Lindgren likes me.*

Tina! moans Cilla. It's me he likes.

Shit, you always have to spoil things! Tina scolds. You can't stand it that the boys go for me, you're so jealous that you'd do anything to . . .

**O my God, what am I saying! Forgive me, Cilla, forgive me!**

*I'm scared! Cilla, can you understand that!*
*Are you thinking of taking revenge on me for something?*
*That wouldn't be like you, I think, but what do I know?*
                    *Forgive me, Cilla!*
                    *Give me a sign!*

A sign? That night I dream about Cilla for the first time since that strange dream I had just after she died. This is a very different sort of dream. It's strangely shadowy on the porch when she comes walking toward me. She comes the way she usually does, but doesn't pay any attention to me. Her face is angry, but she doesn't say anything. She has a letter for Sandra, but for me she has nothing. She pretends I don't exist. When I walk up to her and take hold of her to make her talk, she fades away.

■  ■  ■

A new bout of hell has begun, as if Tina hasn't had enough already. Her sleep is disturbed by bad dreams. Cilla comes at night, and in almost every dream they quarrel with each other. Cilla is angry and Tina is angry and hate flashes between them in dream after dream. Sometimes Cilla wants to be treated normally—they're not supposed to mention that she's dead—but at the same time she's so nasty that Tina screams at her to go away. At other times she's small and lonely and sad, and she weeps and weeps, so Tina starts crying too and wakes up with her cheeks wet and her palm stroking the empty space above the pillow where Cilla has always been—always, always, but not now.

In the end Tina doesn't dare to go to sleep. She lies in bed reading until the words start spinning before her eyes, she sits up, roams around, plays music, and keeps herself awake, anything to ward off the nightmares. When Cilla comes anyway, it's twice as bad, since Tina believes that she's awake and persists in that belief as Cilla fades away and she wakes up for real. Then she has to go and check Dudde, in case Cilla has really cut his ears off. Dudde looks up, startled from his sleep, when she comes and hugs him. He's sleeping peacefully, and he's still got his ears. Thank God—it was only a dream!


One night when she's wandering around the house, she runs into Albert. He has the same problem, she discovers from his slow words in the night. He quarrels with Cilla, hits her, and drives her out of the house almost every night. Wakes up with the anguish high in his throat and can't get rid of it.

They sit in the kitchen in the morning twilight, close to each other and crying together in their misery.

I know I've been horrible to both of you, Albert says. *Terrible!* he adds in French. Now I'm getting paid back. In the daytime I see you, and then you have Cilla's face. You conjure her up inside me, your sad face blames me for the despair she felt when I was nasty to her, no matter how hard I try to convince myself that you're you and that your grief is your own. At night she comes and blames me herself for all the pain I caused her.

You weren't *that* awful, Tina consoles him—yes, she can see that these words really do console him.

But that she can't leave *you* in peace . . . he muses.

We quarreled too, Tina explains. Though not like we do in these dreams, of course. And I said terrible things to Cilla. Maybe she wants revenge?

But Cilla was good-hearted, wasn't she? Albert asks in a pitiful voice. *Le cœur sur le main.* Why would she suddenly turn spiteful after death? She must have understood—at least, by now she must surely see and understand that deep down we didn't mean any harm, no matter what we may have done, don't you think? Surely it's what you mean deep down that counts, isn't it? Isn't that what God takes account of?

Do you believe in God, Pappa?

Albert straightens up. I didn't say that! *D'ailleurs*, we can't sit here blaming Cilla for our dreams. We cook them up ourselves, after all.

To cook something up, you have to get the ingredients from somewhere, Tina points out. When I'm awake and think about it, I can only remember good things about Cilla. But these dreams that I cook up—where do I get the ingredients for them?

This is tough, Albert says. I think we should get in touch with a psychologist. For your sake, at the very least. I'll manage well enough, but you need someone to talk this through with. Things can't go on like this.

■ ■ ■

No, things can't go on like this. Tina isn't at all well on the inside, but it's impossible to get hold of a psychologist at the beginning of the summer vacation. Instead, Monika and Albert decide to rearrange their holiday plans a little and set out on a two-week sailing trip with Tina. That way they'll be away from Rosengården for her birthday and Midsummer, they've figured out. They think this will be better than staying at home for those days and pretending to celebrate, as if everything were the same as usual.

At first Tina agrees, but when they've gotten well out onto the water, she realizes with horror that she, at least, is not going to have a moment's vacation in the next fourteen days. You can't call it a vacation to be sitting in the same boat as two terrifically depressed people! She has to watch over them, keep watch day and night, she doesn't know what they might decide to do.

For their part Monika and Albert probably think they're doing everything they can to relieve the pressure. They hold a stiffly cheerful birthday party for Tina on the open sea, and on Midsummer Night they join in the dancing on a pier where they're strangers and where, amid much laughter and high spirits, they match Tina up with a cute guy whose tan is deeper than the water. And Tina plays along with their comedy—she especially approves of the guy—but still, still, the grief still weighs heavily on them and won't let up, will not let up.

They don't mention Cilla once, don't let her into their pretend happiness. But in the long silences that arise, she is close to them, is sitting in the boat, invisible herself, though she casts an enormous shadow that covers all three of them. They sit there, each in a separate space, and remember other summers, when Cilla was with them and she and Tina darted around pretending to be deckhands. A ton of photos at home show what they looked like. Now not a single photo is taken; it's not clear whether the camera has even made it onto the boat.

And Tina keeps up her vigil. There are many ways to leave this life, but disappearing together with Monika and Albert into the silence and oblivion at the bottom of the sea is not the way Tina wants to go. Nor does she want them to depart without her. God knows what they might decide to do; Tina alone bears the burden of making sure they don't do it.

Maybe it's because she's been keeping watch, or maybe it's because they're more sensible than she thinks, but in any case, they anchor in their usual berth in the harbor after fourteen days of sailing, and Tina can breathe again. The harbor master, Börje, is watching them as always when they sail in. Your boat looked empty! he says as they climb ashore.

At that, Tina plops down and weeps. But Börje's right, of course; that's exactly what they've all felt during the whole sailing trip. There have been three of them in the boat, where there used to be four. And what occupied the most space was the emptiness left by the missing one.

# 10

Tina leafs through the mail that's piled up while she was away. Lots of birthday cards. Thanks, thanks, but she can't bear to read them right now.

Grayn, a neighbor just to the north, arrives with Dudde, who's overjoyed at seeing them, races around and doesn't know whom to lunge at first.

Nice to see there's some life in the mutt after all, Grayn says. He's done nothing but lie there staring out into space the whole time. I thought he was sick and about to kick the bucket.

Not Dudde, naaaaaah, says Albert, while ruffling the dog's coat.

Tina walks around the house for a while. Comes to her stifling room, opens the window, and sits down at the desk. Is a little startled to see Cilla sit down opposite her. Shit, I'm never going to get used to it, Tina sighs, but then she tells Cilla: I've been out sailing. What an ordeal!

Cilla nods. Tina opens her diary, fills facing pages with her only thought:

Cilla, Cilla, Cilla, Cilla, Cilla,
Cilla, Cilla, Cilla, Cilla,
Cilla, Cilla, Cilla, Cilla,
Cilla, Cilla, Cilla, Cilla,
Cilla, Cilla, Cilla, Cilla,
Cilla, Cilla, Cilla, Cilla, Cilla,
Cilla, Cilla, Cilla, Cilla, Cilla,
Cilla, Cilla, Cilla, Cilla, Cilla,
Cilla, Cilla, Cilla, Cilla, Cilla,
Cilla, Cilla, Cilla, Cilla, Cilla,
Cilla, Cilla, Cilla, Cilla, Cilla,
Cilla, Cilla, Cilla, Cilla,
Cilla, Cilla, Cilla, Cilla

I miss you, miss you, miss
you, miss you, miss you,
miss you, miss you, miss
you, miss you, miss you,
miss you, miss you, miss.
you, miss you, miss you, miss
you, miss you, miss you,
miss you, miss you,
miss you, miss you, miss
you, miss you, miss you,
miss you, miss you,
miss you, miss you, miss
you, miss you, miss
you, miss you, miss you

You can't keep moping around like this! Albert says, suddenly hard and unsympathetic. Find something to do! Clean up your room! Cilla's things can't stay there for all eternity. Sort them, dump them, save them, whatever, but *organize*, make an effort!

Clean? Organize? Tina looks around. This is how their room has looked since the second of May; the calendar pages haven't even been torn off. But it's true, Albert is right: who's to go through Cilla's stuff, if not Tina? You and I, we kept no secrets from each other, after all, did we? Whatever I find when I start digging through your stuff, I'm sure to know about it already.

Your diary, your poems, your thoughts . . . what's yours is mine, isn't it?

Cilla answers her from her space behind the mirror: What's yours is mine . . . but she too finishes with a hesitant question: . . . isn't it?

Who would think it could be so tiring to turn pages and move papers around! Sort and dump, Albert said, but everything has to be saved, of course. You wanted to do so much, Cilla! How can I throw out your stories, poems, film scripts . . . *We* wanted to do so much, Cilla. So much together. Here's the strip about Pia, the Film Star, that you drew when it was raining last summer. Pia is you or me or both of us. If I throw out these papers, I'm throwing out a piece of you. The short story about Linda Nilsson, who commits suicide . . . Everyone's unhappy in your stories, Cilla. All your poems are melancholy. If mine weren't the same, I'd think you were terribly depressed. It's not like that, of course, it's just that even when a person's happy it's somehow more fun to write about sad things.

A cassette turns up in the mess: *Ola and Bahir play Cilla*. Tina reads the little note she hasn't seen before:

> *It's even more magical*
> *that a person*
> *can be certain music.*
> *This is Cilla!*
> > *Bahir*

Tina puts the cassette in the tape deck and plays it. The notes unroll their tapestry in the room. They're familiar now, and not just to Tina. The summer has barely begun, but Ola and Bahir are already a smashing success. The public and the critics lie at their feet. If that happens, this cassette will be worth a fortune, Tina said in the spring. And now it is, yes, it's worth even more than a fortune. Now it can't be valued in money at all.

*Cilla Suite* in particular has attracted a great deal of notice. "It's wonderful to see someone dare to rely entirely on music, in this age of miserable lyrics," Tina read in a review. "We get to imagine for ourselves the Cilla that Ola and Bahir paint with their music. It is a loving portrait. There's an ecstatic joy in it but this ends up ringing with pain. A mature work by two young musicians."

A loving portrait. If Bahir only knew! Because surely he doesn't, does he? Cilla could really keep her mouth shut. Not even Tina had the least suspicion. Not until the night after the NVG rally, when Cilla flung out that remark about how Tina didn't seem to get on very well with any of her boys. That was so mean, Tina thought; so she went upstairs and just screamed and punched the wall. And Cilla sat hunched up on her bed and chewed her nails down to nothing because I'd said that no one wanted her because she was gay. But I didn't mean that, of course, I just wanted to get in a jab, but instead she scored a direct hit on me, because I was so hopelessly unhappily in love with Martin and he looked at her much more than at me, I thought.

Finally I couldn't stand slamming the wall and went over and hit her on the knee with my fist, *thump:* You're so *dumb!* and then I went and sat on my bed just like her, though I chewed on my lower lip the way I do when I get sad. Then she came over, after a minute, and whacked me on the knee the same way: You're so *dumb!* and then went back to her bed.

After a while I went over and hit her on the knee again, *Dumb!* and then she came and hit me the same way, *Dumb!* There was one more round before we started laughing at each other and ourselves, mainly at ourselves. And Cilla stayed in my bed and we talked about the evening we'd just had and suddenly I found out that Cilla was in love with Bahir! Completely unexpected for me, somehow she hadn't dared to tell me before, hadn't shown any sign of it at all, not a hint, not even enough so Bahir could have the slightest suspicion.

She was a totally different person when she talked about him. And even though she let me in on her secret, I still felt like I was on the outside and so incredibly inferior. This thing that Cilla was talking about, this was something big, bigger than everything else. Love? Yes, for sure. Compared to what I could glimpse in her eyes, everything I'd been involved in was just a game. Exactly as she'd once said, though at the time I thought she was just trying to calm me down. It was very odd to suddenly feel like a little sister.

We would talk about everything as we lay next to each other in my bed or Cilla's, everything, night after night, no matter how the day had gone, and that's how things always got to be okay in the end. But this was in fact the first time we realized how we would one day be forced to separate. Unless we found two indistinguishable twin guys, someday we would have to be separated by love—isn't that odd!

We fantasized for a long time about the twin boys, how the mix-ups would go in all directions, but we didn't really believe in that future. For me it was Martin that counted, for Cilla it was Bahir. No twins at all! The only thing they had in common was that they were both much too old for us.

That doesn't mean anything, Cilla said. Age doesn't mean anything. Love knows no age limits.

You don't have to tell *me* that, I said. I'm the one who loves you even though you're so young!

She hugged me. Auntie ith tho thweet! she lisped. Hope I can grow old jutht ath grathefully ath you!

■

Everything that Cilla wrote has been seen by Tina before, her
film scripts and stories, her poems and her diary, though the
diary's been read mainly on the sly. So Tina is not prepared for
any surprises when she starts leafing through a notebook that
looks like one you'd use for doing homework. *SECRET!* is written on the first page, however. And the second page starts: *I can
talk to Tina about everything—everything but this.*

Tina slams the notebook shut, shouts inside herself the disturbing discovery she's made: Cilla had a secret diary, an extra
one in addition to the one she'd let Tina read on the sly! And
I find out *now*! Sister, my darling sister!

Tina can feel that she hasn't got the strength for this yet. In
the notebook there are sure to be things that will be painful to
read. Tina's in enough pain already. She hurts just from suddenly finding out that Cilla couldn't talk to her about certain
things.

Is it really all right for me to read it, she asks, or is it still secret from me?

Cilla doesn't answer. Holds her secret in her hand and looks
back with the same question on her face.

Can I? Tina repeats, and sees Cilla mimic her.

Hell! Tina bursts out and falls forward onto the desk, crying.
She's suddenly realized that she's seeing herself in the mirror.
She knew this already, of course, knew it in a way, but she succeeded nonetheless in imagining that Cilla was there. But then
Cilla mimicked her instantly and more exactly than she'd ever
done in their childhood mirror game, so the fantasy ended on
the spot, and that hurt—it hurt, it hurt, it hurt!

It also hurts to have to decide myself if *SECRET* means secret forever and for everyone, for me too, so secret that the

diary should be destroyed. It hurts to decide if I really want to read it, and if so, whether it's from love or curiosity that I want to. I feel so *dirty* going through your things, Cilla!

■ ■ ■

Two packages have arrived, one for Cilla, one for Tina, with materials for the Literature and Drama Camp in August. Tina leaves Cilla's alone but opens hers and takes a peek. She can see from the detailed program that there won't be any dead patches at this camp.

She leafs listlessly through books and pamphlets. Should I send word that I'm not coming, maybe? After all, it was you who really wanted to go; I don't think this looks like much fun. Not without you, anyway.

One photocopied page catches her eye:

A: *The fairy tales lie, Beloved Sister. In reality there is no Salikon, no flowering rosebush to crawl behind, no hole in the ground leading to you. You're surely a queen there, but no entrance to that place exists.*

Salikon! Beloved Sister! Do you remember that book, Cilla!

What a question! Of course I remember. That was our favorite book, after all.

And when I told the story at day care, everyone said, But you have your sister. Yes, I certainly did! We went around calling each other Beloved Sister. We had exactly what all the others wished for. How many times I've thought about that . . .

. . . and said it too, Cilla points out.

. . . every time we lay talking far into the night about everything, absolutely everything, I thought . . .

. . . and said . . .

. . . that the best thing a person could wish for—is what I've got! No one can try to say I didn't realize how lucky I was before I lost you.

You haven't lost me, Cilla reminds her. We're just as close to each other as always.

Tina looks thoughtfully into the mirror. I think I'm going nuts, she says, talking more to herself now. I see you and hear you, even though you don't exist. Can grief drive you out of your mind?

You *know* I exist, Cilla says. There's nothing nuts about it.

Tina stops reasoning and reads on. What sort of script is this anyway, the one that builds on *My Very Own Sister*? She finds this:

P: *I wonder . . . If I could ask you?*
A: *Ask what?*
P: *Do I look like her? A little?*
A: *Who?*
P: *Her—your . . . sister.*
A: *(examines P closely; P turns away slightly, embarrassed):*
  *She looked exactly like me.*

Now Tina is hooked. This is a film script that deals with a single twin! It's even called *The Single Twin*. She forgets everything else and reads, keeps reading. Toward morning, when she's read to the end, she knows that she's finally received the sign she's been waiting for. The film script was written by the Director, the one who's coming to the camp. This script will be discussed there. It's only a draft, the program says. Something to work around; and the Director would be grateful for any comments.

Of course I have to go to the camp—of course! Thanks, Cilla, you knew this when you arranged for us to go.

Tina sits down in the early morning and writes a letter to the Director.

*Hi!*

*I'm a fourteen-year-old girl. Two months ago the impossible happened. My twin sister Cilla died in a traffic accident. I was with her when it happened. She got hit by a car when we were trying to catch the bus to school on my mamma's birthday.*

*I've just read your script* The Single Twin *and I'm sure you can understand why it speaks to me. In August I'm going to the camp that you're going to be at too. I'm wondering if you could give me a few hours then, because I'd very much like to talk to you. From the program it looks like there should be two hours free on Thursday between 12:30 and 2:30. Can you meet me? It's very important to me, so I'm hoping hoping!!!*

*Tina Dubois*

She writes her address and encloses a stamp so the Director will understand that she wants him to reply. Then she dashes to the mailbox, mails the letter, and is back before anyone has woken up. They're lying there asleep and don't have the slightest suspicion that Tina has received the Sign!

*11*

For the next few days life consists of feverish waiting. Tina reads the rest of the material in a snap and becomes more and more certain that the camp is going to be her great experience of the summer.

In her enthusiasm she sometimes forgets to keep watch over Monika and Albert. But only briefly. Then she comes to herself with a start and rushes back to her sentry post. Nothing happens to give her grounds for her anxiety about what they might decide to do. Nothing happens, but their eyes avoid hers, glide away, hide their dark secrets. Secret black thunderclouds hang threateningly above her days, yes, above her nights too.

I can't stay interested! Monika weeps, her voice wild and heartrending, when Albert reproaches her for neglecting her work. Can't you understand that!

They don't mean for Tina to hear them quarreling, but she does. Albert complains, as if software were something that rots if it lies around. For his part, he escapes to the office, to the computers' air-conditioned rooms, where he can soothe his overheated thoughts with cool routines.

He comes home and blinks at the rosebushes. Monika is standing at the window and staring into space. Tina is tense, locks the fire of grief inside her. She doesn't dare to let any of it out, everything's so flammable here—just now it isn't true that the stuff of sorrow is tears.


Even though Tina waits eagerly, she's surprised when the Director's answer arrives so fast. And even though she's been hoping for a positive response, she nearly bursts with joy when he writes that he'll gladly give her as much time as she likes—there's sure to be much more than two hours free in a whole week.

Only after a few euphoric days have passed does the cold light of reflection make her ask herself what she really wants to talk to the Director about.

My God, what am I gonna say? she asks Cilla. This is gonna be the biggest flop of all time! I've made a complete fool of myself!

You have to tell him about our lives, of course, Cilla explains. And about your life as a single twin. I'll see to it that he's interested, so he'll agree to make a film about it together with us. You'll win an Oscar, the first teenage actor to get one . . .

. . . and all the money will go to the National Association for Traffic Victims, if there is one, Tina fills in.

Yikes! There's a crash on the ground floor and Albert can be heard swearing. He stalks around, throwing things and screaming, *Allez au diable!* Finally, one of his fits of anger; finally, something that's the same as before, when they dared to live! He hasn't raged like this since that time in the spring when he was supposed to be helping Cilla with her math. Helping was the word, but he got furious because she couldn't do it, screamed that she was an imbecile, and forced her to calculate in her head, which of course didn't go any better. Cilla cried and Albert roared about lazy girls with nothing but fluff in their skulls. Count on your fingers, at least . . . no, that won't work either, since you've eaten them up. Tina ran to Monika and begged her to step in, but as usual she thought it was best for the girls to cope with this sort of situation on their own. But they couldn't cope with it at all. Everything froze up and went from impossible to hateful. I'm going to murder him, murder, *j'en jure*! Cilla promised and bit off yet another piece of fingernail. Responding with hatred can't be regarded as coping with your pappa's anger. You can't bear to hate someone you love, you can't cope with that at all. And so you bite your nails . . . It's odd, but I'd almost *forgotten* you did that, Cilla!

But when Albert blows up again now after all the silence, to Tina the outburst feels like a relief. Strange, strange, because before she always felt afraid. But why is he so furious? *Diantre!* he shouts, and something smashes.

Get out of here! Monika yells. Go outside and chop wood or something!

If they were here, I'd wring their necks! Albert roars, and kicks something.

Go lift that boulder in the garden and carry it away! Monika suggests.

Damned bastards! Vultures!

Little by little they piece together the fragments and begin to understand what's made him so mad. A woman phoned and offered him the opportunity to buy return-address labels, the kind you stick on your letters, the proceeds go to mumble-mumble.

To what?

The association for traffic victims. It's a national organization. The National Association for Traffic Victims.

I see. Albert weighed the matter, thought for a bit, and said: That certainly sounds like a worthy cause.

Yes, I was sure you'd think so. After what happened.

That set the bomb off. The woman no doubt thanked her lucky stars that there was a long telephone wire between her and the raging Albert. She'd said her name, but it vanished in the hurricane that ensued.

Disgusting, Tina agrees, but she's also thinking about something else, feels a shiver down her spine at the thought: It happened exactly when I promised Cilla to give all the money to that association!

■　■　■

The telephone rings and Tina answers with a flat Hello.

Hi!

Hi?

It's Lotta!

Lotta? No . . . Tina gropes. Do you want to talk to Tina? This is Cilla. Tina's out just now.

She hears a gasp from Lotta, then it's silent for a long while.

Why did you do that? her voice asks; it's small and thin, barely manages to make it out of the receiver and into Tina. I wanted . . . I'm wondering . . .

Lotta stammers for a while but finally gets to the point and asks if she can come out to Rosengården and . . . and talk a little. In the meantime, Tina's head has cleared. Yes, why did I do that? Of course Lotta can come over. *Lotta is my best friend!*

And Lotta comes over; her pappa drives her and disappears as soon as she's gotten out of the car. At the same time, Sandra comes walking down from the bus stop. I was thinking . . . she says, with the same hesitancy that made Lotta stumble. Even though it isn't . . . may not be the right time . . . but then I can . . .

But Tina has a smile on her face that's big enough for both of them. She'd almost forgotten that people existed. And then two of them arrive from the distant real world, classmates from the seventh grade a long, long time ago. Without having consulted each other, they happen to arrive at the same time, each from her own direction—so Fate must have wanted it this way.

Fate wanted—but what did they themselves want? Tina sits there trying to interpret their silence. The juice in their glasses grows tepid by the time she realizes from their quick glances and cautious words that they've come to see her and talk to her— her, Tina; to make sure that she's making progress, that she's alive; to hear that her voice is the same. Yes, when everything's been changed and turned upside down, you want something to be the same as before.

These days Tina doesn't feel much like the person she was until recently, or rather, the person she was a long time ago, back in the seventh grade, but when she senses their awkward concern she's so moved that tears catch her off guard and overflow. Sandra's there with a hug at once; she's crying too. Lotta hugs them both, puts her arms around them but doesn't cry, not this time. Now she's a comforting murmur that says, It's good for you to cry, Tina, you were so hard before, so unnaturally cheerful that I was afraid; now I'm not afraid anymore. Jesus, it must be awfully tough for you! And for you too, Sandra.

It's not much, compared to . . . Sandra sniffs, close to Tina's ear.

Compared to? Cilla was so fond of Sandra, doesn't that make it tough enough? Yes and no, because that's not really where the pain comes from. What's tough for Sandra, as Tina and Lotta can understand, is that she let Cilla down, or feels that she did, when she finally caved in to the pressure from the many students who wanted to freeze Cilla out. Conscience, in short: that's what's paining Sandra. She came here today to compare her torment to Tina's, and maybe to get some relief by seeing that Tina's was greater.

They stroll down to the churchyard, to Cilla's grave.

I think this is exactly the way Cilla wanted it to be, Tina declares as she waters the flowers: pansies above Cilla's face, roses above her chest and belly, more pansies above her legs. Water for all the flowers that watch over my sister . . . Sometimes, when Cilla was depressed, she used to ask if we would cry at her funeral. Everyone says things like that, I guess?

Everyone says things like that, Lotta hastens to confirm.

Sure, nods Sandra. Though I've stopped talking like that. Now.

Exactly! Lotta seconds that, too.

We certainly cried enough, Tina thinks aloud. I wanted the grave to be a little different at first. With lots of things written on the stone. But now I think it's fine like this.

They read the stone: Cilla's name, the date of the beginning and the date of the end of her short life.

Imagine dying before you've turned fourteen, Lotta ponders. Before you've, like, managed to *do* anything.

Tina feels the objection rising in her even before Sandra says it: But Cilla really managed to do a lot. Project U—wasn't that something?

Yes, sure, but I mean . . .

They know what Lotta means, of course. It's just that you have to express yourself very precisely when you're standing with bereaved people at a fresh grave. Have to say exactly what you mean. Preferably not say anything at all. *The deepest feelings hide furthest inside you among the unspoken words.* If the words are uttered, the feelings from that secret place may not be able to cope with being suddenly exposed to the harsh light.

Now the girls sit on a bench near Cilla's resting place and look at the beautiful view she has.

Although, it's largely thanks to you that Project U turned out as it did, Tina says, looking out over the slope.

Nah! Sandra says. I just put on the final touches. Cilla had it almost ready, after all . . . Sandra interrupts herself: Shit! Can she ever forgive me, do you think?

She had a letter for you, Tina answers, still talking into the air. She didn't want to talk to me, but she had a letter for you. She pretended I wasn't there.

Lotta puts a hand on Tina's shoulder, a reassuring pressure.

Did you read it? Sandra asks.

It's all just one long nightmare, Tina says. I'm just waiting to wake up from it.

I think Cilla will forgive everyone for everything, Lotta declares. She's an angel or a star now and understands everything in exactly the right way. She's not angry at anyone, she's our guardian angel. That's what I think, anyway.

*Lotta is my best friend!*


They come over several times. One day Lotta, another day Sandra, sometimes both on the same day, without having arranged it with each other. They want to talk about Cilla, they want

Tina to talk, they want to compare their thoughts, they want to be with Tina. And more important than all these things they want is the joy they feel when they see that their warmth is doing Tina some good. To talk and talk and talk—that's good for Tina. It does her good to be able to say, after a night full of nightmares: I'm so scared that Cilla will take revenge for something I've done!—to say it without immediately being reproached for thinking bad thoughts about her sister.

No one will ever be able to give an account of everything the three girls said to one another during this period, how they could find the right words so that one became a comfort for the other who became a support for the third who became a joy for the first again and again. No one was there to take minutes at their meetings, and the girls themselves were too deeply absorbed in their own and one another's hearts to be able to give any details to the world around them.

Long afterwards, Tina sums up her impressions from that time—that is, July, roughly speaking, the time between the sailing trip and the camp—sums them up in the thought that two people really meant something to me then. Not Mamma. She was so busy with her own grief. I had to play a role for her the whole time, play Cilla's role in order to cheer her up. Not Pappa. He was good now and then, when he dared to show his feelings, talk and cry with me. That meant a lot to me, of course. But then he'd have spells when he took it into his head that I had to pull myself together—much, much more than I had the strength for. No, the two people I mean are Lotta, my best friend, and Sandra, who had been Cilla's best friend. Now she became mine—together with Lotta, that is. They listened—yes, that was it exactly: they listened, they let me talk, they let me say absolutely anything I wanted to, they always had the right answer and always sensed when it was better to be silent, they were grieving together with me, and suddenly we could laugh at something, laugh all together. Oh! it was so good to be able to laugh again, to be childish! Sandra has the prettiest face in the world when she laughs and smiles, I'm not exaggerating when I say that. And she's pretty when she's serious, too, she's so fervent and intense. It's really not strange that she was Cilla's best friend. Lotta's a bit more moderate; she doesn't have such great eruptions of joy and doesn't cry so often. But she too has a laugh so beautiful it's contagious. It was only with Lotta and Sandra that I could both grieve and be happy about whatever, and feel that no matter which of the two we did, it was exactly right. I don't think I would have gotten through that summer, the time leading up to the Literature Camp, if they hadn't been with me. I really don't think so.

# 12

*I*n a gym reeking of sweat—
and slickly named the Hall of Sport—the twenty-six girls pass
their nights. Their bunks consist of lumpy mattresses on the
floor. In the building next door, the five boys sleep on back-
breaker cots in a small room even smellier than the gym. In the
morning they all climb onto crummy bikes and pedal a couple
of miles down the main road to an improvised breakfast in a
school unused since the dawn of time, where a classroom is
called a dining hall and also serves as a reading room and a rec
room for group activities. At midday a meager lunch is served
on paper plates, with drinks in plastic cups. Its contents de-
pend on which of the four librarians is responsible for the meals
that day. None of them has mastered the culinary arts, nor does
any of them seem to possess the slightest imagination when it
comes to preparing food. Their flat stomachs must have for-

gotten, early in their lives, all cravings beyond the world of books. Cookbooks can't ever have interested them.

Around five o'clock they all pedal a mile through the wilderness in the opposite direction to a proper restaurant and a proper dinner on tables with proper tablecloths, porcelain plates, and real glasses. There they soon learn how to make up for the damage, if any damage has in fact been done. They relish dishes that they had foolishly rejected in their spoiled lives back home, experiment adventurously with spices, and decorate their plates skillfully with lettuce, cucumber, and tomato.

Cycle back and gather in the school again for a few hours of conversation, during which five participants talk about their favorite books each evening. When the fifth one has fallen silent, nighttime snacks appear and the talk wanders off in whatever directions it happens to take. No matter how late it gets, the leaders say nothing, except to announce firmly that you can use your free time however you like as long as the scheduled activities don't suffer for it. If you want to skip a night's sleep, that's up to you, but don't be one minute late the next morning. If you're too tired to take an active part in discussions and exercises, then you'll have to accept our making rules about free time.

In the beginning, at least, the participants respond with common sense. Break up before midnight and bike through the August darkness to their quarters. Doze off, exhausted, in no shape even to make attempts at cozy small talk. Are called back to life by Barbro's god-awful alarm clock. Swear heatedly under the stingy sprinkle of cold-water showers and for the first hour of the morning hate everything to do with camp and drama and literature, until their hatred evaporates together with the morning dew when they're on their bikes and heading for the school.

But as friendships develop, common sense recedes. The

darker the rings under their eyes become, the more the enjoyment of the participants increases. The many unknown faces acquire names, and soon the lovely stars of new friendships twinkle above heads that have lost interest in hour-long lessons on theatrical coiffure. Familiarity helps them find oases in the days' tight schedule, resting spots in the intensive program.

Tina enjoys herself to the depths of her fervent heart. She had almost forgotten what it was like to meet people who don't avert their eyes and draw a sharp breath just trying to find something suitable to say. Perhaps the leaders know, but none of her companions is aware of the sorrow she's carrying. Here no one is startled by coming face-to-face with a living mirror image of someone who's just died. At the camp she's treated like a completely ordinary person. And it's wonderful to be ordinary!

What does it mean to be ordinary? Normal behavior in the circle where she now finds herself: as soon as the bell announces free time, to nibble through a poem or polish the dialogue in a play or exchange volleys of extraordinarily well-thought-out and significant pronouncements. God, does a person get so terribly deep in the eighth grade! Here it's normal to be convinced that the meaning of life is to be found clearly formulated somewhere or other. All human exertion is aimed at finding that formulation. Four librarians, a drama teacher, one author, and one director have come here to point the way to the place where it can probably be found.

She gets a chance to have a talk with the Director on Tuesday, the second day of the camp. By then her pleasure at living and being normal has already grown so great that she doesn't want to dispel it. She tells him briefly that she was very unhappy in the beginning of July, when she wrote him that letter.

The light that surrounds her now explains better than words that she doesn't need the Director to take care of her. If you change your mind and want to go into this again, just let me know, he says in a friendly way when their conversation has stalled.

Barbro, the drama teacher, builds her exercises around *The Single Twin*. The Director goes from group to group but doesn't give any directions at all—Barbro and any participants who are interested have to take care of that. It's hard to figure out what his job is here; the things he says suggest that for the most part he's pondering the difference between theater and film. Once, though, he remarks briefly to Per Sjöberg that *direction should not force* your interpretation on the actors. Another time, he informs Camilla Faager just as briefly that you have to *use direction to force* the actors to discover for themselves the proper way to express the interpretation that you never make explicit.

Why can't you make it explicit? Camilla wonders, but by then the Director has moved on, so his comment, too, is something she'll have to interpret on her own.

He gets several Why's from participants interested in directing, but the questions he hears must sound completely different from the ones that are asked. He answers that in film there is only one correct solution, dictated by the script and the footage that's been shot; it's the editor's job to find it. Onstage, on the other hand, the correct solution varies from performance to performance—the basis for it is only partly written into the play. It's dictated above all by the audience sitting in the darkened theater: vibrations from the audience determine the actors' gestures from the first moment.

It certainly sounds interesting, what he's saying, but seems to have absolutely nothing to do with Carro's question: Why did you write that Annette should turn her back to the camera when Pia says that bit? Are directions like that usually included in the script?

Much more goes on between the participants and the Author. Their first session is almost painfully hesitant and stiff. Tina wonders how many of the others think, as she does, that the Author's books are completely uninteresting. Maybe a book doesn't have to be funny, romantic, or thrilling. But it's still got to have *something* to rouse readers from their own thoughts.

At the first session the Author himself seems just as deadly boring as his books. Drones on about God knows what, and surrounds his droning with long silences. Did he ask a question; and if not, why did he fall silent? Has he been struck dumb; and if not, why doesn't he start talking again?

Toward the end of the two hours he reads aloud from the book they're all supposed to have read in advance. Drones his way monotonously through a passage that Tina had yawned at and put aside at home. Mull that over, he says afterwards. Tomorrow I'll show you something.

Mull what over? Tina doesn't dare to ask. The others look so interested behind their smiles; they might think, they might realize, that she's stupid.

When the next day's meeting starts, the Author again reads aloud the passage he read the day before. Something has happened overnight—today sparks fly from the text! Tina opens the book and follows along as he reads. The same words put her to sleep before, but today the Author's voice brings them alive. How is it possible!

It turns out that Tina hasn't been alone in her view. Now that they've changed their minds, her new friends dare to reveal what they thought before. The Author laughs, pleased that his trick has succeeded, then explains that he believes the book gets written inside the reader. That's why one can write the way he writes. Then the reader has to give meaning to the writing. Now the Author, with nothing but a new intonation, has given us the key to the book. That we couldn't find it ourselves doesn't prove that there's anything wrong with the text. What it shows, says the Author, is that we lock ourselves into our view of the text as soon as we read the first few words. The idea that it can be read in a different way is something they haven't taught us in school. And away he goes, expounding on this, that, and the other in lesson after lesson, gesturing energetically, handing out assignments, and praising us no matter what we do. I can't remember a word, and barely understood half of it, but somehow or other it was all enormously interesting.


There's a reason why Tina vanishes upward into a cloud where everything stands out clearly before her but is nonetheless incomprehensible, where every conversation rushes in on her with great import but at the same time remains beyond the reach of explanations, where each moment is intense, incandescent, and gone as soon as it's begun yet manages in that brief instant to fill her like the particle of Eternity that it actually is.

That reason is called Stefan Juhle. His last name is pronounced Yul, with a vowel as in English "good," they all learned when he corrected Barbro at roll call. A more beautiful name could not be given a human. Nor more beautiful hair, eyes, ears, lips, neck, arms, hands, chest, belly, hips, ass, thighs, shins, arches, or toes—according to Tina's cool and objective judgment. No one could move more beautifully, no one could smile more beautifully, no one could have a more beautiful voice that breaks as adorably as his when he gets excited. And that happens at almost every teaching session. He's excited, he's animated, he's the most beautiful creature on earth!

He breaks into her existence on Tuesday by pedaling up beside her on the bike trip to dinner (O, his leg muscles when he pedals! the wind in his sun-bleached hair! his slender hands on the handlebars!) and asking (O, that voice! that voice!) if she's hungry.

A bit, Tina says vaguely, and swallows something that's growing and turning sweet on her palate while she tries to remember the name of the god she's beholding.

A bit? asks the god (O, his voice! his smile around the words! his lips! his teeth! I can't ride this bike!).

Not at all. Tina realizes what the answer should be and corrects herself.

She stops a second before she would have fallen off the bike, plants her jelly-legs on the road, and leans against the handlebars to give the dizziness a chance to settle down. But it grows, it intensifies when the god looks at her with his eyes, smiles with his lips, and speaks with his voice—yes, every feature is his, and every feature that is his sets her head spinning and is pure and noble, and he speaks and says: Neither am I.

Neither am I, neither am I, what about Neither am I? O, his voice! O, the golden down on his arms! O, the line of his cheek! what about Neither am I?

Stefan Juhle, she reads on the name tag he has on his chest, Stefan Juhle, yes, of course, Yul as in "good," Stefan Yul, Stefan, Stefan, what a wonderful name! O, chest where that name resides! O, name! O, Stefan!

Well in that case can't we . . . ? he says and tosses his head (O, the grace of that movement!) obliquely back toward the right (O, the swing-flick of his hair as it follows the movement!).

Obliquely back toward the right, there's a strip of spruce forest, after that a beach, then the sea, then islands and the horizon before infinite space begins obliquely back toward the right.

Sure we can, Tina agrees, and bows her head in a nod, a slow movement that makes it possible for her to swallow, swallow again.

No one sees them veer off the road. Silently they walk their bikes through the strip of forest, out across the sea, past the horizon, out beyond eternity, and come to themselves again on the beach, sitting with their feet in the mild lapping water, and Tina hears a voice from far beyond the horizon, the clearest solo voice, singing, *O, never was the sea so shining . . . as when you walked by my side . . .*

Now begins the virtually impossible task of creating words between them, sufficiently large words. Tina decides that Stefan will have to speak first. He's the one who's brought this situation about, he's the one who'll have to explain it.

I've been watching you for a long time, he offers as an explanation, when the sound of the sea can no longer fill the silence.

Tina looks out over the water . . . *and never was the shore so comforting . . .* The god has been watching her! For a long time—when they've only been there two days. Been watching Tina! He's doing it right now too. She feels his gaze and knows how her profile on that side looks from his point of view. That profile is the best feature I've got; that's a fact, not a boast.

I've been watching you since the bus trip out here, Stefan reveals. But you don't notice, he charges. Or pretend you don't, he suggests.

Don't notice, Tina confirms in a voice that doesn't carry very far, but then, Stefan isn't very far from her, no, he's sitting close, even closer than when they sat down, though she has no idea how that's happened.

Tina Dubois, he says, trying out the name. Tina, Tina . . . is it Kristina or Martina or what?

Just Tina. Well, really Martinelle.

Martinelle, Martinelle. He gets the taste of it. Can you *tell* you've cast a *spell*—I'm in your hands, Mademoi*selle*, because you are *si belle*.

And he actually lays his hands in hers. She has her hands on her knees, so she suddenly finds his hands on her thigh, at the edge of her shorts, bold contact that sends flames shooting down between her legs, the heat so strong that in pure reflex she uses her hands to push his away. She laughs as if his silly little poem has her full attention and approval, laughs out, "Stef-an, carry *on*!"—laughs and turns more of her neck toward him so he can't see how she peeks downward. She feels wet between her legs; is anything visible, or is she just imagining it? Nothing's visible, though it's not her imagination either; but his hands are gone now and she can turn her head a little further toward him, laugh some more so he won't think she's angry.

What? he asks. What're you laughing at?

At our poems, she claims.

He laughs too. No one could have a more beautiful laugh! She looks at his teeth and at his eyes that narrow as he laughs. He has light-blue eyes, lighter than hers.

You have blue eyes, he tells her. I've never seen blue eyes that dark. They seem almost brown until you take a closer look.

I've never thought so, Tina says, confused.

At that, Stefan breaks out in a huge laugh. You're fun, you know, Martinelle-gazelle!

He rocks, as if accidentally, against her shoulder. The fire runs along her skin there, too, then leaps inward, into her depths. Everything happens so quickly. Surprisingly fast, Tina is flooded by something that overflows and runs out of her in a moan.

Stefan stops laughing and looks at her, alarmed. What is it?

It hurts so much! Tina's face complains, blinking at the sky.

Where? Stefan pants, with fear in his breathing.

Tina puts her hand on her heart and falls over backward.

Wh-wh-what's happening! Stefan's teeth are chattering as if he's freezing. Y-y-your face is g-g-green.

I'm dying now, Tina thinks. How could it happen at a moment like this?

Cilla! she says, and grows faint. I'll be right there!

The last thing she feels, before it all goes black, is Stefan's hands, shaking her.

# 13

You scared the hell out of me! Stefan is patting her face with wet hands. He's got the sea to scoop from; he's scooped, and she's come around. Do you get attacks like that often?

It's never happened before.

She feels like lying there for a while. Lying there and feeling, without being able to prevent it, how the memory of his hands evaporates from her skin along with the water. He has shouted over her lifeless body; the echo of fear is still ringing above them, but it too is slowly fading away.

He sits looking out over the sea. She can see he's biting his lower lip. The dark-red lips, the white teeth, the blue faraway gaze—everything about Stefan is perfect, one detail after another in a painting by a master.

Who's Cilla? he asks, facing the horizon.

That's me, Tina answers. That's my name.

Stefan ponders this.

Tina ponders it.

But you're called Tina? Stefan tries to clarify the notion.

The sound of her name gets Tina to sit up. She moves over to him, up close, right arm grazing left arm. He doesn't move away. Slowly, perhaps unnoticeably, she changes the graze to a firm touch. And she feels an answering pressure. Graze or pressure, what matters for two people is that they both take part in the touch.

I was just kidding, Tina says. My name is Tina. Martinelle and Tina.

I don't get the joke.

Stefan sounds somewhat hurt. She's fainted, he's brought her around, and now she's pulling his leg.

Look at me! Tina commands.

He obeys—gladly, it seems. Turns his head and looks at Tina close up. Her eyes! No, she's not pulling his leg.

What do you see? she asks.

He gives a quick laugh, confused. Dark-blue eyes, he says. Suntanned forehead reflecting the sky. Raspberry lips. A chin that fits in my hand.

It's Cilla you're seeing, Tina says.

Oh! Stefan draws back his hand. I could have sworn it was Tina.

We're twins. Identical.

Lucky she didn't come to the camp too, Stefan says. It would almost have been too much. Overwhelming, as the Author says.

She's here, Tina assures him, and points with her hand at her chest, where it has just hurt so much. I've got her in here.

Stefan keeps looking at her, but an uneasiness wanders across the bottom of his light-blue gaze. She makes him uncertain.

She died three months ago. Three months and five days.

Oh! Stefan exclaims and turns toward the sea. Now I understand.

I think she gave me a warning just now, Tina says to his back. I'm not sure, but maybe she wanted me to understand that . . . um, what?

It's as if time itself ponders this for a while. Everything stops and turns into waiting. Then Stefan stretches out his arm and lays it across Tina's back. Poor you! he says softly. It must be horrible.

His voice! He's crying! The god is crying! The painting of the master may be damaged! Tina lifts her hand and tries to dry his tears. It doesn't help. On the contrary: she starts crying too.

From that time forward, the activities at the camp are a routine that goes on around Tina, outside her. It's a matter of participating, of acting onstage and reading poems and writing and taking part in discussions. It's a matter of making notes about what to read and about how to find things to read when you're in this or that mood. It's a matter of standing there among the others without betraying that you aren't really there. It's a matter of knowing what's going on in that world, so you don't say anything to reveal that it doesn't exist.

The only thing that exists is Stefan. Wherever he is, that's where Tina is too. Wherever she is, that's where Stefan is. Cilla is with them: stands between them at first, but gradually moves to hover above them . . . *fields and meadows and trees never lovelier than now* . . . It's Marie Fredriksson's voice, Tina realizes, of course it is—so clear and floating in space.

Naturally, they are discovered; obviously, the others see what's going on between those two; of course their companions send one another knowing looks and make gestures for Sure is hot around here! But who cares—they don't really exist, these gesturing companions. They're parts in a play. The camp is a stage set all around them, a set they call reality. Only Tina and Stefan know the true reality. It fills them, and they allow themselves to be filled. The rest, everything that happens and flows and splashes around them, will have to serve as shadows, as tinsel and playthings for the others, the nonexistent ones.

They go off during their free time, away from the others. The beach, the woods, and the roads listen to their conversations *. . . and flowers were never so sweetly fragrant . . .*

In the evening they're the first to break away from the gathering. Do whatever you like with your free time, is the policy. They do what they like, they vanish and let the others sit there guessing what they're up to *. . . as when you walked by my side toward the setting sun, the evening a magical twilight . . .*

There's so much to do when two people need to explore each other. Every second is filled with treasures *. . . when your tresses hid me from the world, smothering all the sorrows I surrendered . . .* The first time Stefan kisses Tina, she realizes that everything else of this sort has been only a childish game. She reciprocates, and wishes these moments would never end . . .

       *sweetheart,*

              *in your*

                      *very first*

                              *kiss.*

But the moments end, of course they do. Stefan suddenly pulls back. Sorry! she hears him whisper.

What's he apologizing for?

It's okay, she says, and pulls him close again, *the music build-ing up.*

But now he doesn't want to, he resists, pulls away, slightly but noticeably. Didn't she taste good?


It takes her a whole day to mull this over, a day when she mind-lessly acts in a play and doesn't even care that Camilla Faager gets a lot of praise for a miserable interpretation of her role.

When evening comes, Stefan is bolder, stands with his mouth close to her lips *and Marie Fredriksson is singing again, this time with full backup by the Roxettes.* Tina is cautious now, doesn't show her eagerness so openly. Her day's pondering has told her that she'll scare him off if she's too eager. She lets her-self be kissed, strokes his hair, and plays the part of a girl who doesn't know what's going on. That seems to be roughly what he wants, *whether it's the backup's fault or just that it isn't the very first kiss anymore, the Song won't take off.* Her hands are in his hair when he leaves her face and tastes his way down her throat. She whimpers a little without wanting to when he reaches her breast; she turns slightly so he understands that he should pull up her T-shirt and go in under it. He kisses and sucks, and she lets everything happen the way he wants, is care-ful not to reach down to respond. In the morning she sees a hickey, a small blue-gray smile on her left breast. She smiles back at it but is quick to cover it—there are so many prying eyes here.


Later they talk; they talk and talk. Two lives to be explored—there's a lot to talk about. Stefan gets to hear all about Cilla. As for him, he's got a younger brother and sister and seems to have lived a life without major worries. Now, though, the magnitude of life has hit him.

But despite its magnitude, the life that remains is brief and can't just be sipped. Above all, this week is short. Letting yourself be kissed is pretty good. Still, answering in kind is much better. There comes an evening when Stefan isn't scared off by how hot she is. Then the night is on fire around them, they're aflame themselves, Tina presses her burning body against his. Through the cloth of his shorts she can feel his . . . hell, what can you call it that doesn't sound ugly! It's hard now, the only hardness in all of Stefan.

He's embarrassed that she's discovered what he has so far managed to hide. I love you so much, he declares, but it's not that I want to screw. It stands up on its own.

I wasn't thinking that, Tina says, wanting him to stop worrying and come back to her. I love you too, and a person can feel that way without screwing.

He dares then to come close to her again, to kiss and caress her. And her hands fly over his body again, just as his hands travel over hers. She finds her way down into his shorts, responding to his hand, lost in hers.

At that he gasps No! beside her mouth and pulls her hand away. I'll come if you touch it.

Nothing wrong with that, Tina offers, but the spell is broken.

Stefan sits up. It's not fair, he says. Girls can get as excited as they like and it's invisible.

It is not! Tina protests. Would you say I seem cold?

It stands up on its own, Stefan says. Don't think it means I want to.

I wasn't thinking that, Tina assures him again.

I'd rather just lie next to you, feel you, kiss you. Nothing else.

Come on, then! Tina urges him. I want the same thing.

But the spell is broken.


The final evening arrives, with entertainment, summing-up speeches, and talk that's impossible to get away from. When they're not onstage, they sit next to each other with eyes all around them, and the precious hours pass by. The evening doesn't finish until way past midnight, and then the whole group bikes to their quarters.

But Tina knows what Stefan wants, and he feels what she wants. They both want to be left behind by the other cyclists, so they're soon trailing at the rear.

Their friends are gone. The night stands silent around Tina and Stefan as they slowly walk their bikes along the road. It's awkward to hug and kiss while walking two bikes, but where there's a will there's a way. And the will is there.

How the hell am I supposed to manage with just letters from you from now on? Stefan wonders.

Hard work and lots of exercise, Tina suggests, struggling for a cheerful tone. And you could always come and visit . . .

But there's no way until Christmas break, Stefan laments. Hell, I'll die of longing before then.

They make their way down to the beach. Night hides them from the whole world but gives them just enough light to see each other. They take off their jeans and jackets, spread them out, and lie down. At once the song begins, the clear solo voice: *O, never was the sea so shining . . .*

Take that off too! Stefan plucks at her T-shirt.

You can do that. Tina stretches her arms above her head.

He lifts it off her. She in turn pulls up his jersey. Traps his head in it and kisses him on the chest and stomach. He soon gets out and brings his lips to hers.

What does it do to girls? he asks suddenly.

Feel for yourself! she whispers, and when he hesitates she leads his hand downward. As for me . . .

After that she says no more, because he's touching her and his hand stays there and plays and strokes her into space, and then a person can't talk, not with words but with your body you can speak, with one body, with two bodies, my body to your body to my body ever higher toward your body ever higher toward my body, and when the night bursts into fireworks around Tina, she twists aside his briefs and wraps her hand around his hard and eager sign of love, and he lets her, yes he wants her to, yes he cries out and her sparkling starry sky is joined by his.


This is what they've been longing for all week, without knowing it. Now they lie still and listen to the sea, each with the other's hand left resting in a pleasure-filled secret place.

I love you, whispers Tina, afraid that something fragile will break.

I love you, Stefan answers, and nothing breaks.

It's lucky that we have to part now, Tina says, and continues at once: Because it's irresistible. The next time, if there had been one, we would have made love. All the way, I mean. I can feel it. And I don't really want to do that. But I would have done it anyway. That's just how it would go.

Stefan nods. The mind says no, but the rest is all for it, wants it more than anything. You're right, it's lucky we won't be meeting anymore. Though it's really horrible, too.

They lie there, two explorers. Contemplate the beautiful

kingdom they've discovered. Millions and millions of people have discovered it before them. Yet the two of them are alone there.

Cilla said once that I needed to be so much in love that I would forget about myself. It's true. Just now I really forgot about myself. I was you, somehow. I didn't exist.

You existed, Stefan affirmed. I was the one who became you. I don't know—we sort of switched places. I've never felt like that before.

Tina forgets to agree that she's never felt like that either. She lies there wondering what Cilla really knew and what she'd just repeated from some book. So neither of them speaks until Stefan has finished interpreting her silence and asks: Have you been with many boys before me?

Never like this! Tina is quick to answer. It's just been childish games. I've fluttered from one to another like a butterfly. Nothing that meant anything. And you? Lots of girls?

No, none, he claims.

Someone as gorgeous as you! Tina sighs. Am I supposed to believe that?

If I believe you, he answers. No fluttering at all for me. The first time I fall in love, it turns out to be with you. Talk about luck!

Tina points upward at the sky. I believe Cilla is sitting up there. It's Cilla who's led me to you.

Tina waves at a star and calls out: Hi, Cilla! Thanks for Stefan!

Cut it out! Stefan snaps, and sits up. But his voice gets kind again at once. I'm sorry, but I'd rather be alone with you here. Shit, I'm wet all over . . .

He goes down to the water and she hears splashing sounds.

While he's away, Tina discovers that she too is wet from his explosion. She didn't feel it as long as he was still lying there. She smells her hand, sniffs and smiles. *My beloved!*

She too goes down and washes herself. Then she stands next to Stefan and strokes his naked belly, strokes and plays a bit between his legs. Now it's small and soft again, so small and soft!

It's really unfair, says Stefan. A girl can keep going as long as she wants, but not a guy. Once he's come, that's the end for him.

You can wait a while and start again later, can't you?

Stefan doesn't answer this question, but Tina can see and feel that she's right—her stroking and playing have roused his desire again. He surely *could* start again, but now maybe they'd better be a little sensible.

Sensible! What a sad, gray word.

Tina pulls her jeans on. Stefan does the same. It's grown noticeably lighter, so it's easy for them to make their way up to the road with their bikes.

The sleeping quarters lie silent and give no clue that so many people are staying there. They say goodbye at the entrance. Each kiss has the bitterness of the Last Time.

Come with me and sleep in my bed! Stefan whispers suddenly.

You're crazy! Tina giggles.

Crazy! What a sharp, red word.

Doesn't matter! Stefan says. What can they do about it? We're going home tomorrow anyway.

You *are* crazy, Tina whispers fondly, and sneaks along behind him.

But when they open the door to the boys' cabin, she stiffens and has second thoughts: This stench is suffocating! I can't stand it.

Then I'll come with you instead, Stefan decides.

They pad off in the other direction, to the gym. Tina's mattress is near the door, so they don't have to risk any embarrassing encounters in the dim light. The air is considerably better here. This place is bearable for a night, Stefan sighs as they get comfortable.

Tina smiles and sniffs the air. Yup, I think you'll survive, she says. But now we have to sleep, Stefan, be sensible people—be good children and just sleep.

He doesn't object. Just to lie close to Tina is what he wants, after all, even if there's a stubborn agitation down there that's clamoring for more. And just to rest her head on Stefan's chest is what Tina wants, though she, too, feels the call of a greater longing.

God, imagine the looks on their faces in the morning! she sighs, then falls asleep.


In my dream Cilla comes and reads me her poem about the meadow with the flower in the middle. *That flower is called Love.* If I was a fluttering butterfly in the meadow before, now I've finally found the flower where I can settle.

Thanks, Cilla, for being there and showing me the way to Stefan! I love him, you know that. And you know that now it's finally serious for Tina.

Thank you, sister, my beloved sister! Now help me to keep him.

# 14

One month later, the summer is long gone, and Tina is in the eighth grade. All at once life is much, much more difficult than she'd envisioned. Or perhaps the difficulty arises because she didn't envision anything, because she neglected to think about what it would be like to return to school, to classmates who've grown a couple of years older at a stroke and at the same time forgotten their past, forgotten the children they were in seventh grade, forgotten their whole childhood, which ended yesterday. Yet they haven't forgotten. They remember, but they pretend not to.

Quite simply, they can't be natural anymore, not even with themselves: it's as if they constantly have a mirror in front of them where they check to make sure that a living face can't be glimpsed behind the layers of makeup, their clumsy paintings that take so much time to frame and mount. Nor can they be natural with one another: between them that mirror turns into a plastic shield with a microphone in it for flimsy filaments of talk and affected laughter. Above all, they can't be natural with Tina. They get nervous in her vicinity, they hold their breath against grief's bad odor, they evade any attempts at conversation; and if they do have to approach her, they're nauseatingly considerate or so exaggeratedly natural in their gestures and choice of words that they're positively slathered with naturalness.

Tina would gladly talk with all of them about everything, the way she could before, but she's silenced by their desire to get away from her, by their exaggerated concern, by their fumbling for "suitable" topics of conversation, by their tendency to squelch their idle talk when she approaches. Above all, she's silenced when she notices that they're shocked if she dares to laugh. Then she breaks off her laughter. To her friends, the interruption sounds as if she's realized how brazen she's being and is embarrassed. So they're ashamed for her; they flush so intensely that the heat cracks the makeup on their masks.

Lotta and Sandra are the only ones who can behave naturally toward Tina, but they're so popular that someone often comes and drags one or both of them off to company more cheerful than Tina's. More cheerful? Well, not so serious, anyway. *Shallow* is no doubt the correct term for describing that company. The girls in the eighth grade are so shallow it's scary, Tina thinks.

And the boys—yes, they're even worse, if that's possible, though their shallowness takes a different form. They don't preen their feathers day in and day out. But they stand around in their guy-huddles, cracking up about nothing at all and punching each other on the shoulder or in the stomach. What are they talking about? Heh-heh! is all you ever hear. If you say anything to one of them, all you get is a guffaw, while the others smirk and make lewd gestures they think you can't see. In the seventh grade they were all so sweet. Just ask me—I've been in love with every last one of them! They were childish, but in a sweet way. Now they're transformed. Childishness transformed into a guffawky façade. The sweetness has run away and hidden somewhere.

Going to school doesn't just mean withdrawing from your friends or trying to get through to them. You have to manage the schoolwork, too. Tina tries, pulls herself together, pays attention, concentrates, behaves herself, wants to, wants to, wants to, but can't find the strength. The teachers treat her as if she had a bout of toothache in the spring, okay, but surely it must have passed during the summer break, so by now Tina should be just fine. They're entirely unsympathetic when, after the first two weeks, she becomes less conscientious, stops showing the slightest interest in school, lets her homework slide—in fact, doesn't give a damn about it—comes late, leaves early, or on some days doesn't show up at all.

A person who's been stricken to the core can't manage to sit in a classroom and keep plugging away, can't force her ears to follow the small-minded monologues up at the blackboard, can't focus her eyes on handouts full of inane questions, and naturally can't answer those questions either.

What she's been stricken with, at the core, doesn't really matter in this setting: numbing grief or dizzying happiness, a dear sister's death or a love beyond all reason—stricken is what she is, and she can no longer resign herself to all the trivialities that school requires.

These teachers who don't understand her silent language—

have they ever been stricken themselves? Tina doubts it, since the blindness they display suggests they have no depths at all. But is it really possible that in such a large group of grownups every last one has been spared misfortune? A creepy thought: is it precisely the people with charmed lives, the shallow ones, who choose to be teachers?


Well, Cilla? says Ingvar, the math teacher.

He's waiting for an answer; he's so immersed in the question that he doesn't notice how a heavy blanket descends from the ceiling and covers the class, sinks it into the deep, echoless silence that results when twenty-five people stop moving their limbs, stop blinking, stop swallowing, stop, stop, totally stop. He doesn't notice it, is aware of nothing but his question and his little ironic grin—yes, he's certainly amused at having directed his question to Cilla, since she has never managed, in a single math lesson, to give the correct answer to anything at all, neither she nor her sister . . . good God, her sister! Now Ingvar wakes up, for now Tina has broken free of the silence, has rushed up and is standing right next to him and screaming: My name is Tina! Goddammit, my name is Tina!

She attacks him, hits him with clenched fists. Cilla is dead, *dead, deahhhd*! I'm alive and my name is Tina! Can't you understand that, you goddamned . . . goddamned . . .

I'm sorry! Ingvar whispers. I'm so sorry!

But Tina doesn't hear that, she's already out the door. Away, away!

Lotta races after her. Tina doesn't have the strength to run very far, and Lotta soon catches up with her, hugs her, soothes her, weeps together with Tina.

I'm so scared! Tina sobs. Am I Cilla—am I?

No, Lotta assures her. You're Tina and you're alive. He just misspoke.

He just misspoke, Tina repeats after her.

Anyone can misspeak, Lotta explains slowly and patiently, wiping the tears away from Tina's cheeks. You could too.

Tina nods. It's only two days since she saw Cilla coming down the stairs and thought it was entirely natural. Cilla, you can . . . she began, but she broke off, because in reality it was Sandra on the stairs. And Sandra got so scared that she sat down in a heap.

Anyone can misspeak, Tina grants, but she doesn't tell Lotta that she didn't just misspeak in the stairway, she also mis-saw. It happens so often: Tina sees Cilla, hears Cilla, but then the scene changes a little, just a little, and it's not Cilla. Every time it hurts, hurts.

When will it end? Cilla will never come back, after all, so when will I stop seeing her?


Tears and outbreaks of rage. Cuts classes or runs out of them. Such behavior produces phone calls from School to Home, where Monika and Albert then rebuke Tina for not getting her act together. Surely you don't imagine that you're somehow *honoring* Cilla's memory by neglecting your schoolwork!

All summer I kept watch over my depressed parents! Ignored myself and helped them with everything. Now they thank me by denying me the right to grieve. Death and grief are of course things that only grownups understand. A fourteen-year-old should keep her chin up and look cheerful, fuss with her makeup, paint over her pimples three times a day, and at the very least attend to her schoolwork.

All this—the lack of understanding, the loneliness—absolutely all of it might have been bearable, but on top of all her sorrows Tina has placed the flickering flame of her heart's longing. That flame is burning, and the pain is not sweet. Week after week goes by without a letter, without a line, without any sign of life from Stefan. Week after week, when he promised to write at least once an hour! Even with one letter after another, the fall would have been long and difficult. What it's like now can't be described in words.

Tina has told Lotta, told her everything about Stefan and shown her his photo. Lotta hugged her and cheered—because love is so wonderful! Congrats! What a catch! But as time passed, Lotta realized she should tone it down, because unhappy love—that's something Lotta knows about. Her romance with Micke Englund fell apart, to name just one of her encounters with that kind of sorrow.

Micke Englund? Tina muses. Micke Englund—what became of him? Last spring it sounded almost as if he wanted to go with me. "I care about you," he said. "Although of course I'm seeing Lotta now." Now Lotta says he's not around anymore. Where is he, then?

Don't talk to me about Micke! Lotta defends herself. It was him who came on to me, you know that. And I trusted him and fell in love, helplessly in love. And then he's the one who splits. Not a word about why. I can't bear to talk about Micke, can't even think about him.

Yeah, what a drag, Tina commiserates. Though he really is attractive. Not like Stefan, but attractive. In his way. Although Stefan . . .

Give your damned Stefan a wake-up call! Lotta advises. Go

out with Fredde Lindgren, and you'll see how fast he comes around.

He would never hear about it, Tina points out. And Fredde is . . . such a wimp.

Tina has already rejected Fredde. It was almost the first thing that happened this term, the first thing that was at all amusing. Lotta came to her with the message that Fredde Lindgren had asked her to ask Tina if he could go out with her.

Tina sent word that she thought Fredde was big enough to ask for himself. He came to her then, so embarrassed that he really must have been seriously in love. But between her and him hung the image of Stefan Juhle. I can't, said Tina. Actually, I'm practically engaged.

This answer was a slug in the jaw for Fredde, you could see that. But he was brave about it in his way. He pulled himself together, gave a pained laugh, and said: Well now, engaged! That calls for congratulations, then, doesn't it!

*Practically* engaged, corrected Tina, looking at his pained expression, feeling that his hurt was like her own, pitying him, almost taking pity on him—but you can't go out with a guy just out of pity. You need a little more reason than that.

You certainly could have let me tell him that, Lotta reproached her. Poor Fredde, he was so brave and thought for sure that you'd say yes—since you wanted to tell him yourself. What a blow!

He's a wimp! Tina decided. You should see Stefan, then you'd understand that I can't even talk about Fredde on the same day.

Stefan would never find out anything where he is, Lotta said on that occasion. Unless you wrote and told him, of course.

Besides, I know that Fredde thinks I'm Cilla, it occurred to Tina to say. But I'm not. I'm me. He would just end up comparing. Suddenly he'd discover that we're not at all alike. Then he'd end it. I know that.

Weird things you're saying, you know, Lotta snorted.

It's Cilla who led me to Stefan. You think I should thank her by taking her guy instead?

That's not what I meant at all! Lotta defended herself, and at the same time attacked: You're the one who's thinking things now. I can't be bothered explaining it all, but the point is you're wrong, and you know it!

Lotta turned angrily on her heel and went off to find more sensible company. But her anger didn't last long—luckily enough, since Tina can't do entirely without Lotta. And now Lotta's suggesting Fredde again, so her anger must truly be forgotten. Which doesn't change the fact: never Fredde Lindgren for one who's been kissed by Stefan Juhle! Stefan, Stefan, why haven't I heard from you!

■ ■ ■

Tina's neglect of her schoolwork, her truancy, her crying jags and general moodiness gradually remind Albert that he had meant to find a psychologist for her. They rub me the wrong way, he says when psychologists come up. Their main goal is to prove what fine educations they have.

Be that as it may, a psychologist will have to have a look at Tina. Her teachers have also realized that she's a case for the guidance office.

As long as it isn't Carina! says Tina, making her wishes clear. Carina is just impossible to talk to.

She has some luck in that a new person has just taken the post of assistant school psychologist for the district. His name is Georg Jansson; he comes from a distant place and is an unknown quantity around here; he has no record to defend himself against, none to help him either. Tina likes his way of shaking hands, of looking her in the eyes from time to time, of looking somewhere else when she needs a rest from his gaze, of not asking questions. He lets her talk.

And Tina talks. She likes that Georg doesn't dismiss her grief, that he doesn't interrupt her melancholy accounts with some grownup machete blow that means she should pull herself together and understand that everything will be better when sufficient time has passed. Tina has promised herself that the next person who says that time heals all wounds will get a punch in the mouth. If he complains about his fat lip, she'll tell him what he told her: That'll heal soon enough!

But Georg doesn't say anything that would force her to keep her promise. Without asking questions, he's soon found out what's oppressing her. The summer was just awful, he hears. Mamma and Pappa were suicidal the whole time, so I was forced to look after them. They think they're more entitled to grieve than I am. But we were twins, Cilla was like a part of me, no one was closer to her than me, yet it's like I'm not supposed to grieve. It's wrong.

Georg nods. Grief is infinite, he mumbles, or something to that effect. There's enough for everyone.

And Jonny's moved out—no, run away is more like it, because he couldn't stand being there. That he may be grieving is something no one's thought about at all, though I know he is. And then he got a job at a drafting firm—I guess that's the main reason he moved out, if you want to be precise about it. Now that he's not home anymore, I notice that I actually needed him to talk to—I'm so terribly lonely. Here at school everybody's busy polishing their nails and putting makeup on and fixing their hair. They've got to have everything in the latest fashion, from their hairdos and earrings down to their shoes.

They're so shallow it's just impossible to make any contact with them. And the teachers think I've forgotten Cilla. They think I'm too young to understand death and now that the summer has passed I've forgotten. A pretty dumb idea from some not very smart grownups. They're the ones who've forgotten what it's like to be young, what you think and understand and feel. How can they become teachers if they've forgotten that? How can they be teachers without being reminded of it every single day, and without finally waking up?

She pauses briefly, but Georg makes no attempt to answer her questions. Which aren't really questions, strictly speaking.

And then at a camp this summer I fell in love with a fan-TAS-tic boy who doesn't give a shit about me now.

There, it slipped out after all. She'd meant to keep her mouth shut about Stefan, since grownups always think that teenagers' love affairs are like cheap romance novels. And maybe hers have been that, until now. But with Stefan it's serious, that's something no grownup can understand.

Georg doesn't let on what he thinks. So there's static on every channel, he says without a question mark, and it sounds like understanding, that bit about the channels—it sounds like he understands that Tina's not feeling up to much right now, that it's pretty dark and silent in there behind the flood of words.

We slept together on the last night, she says. But he hasn't answered a single letter, and I've written I don't know how many. Thousands.

Sounds tough, Georg nods. I could never manage to write a thousand letters to someone who didn't answer. Not even ten.

I think Cilla led me to him. But if he lets me down now, then I don't know what I should think. She can't be that badly mistaken, can she? Or did she get jealous?

I'm sure your sister is above such base motives as jealousy, Georg says.

Maybe Stefan is too far away now, Tina muses. So far away that Cilla can't get through to him?

The psychologist says nothing about that theory. Keeps quiet and waits for her to continue. But Tina has broken off. The silence that arose in the wake of her question made room for a warning voice beside her ear: Don't give him anything else now! Wait and see what he does with what he's got.

It's so clear, this voice, that Tina turns her head. But by then Cilla has already vanished. Why couldn't she stay!

Tina faces forward again and performs a quick little smile. Georg has been watching her, saw her listen, turn her head, and come back again. Was she behaving strangely? It wouldn't surprise her if she was going nuts. It's as if a shield inside her head has begun to give way under the weight of all her burdens. Sometimes it starts spinning in there, and she gets dizzy for a minute. And now there was Cilla's voice.

Can you go crazy from grief? she asks herself more than Georg.

People are fragile things, comes the answer from Georg. If you let the sorrow out, then there's most likely no danger. Keeping it under control—that's something you have to give up on.

Tina recalls that she's already had that idea, or something similar. Sometime during the first period of grief, when she cried together with Albert. She understood then that self-control didn't mean strength. Later she forgot. Albert, the one who showed her what strength looked like, has forgotten it too and now preaches about shaping up. But how can you dare to let go of your self-control when everyone's afraid that you might unleash the howling of your heart?

How do you feel in the morning? is the first question when Georg finally starts asking her things. Do you feel ill?

Tina looks at him. What did he say? Mornings, he asked about the morning. I feel bad all the time, she decides to answer.

I mean, Georg says, and falls silent for a moment, turns his pen over, resumes: I mean, do you throw up and so on? Is it possible you're pregnant?

Pregnant?

That often makes people very depressed. It's just chemistry. Glands and such.

The thoughts go rushing around and turn somersaults in her brain as Tina tries to understand what he's saying. She's on the point of laughing in his face when she realizes what he's heard her say. But she keeps a straight face, or at least she thinks she does; keeps up her mask and decides on the spot to play along with his comedy, to make it even richer.

Not a chance, she says. He used a condom. Two of them, just to be sure. And I've been taking the pill since . . . right, since I had an abortion two years ago. And by the way, I didn't get at all depressed that time, I'm not the type. I was ecstatic. Though Mamma thought I was too young, so she went along with . . . especially since Pappa would have beaten me to death if he'd found out. So don't tell!

I can't. Confidentiality, Georg reminds her.

Tina relishes the sight of him maintaining a poker face. So that's what a shocked psychologist looks like when he's not allowed to show that he's shocked. Serves him right! "Maybe you're pregnant"—he was begging for a tall tale! How Cilla would have appreciated the one she'd just spun! Cilla would have gotten a real kick from lying her way out of the school psychologist's office. She didn't have Tina's ability to talk to almost anyone about what was closest to her heart. Whoever wanted to hear Cilla talk about herself would have to be willing to spend a long time being weighed in her scales. There weren't many who managed that. There weren't many she cared enough about to bother weighing them, either. So she'd come out with some wild story, fantasies that her listener believed because they flowed so effortlessly and sounded like confidences. And she got help from Tina, who even without being tipped off in advance would often confirm that Cilla's story was true. Actually, the truth was even worse, Tina would suggest. 'Cause Cilla didn't tell you that . . . and then Tina would spread it on a little thicker, without exactly knowing all of Cilla's story. But it always worked out. Without any consultation, they could work in tandem on a complete fiction, just as flawlessly as in their mirror routine, when they'd followed each other's movements until in the end they couldn't tell who was leading and who was following. They could lie and back each other up so fairy tales became the truth and night turned into day for whoever got lost in their ingenuous eyes. When they were alone with each other later, the girls would giggle as they unraveled the threads of their story, discovered how their parts had succeeded in meshing like the parts of a well-planned farce. That's what real-life theater is like, Cilla said. Playacting at its best. The spectators don't even know it's theater, they think it's real life and they're in it. But Cilla, who started and directed the play, never stepped out from the wings.

Well, it's a shame about Georg, because he meant well, of course. If his name were Carina, the whole teaching staff would know all about this story in ten minutes. Tina can just wait and see now. This will be her little test of Georg's trustworthiness.

If the faintest little rumor about her abortion comes trickling in from some other source, she'll know who's been gossiping. No one else has ever heard so much as a mention of it, no one—not even herself until this very moment. And she can keep her mouth shut about what she's found out.

She gets up. I have to go now.

Georg looks at his calendar. When are you coming again?

Tina shrugs.

I'm here on Tuesdays, Thursdays, and Fridays, Georg informs her. But if you feel you need to talk, just give me a call—he stretches out his hand and gives her a card with his phone number—and I can rearrange my schedule.

Don't you have anyone else but me to . . . to . . .

No one as important, in any case, says Georg, and walks her to the door. Come whenever you need to. And no matter what happens, come back at the same time next week, is that okay?

Tina nods. She's a little ashamed at having taken him in. But that wasn't her. It was Cilla. Tina just helped out a little— the way she used to, before.

# 15

For first prize in the category Weird Behavior, the nominee is . . . Einar Roxén, the music teacher who gave Cilla and Tina flute and violin lessons. Since Cilla's death, he hasn't said a single word to Tina. Her classmates avoid her, they're self-conscious if they're forced to be near her, but at least they say something if they have to, even if the words come out stiffly. But Roxén refuses to speak with her.

At first Tina didn't notice it. She couldn't bear the thought of picking up the violin, stopped playing, and for a good part of the fall term thought she would never start again. To play alone—how could she? Music, like theater, is something you do with others. Music was something she and Cilla had taken up together.

But then along came Bahir! One day he and Ola were suddenly standing there in the garden at Rosengården. They'd gone to the trouble of visiting Tina and no one else, because—

—Congrats on the prize . . . the prizes, Tina interrupted. She could barely stand still. Ola was as bewitchingly good-looking as ever, but it was Bahir who did the talking, and the glow from their summer's successes enveloped both of them.

Thanks, it was mainly because of *Cilla Suite*, Bahir said, and quickly glanced around, as if he was worried about something coming from behind him. It was *Cilla Suite* that really gave us a boost.

With his pronunciation, it sounded like English: *Cilla Sweet*. It was *Cilla Sweet* that gave us a boost.

Ola nodded. Tina nodded. The papers had covered their tour. It must be terrific! she said. I mean: Wham! Bingo! and you were famous.

Baloney, Ola said.

It's beautiful here, Bahir said, and looked around. He saw autumn at its finest. And when he inhaled, he must have smelled the fragrances that were as clear as the colors, all the freshness that, together with the long silence after his comment, moved Tina to say: What a summer we've had!

Bahir's gaze rested on her, he looked at her hair, then he lowered his eyes to hers. She heard his thought, even though he didn't say it aloud. People always looked like that when they were thinking: My God, how alike you are! Then they usually said it, but Bahir said: You play the violin, don't you? No, he said it without the question mark. It was Tina who heard a question mark. How did he know? She got no answer to that.

When we played *Cilla Sweet* for the umpteenth time, Bahir explained, we heard that the synthesized strings were wrong.

Wrong?

Ola nodded behind Bahir, a bobbing up and down with his head that meant she'd heard correctly. The synthesized strings in *Cilla Suite* weren't right.

A single violin, Bahir said. A real stringed instrument. That'll make it perfect.

I'm not good enough, Tina declared. And I haven't practiced since . . . well.

What the hell is practice? Ola asked.

Think about it, Bahir said, then turned on his heel and walked toward the car. I know you can do it if you want to. If you want to, you can. We'll take care of the rest. I'll come and ask one more time. Just one more time.

You haven't actually asked me anything, Tina pointed out.

Ola kept walking, got into the car and sat behind the wheel, but Bahir stopped when she said that, turned around, and stepped up close to her. He raised his hand so she thought he was going to lift her chin, but somewhere along the way the gesture got stuck, his hand remaining in midair, and his brown-black eyes went straight into her when he told her that everything, the whole summer—do you understand—everything was Cilla, it was just for her sake I was playing, and the prize and the money and the whole damned routine didn't mean shit, because Cilla is the only thing—can you understand that—absolutely the only thing, ever since that first time, when she came and asked if we would do the music for that play, only Cilla, no one else, and then she died.

Tina couldn't see him anymore, something was dimming her view, she heard him, that was all, heard the pressure under his voice, heard that he was driven to speak, that he was forcing himself to tell her something, that every time he paused he was convincing himself to trust her, trust that the girl in front of him understood what he was saying, surely she had to understand—she was the spitting image of Cilla. And he kept on forcing the words out: To suddenly hear that the music is wrong there, when it's too late to do anything about it—that's hell itself, I swear, it's hellish to have a success with something that isn't right. Don't say again that I haven't asked you anything. I've asked you for something, and I'm going to come here one more time, and when I do, it still won't be about me, or Ola, or you, it won't be about anyone but Cilla. Or—it'll be about me, too, because I can't do anything else until I set this right, if you understand what I'm saying.

Of course I understood! And I was so ashamed that I didn't know where to put myself. Here he was, he'd come here virtually fractured by that pain and asked me for help, and I tried to make light of it all, pick at his words, throw him "You haven't asked anything." God, how ashamed I was! I understand well enough, I said. Cilla was my sister, after all. My twin sister. "And then she died"—exactly. I know what grief is.

Twin sister, Bahir repeated, and looked at me closely again in his way—no, he hadn't stopped looking, he kept it up, just sharpened his gaze a little. And he sharpened his voice too— good God, I think he hated me at that moment: Twins? Hell, you're so different from each other it's hard to believe you're even related!

With that he let Tina go. His hand no longer hung in midair; his voice no longer held her suspended above the ground—yes, before she quite knew how the change of scene had happened, the car had taken him away.

And Tina went inside. I'm sorry! she said to the walls and floor and ceiling, and to Cilla. I'm sorry, I'm sorry, Cilla! He loved you, he loves you and doesn't have a clue that you loved him. Jesus, what kind of mess have I made now!

She lifted the violin from its case, tuned it, flexed her finger joints, and got the strings to play a little melody. Didn't she hear at once how the flute took up its part?

Yes, of course!

What she'd been so afraid of suddenly became a wish fulfilled: Cilla came close again, stood beside her and followed her arabesques. Afraid—why should she be afraid? Tina let the notes rise and flow out into the house, fill it up.

When she paused, she discovered Albert outside her door. He was crying, sitting there crying with joy because the music had finally come back, when he'd given up hope, believing that music too had died for Tina. Crying also from the memories brought to life by the familiar melody. Perhaps crying for ten other reasons as he thanked Tina with a wordless embrace.

That's the sort of language that releases Tina's tears. Now they cry together again, she and Albert. And all the hardness he's shown her is gone and forgotten. Their whispers crisscross the room.

My little girl!

Pappa, Pappa!

■ ■ ■

Once Tina had made up her mind to resume her lessons, she naturally turned to Einar Roxén. But no sooner had she set off to make the appointment than a little alarm bell rang in her head. Hadn't they almost crashed into each other in the hallway a couple of times? Hadn't she automatically said hi but gotten no greeting in return? She didn't think these questions through, but they made her alert to how he might behave when she stood before him and asked if she could start taking violin lessons again, twice a week would be fine to begin with. To get going. If that would be okay?

He stared at her, that strange girl who always accosted him

in the hallways. No—he stared behind her, straight through her, since she wasn't really there.

Isn't that okay? she asked, and felt that she was blushing. She was ashamed for his sake, because he was acting so strangely—no, so incredibly stupidly. But he didn't blush. If he had changed color, he would sooner have gone pale. Isn't that okay?

He gave a snort and started moving. Tina barely managed to step aside. *What a fucking boor!*

The way he treated her suddenly hurt so much that Tina screamed from the pain that went through her body, a piercing shriek of rage straight out into the long hallway. Everyone turned and stared, everyone except Einar Roxén.

What happened? What did he do? they asked, horrified by the cry of an animal.

Lotta came rushing over and shook Tina, while Sandra came from the other direction. What's the matter? Calm down!

She could tell Lotta and Sandra. Stammering and sobbing, she managed to tell them what had just happened.

The guy's got a screw loose, Lotta agreed.

Cilla was his favorite student, Sandra said. You must have noticed that.

That's no reason! Tina said.

But Sandra understood something that Tina didn't. You're so like her, after all, so terribly like her, she said. And it was clear that was supposed to be an explanation.


Albert was furious when Tina told him about this. He phoned Roxén and bawled him out, but it didn't seem to help. Now Tina's taking lessons from Evy Andersson, who thinks Tina is so good that she, Evy, has nothing to teach her. But that's probably just modesty. If nothing else, Evy is encouraging and inspiring. She's the kind of teacher who shows how pleased she is when her students do well—and also the kind of teacher students want to please.

That is why, while all the other teachers agree that Tina is about to go off the rails completely, Evy sees a girl who is putting intense concentration and work into her music.

Yes, Tina plays, plays for several hours each day, and notices that concentrating gives her peace during those hours. She derives peace as well from sensing Cilla's presence during these musical intervals. Sensing the slight change in the room's light and atmospheric pressure that says now she's come and is standing just behind me. Don't look in the mirror and don't turn around, because Cilla is shy now and will vanish.

If I listen beyond the notes I play, I can hear your flute as always.

Cilla! I beg. Stay with me, even after I've finished playing!

But there are rules for the dead as well as the living. If I'm to keep you with me, I'll have to play forever.

■ ■ ■

Yes, there are intervals of peace, of happiness, one could even say. So Tina is defenseless and unprepared when her sleep is once again disturbed by twisted dream images. Cilla comes and threatens her with her blue, broken hands. Blames her death on Tina and wants to trade places with her. Wild quarrels alternate with inconsolable weeping. Tina knows she is dreaming; she wants to wake up to be free. She struggles with Cilla but can't manage to break out of the dungeon of these dreams.

It's so cold here, Cilla complains. It's peaceful and just fine, but I'm freezing.

Then Tina wakes up shaking with cold. She winds the blankets and covers around her but still can't get warm. Falls asleep at last, or doesn't. Can't tell if she's dreaming that Cilla wants to lie down beside her or if she's awake, so that what's happening is somehow true. I want to warm myself on you, Cilla says, and lays an icy hand on her breast, over her heart. You think you're freezing, but compared to me, you're hot.

Tina tells Georg Jansson that Cilla is haunting her at night. Why is she so angry at me? Why can't we ever have good times like when she was alive?

Georg says that it isn't Cilla who comes at night, but that all dreams are signals from the unconscious. If they're really unpleasant, those dreams, then one can be sure that they're symbolic in one way or another, repressed thoughts that have been recast into dream images. Maybe you're carrying around something you don't want to admit to yourself.

Tina shakes her head. She's thought so much about Cilla and herself during this time that there can't be anything repressed.

I don't know, says Georg, but from those dreams you've described, it sounds like you two quarreled, though now you'd prefer not to remember that. Maybe love wasn't the only feeling you had for each other. Jealousy or hate or something or other that you'd rather not acknowledge.

Georg speaks without question marks, but Tina answers by shaking her head.

When you fall asleep, the barriers against such thoughts are let down, he continues, ignoring her silent protest. And the thoughts are transformed into bad dreams, which you'll never get rid of unless you stop building up a pretty but false image of your life together. You have to accept the ugly parts too. And you have to learn not to feel guilty about them; you really have to learn that, deep down inside you.

But I don't feel guilty about anything, Tina objects.

It would be very strange if you didn't. I've never yet seen a case in which there isn't a whole lot of guilt where grief would be a heavy enough burden on its own. For example, have you understood that at your age, almost fourteen, you were just beginning the process of separating from each other, a completely normal process that involves a lot of quarreling and unpleasant behavior? Normally, kids get through that okay, given enough time. But in your case that process was interrupted by Cilla's death. I think that a lot of your dreams are about your not having finished getting free of Cilla. You don't want to acknowledge the unpleasant behavior. I don't mean you should admit it to me. No, it's to yourself you have to admit it. But you don't want to, don't dare to. And then it comes in your dreams instead, distorted and accusing. That's what I think is happening. But if you believe that Cilla is really trying to make contact with you, I can go along with that . . .

You don't need to go along with anything you don't believe, Tina interrupts him sullenly.

Well, okay. Then I'll put it this way: your interpretation of the dreams—that it's really Cilla who's seeking you out—agrees with my interpretation insofar as I think it's your guilty conscience and your repressed thoughts turning up in symbolic form. In other words, what Cilla is trying to tell you is that your quarrels were nothing but a normal phase in your development as free individuals, that anger, hate, and jealousy didn't mean a thing when it came to the love between you. She has perspective now, after all; she sees the explanations and wants to give them to you. And your guilty conscience is an obstacle that causes the two of you to quarrel in your dreams, especially if you try at the same time to repress the thought that what she's talking about is in fact true: that you argued with each other.

Anger, hate, jealousy, Tina repeats. That's really something! There wasn't anything like that between Cilla and me. Is it so damned impossible that we loved each other!

Of course you did. That's why all the rest doesn't mean anything.


Tina has made it her habit to walk all the way home after her conversations with Georg; she finds it's good for her to have some time to reflect undisturbed. She takes the shortcut through the woods, along the stretch where the highway will run if the powers that be have their way. Death Road is a bottleneck for important commercial traffic. Each application of the brakes, each second lost, translates into unfathomable sums in the debit column. The solution to that problem is called Highway, straight and wide. But every time a start on that solution has approached, the local people have gone out and chained themselves to the trees. The press and the police pay attention to these protests. There's a lot of action for a while, and the highway-building is put off. For how long? The environmentalists won't let themselves be caught napping. Far away, someone is waiting for that to happen. At any moment a remote-controlled battalion of machines can come crashing through the woods.

This fall, however, everything is quiet. Tina wanders through the forest of thinning foliage and ponders Georg Jansson's words. Ponders by talking with Cilla, who's walking by her side: Are you angry at me, Cilla? Georg thinks I feel guilty about something.

I can't turn around toward Cilla to see her when she answers. I've done that by mistake several times, forgotten myself and turned toward her; that's how we always used to talk. But not anymore; she fades away and vanishes and just leaves a gap behind her.

Maybe there's some truth in what Georg says. Maybe I'm carrying all these images—the ones in the dreams and the ones from waking hours—inside me, so that I'm just imagining Cilla's presence. Maybe, maybe it's true, but I don't see how anything will be better if I let myself be persuaded of that than if my imaginings bring me peace because they're so vivid. The proof that I'm right is that you're walking beside me here and answering me, Cilla, I'm not imagining that, after all. But why are you so shy now, why do you vanish, when I want to see you so badly? Is it Georg who's scaring you away from me? All his talk about guilt?

■ ■ ■

Then something new happens. Georg points to the easy chair: Sit there, it's much more comfortable. Like that. And now I'll sit here, so I can't see you and you don't have to see me. How do you feel?

So-so.

Tense?

A little.

Relax for a while.

It's not so easy to just suddenly relax.

No, but you don't need to tense up, either. Think about something pretty. Something beautiful. Tell me about it if you want to, or think about it to yourself, silently.

At first Tina thinks silently, searches a long time inside herself for something beautiful. Stefan flies by; she sees his eyes, lips, and hands. Where is he now? Not with me, at any rate. Well, some pretty sight *that* was.

I had such a wonderful dream the night after Cilla died.

Yes?

We were out biking. And we went swimming. And it was so nice.

Swimming in the sea?

Yes.

Like the summer before?

Yeah . . . no, it was longer ago.

Longer ago. Are your eyes closed now?

Yes. And we're swimming.

Can you repeat after me?

Repeat?

Repeat and then keep going.

Sure, I suppose so.

Cilla is my twin sister.

Cilla is my twin sister.

I love her, she . . .

I love her, she loves me.

The only thing I can't forgive her for is . . .

The only thing I can't forgive her for is dying. I just can't understand how she could do it. How the hell can she go and get run over and die and leave me behind to take care of Mamma and Pappa and friends and life and missing her, missing her, I miss you, I miss you so goddamn much!

Tina suddenly hears what she's saying and goes silent at once. Georg continues, forces her to go further: I dreamt that she blamed me for her death. The worst part is that . . .

I dreamt that she blamed me for her death. The worst part is that . . . Tina interrupts herself, she too breaks off, because she hears the *crump*, hears the undescribable sound when the car gets Cilla, hears the tires screech, hears the bird-rustle of the scattering essay, hears everything happen right behind her back, where she herself had run just a moment before, had run right across Death Road without seeing anything but the bus, but now she sees Cilla pointing at her with broken hands and wanting to trade places: I'll run ahead and you come behind me and take the *crump*, I'll take care of Mamma and Pappa and friends and life and missing you, I'll take care of all of it as long as we trade, because I want to live, Tina, I want to live! And Tina cries out sobbing into Georg's room: I want to live, Cilla, I want to live! Let me live in pe-e-e-a-ce!

The worst part is that you believe that accusation, Georg says. You believe it's all your fault. It's your own accusation.

If only I'd looked first . . . Tina weeps.

If you want to live, Georg says, live in peace as you say, then you'll have to explain to Tina at the roadside that it's not her fault. You'll have to make her really understand that. She was extremely lucky: she escaped death by just a few seconds. You have to explain to her that being lucky that way isn't the same thing as being to blame because Cilla didn't have equally good luck. You have to explain to her that they both acted equally stupidly in exactly the same situation. It's not a question of blame, but of good luck and bad luck. Tina had good luck and Cilla had bad luck. They were both blameless. No one but you can explain this to her, Tina, because you're the one who knows that Tina also ran across the road without looking. You have to do this, you have to free her. Otherwise, Tina is going to remain there at the roadside, get stuck there—I don't know for how long, but any time is too much time; she's already stood there far too long.

Tina hears him through the uproar in her head. She understands that he has a purpose in talking about her as two Tinas at the same time. And she understands that purpose, more or less. Right now, she guards herself against that purpose a little, but his suggestion has nonetheless begun its journey through the labyrinthine coils of her brain. Right at this moment, she won't follow his suggestion; right now, she won't find an explanation that can lift the blame from Tina on the shoulder of Death Road. But when she eventually succeeds, she will remember that it was now, at this moment, that Georg showed her an opening. It will be a while before she succeeds; it will take time to get there with the small steps that Tina dares to take. But she will succeed. Right now, she weeps uncontrollably.

# 16

Yuck! Tina sighs, groans, wails, as she crumples up yet another sheet of paper and throws it among the other paper balls on the floor. She wants to write a poem, two poems, but the words betray her, don't want to become poems.

That the words betray her is perhaps as it should be, because the poems are supposed to be about betrayal. Stefan has betrayed her; she has realized this. Whether he was lying to her face when they were at the camp or something made him change later on, she doesn't know. The result is the same in any case: he's betrayed her. That's what one of the poems is supposed to be about.

The other is for Cilla. Not for Cilla, dear Cilla, lost sister, but for Cilla who betrayed her, damned Cilla who's left Tina alone to take care of everything, a poem for the Cilla that Georg Jansson showed her.

That poem is the hardest Tina has ever tried to write, she can feel this each time she puts the pen on the paper to begin it. The pen won't move, no signal reaches the hand with orders to start writing, her thoughts lie paralyzed in her brain, petrified by the question: Can I really write those things? So she decides to start with the poem to Stefan instead, since his betrayal is easier to describe, she thinks. Thinks—until she reads what she's written. Call it a cry for help, call it a sob of loneliness, call it anything but a poem.

*Why?* stands at the top of sheet after sheet. On a few of them the questioning continues with *Why did you end it?*—on a few others with *Why did you betray me?* When she realizes that Stefan hasn't ended it, he's just slunk away, she can throw out all the drafts that say he *ended it.* When she's stared for a long, long time at the sheets of paper she's kept, she notices that her thoughts are focused more on looking for an answer to the question than on composing a poem that describes the betrayal or the pain in its wake. Why ask questions? He's betrayed her, after all. Let the poem tell, then, not ask.

> *I know that everything comes to a stop*
> *I know that everything must stop*
> *but if it's just barely had a chance to start*
> *you betray it if you . . .*

Yuck! *You betray it if you betray it*—clever thought! Tina rips up the paper. What was it the Author had said at the Literature Camp? Vary rather than repeat. Betray, betray, betray—not very good. Betray, slink away, deceive—better. The word *stop* is repeated too. There are other words. End, completion, period.

Tina starts as before, continues as before, but *varies* where she had earlier repeated; erases, changes, reads, changes. To write poems is to change poems, Tina's heard it said, and now she sees it herself and changes, changes, doesn't give up, until finally she arrives at a formulation she's satisfied with:

*I know that everything comes to a stop*
*I know that everything must end*
*but if its time is not yet up*
*you betray it if you don't come back again.*

I'm a genius! she announces when she reads through the result. And I can rhyme too!

Exhilarated by her progress, she throws herself into the more difficult task. She discovers at once that this poem can begin in exactly the same way; so she writes the same first line. It can continue the same way, what the words are about depends on what you have in mind when you read them, just as the Author said this summer. The poem can even end in the same way!

Tina is absolutely delighted. She's found the Poem of Betrayal, the ultimate poem about betrayal, any betrayal at all. This has given some meaning to Stefan's deception. If Tina becomes a great and famous poet in the future, she can turn to the camera when she receives the Nobel Prize and say: And I would like to thank Stefan Juhle, wherever he is. It's thanks to him I'm standing here now. He betrayed me when I was fourteen years old. That served as an incita—well, a prod. Fourteen is an awfully sensitive age, and his cruel action made me serious about expressing myself in lyric form.

When her delight has subsided a bit, she decides that Cilla is worth a few changes. Certain revisions, made with the intention of distinguishing the two betrayals.

*I know that everything comes to a stop*
*everything must eventually reach its end*
*but if the time is not yet up*
*it's a betrayal not to come back again.*

Tina is so delighted by this verbal carpentry and her success at it, above all her success, that she forgets her sorrow while she's working. That's not to say that the sorrow forgets her. No, the night does come, new long days do come, and the sorrow returns, as if it had learned from the poem and sensed it would be a betrayal not to come back again. You of all things I will allow to betray me, says Tina to the black cloud.


Writing poems is one way out of the dark spaces, is one path to the light, Tina concludes. There are more paths to take if one wants to find words that can overcome sorrow and describe betrayal, or do whatever else one might want words for. At the camp this summer Tina got some tips, which she noted down and forgot; but of course she still has the notes. Now she goes to the library and searches the shelves, seeks out books in totally different sections than barely a year ago. Sits breathless in the reading room with articles about contact beyond the boundaries we usually set for our spirits. Takes books home and devotes the nights to reading about the powers of the self, the meaning of life, the existence of other worlds. Reads everything she can find about how the seemingly inexplicable can be explained.

These books are certainly strange: they give answers that Tina has never heard before. In her experience, if you turn to people and ask for explanations, you always get answers that have to do with God. What is love? God's handiwork. How can people understand each other's thoughts? Because they meet in God. Why are we born? What's the purpose of life? What's the meaning of death? God has the answers, but they are hidden from us. What is it that calls from beyond the mountain? Always, always, the answer contains God. As soon as you ask questions about such topics, it's taken as proof that you believe or want to believe in God. Tina knows there was a time when she accepted those vague but confident answers from believers, though without necessarily believing. Now she realizes that she doesn't believe in God. So those answers are no use. They don't help once you've discovered that they avoid the really difficult part. God is the answer to believers' fantasies of a solution to the difficult equation. And because they fantasize so fervently, they're satisfied, even though the answer is incomplete. There's so much to object to about God that it's impossible to entrust your life to him. It's even more repugnant to use God's omnipotence to explain Cilla's death.

But the answers these books give are different, even though the authors clearly want to find answers to their difficult questions just as much as the believers do. These writers avoid mentioning God when trying to explain difficult problems. In one place after another, Tina reads variations on the idea that we are all parts of a larger whole, that—in a way invisible to our own eyes—we are united on a deep level that we can learn to apprehend, if dimly. Love and understanding between people who were strangers seem perfectly natural from this perspective. Life and death are two aspects, human aspects, of something that in itself is one and the same thing—something that also contains time, space, and all the objects that exist in them. On the deepest level everything is one and the same, it's just we who don't see it that way and insist on setting up our imperfect categories for the parts, insist on giving them names, as if the parts were unconnected.

The books that treat these subjects are often tough going, to put it mildly. The learned author refers to something that someone said in 300 B.C., that someone else connected to in the 1300s, that so-and-so had a theory about in the 1700s, and that we only came to understand with the advent of the theory of relativity. Or the author swings easily from one thinker to another far off in the East, where for four thousand years they've known everything that we've just now begun to scratch the surface of. Tina can scarcely read two or three pages without having to break off and hunt up another book the author refers to, as if it goes without saying that all readers have the whole of literature fresh in their memories. But when the book she's reading is based on quantum mechanics and relativity, she gives up trying to check the sources. Just studies the book and trusts the conclusions that it claims follow from the impenetrable theories. Perhaps you don't need to go into everything. The author probably wrote the book so you wouldn't have to.

It feels important, what she's reading now, but it's difficult and demands a lot of time. Tina cuts school so she can read more, plays hooky because the insights she's gaining tell her that right now school can't offer anything more important than what she's reading. No school subject in the eighth grade comes anywhere close to explaining the mysteries of existence.

The teachers have no sympathy for a girl who holds their teaching in such contempt. That she is troubled surely can't excuse that sort of behavior. Is she going to have fewer problems if she neglects her schoolwork? If she can never answer in class, or isn't even there, and can't produce any results on tests, then she'll have to accept getting graded accordingly. And Tina accepts it—or rather, she couldn't care less about her grades.

■

Tina also searches for more poetically satisfying answers to the big questions. No matter how well written a philosophy book is, it will still be heavy going. Maybe someone's written a poem that casts light on the same issue with a few shimmering words.

The poetry is neatly arranged in a corner of the library. You can pull out one book after another, leaf through, browse here and there, stop wherever you find something you like. In this way, almost at random, it happens that Tina opens a thin volume and reads these words:

> *I saw you dead, no*
> *it was no longer*
> *you.*
> *The body lay there*
> *motionless, void*
> *recalled the person*
> *who moved out*
> *reminded me*
> *that you really were*
> *not there.*

Yes, the poem continues, but here are the words that become Tina's way in. To think one can write poems like that—so simple, so true! That it's allowed!

*I Have Seen Someone* is the title of the collection; Marie Louise Ramnefalk is the name of the poet. Tina browses, sees how precisely all the fine little arrows have hit their marks, unerring words that quiver in the bull's-eye on grief's black target. This isn't exactly Tina's grief, it's another target: a grown woman in the void left by her husband's illness and death. Another grief, but Tina feels even so that her own has been given words.

So language isn't speechless after all, it has words that we can sometimes touch each other with. And in learning about another person's grief, I find that my own is to some degree relieved. *All sorrows that are my sorrows . . .* where did I read that? I browse and search, but find it somewhere else, and then it's not as I remember it, but instead goes: *the songs of all of you that are the same song / and the songs of all people, which are my own singing.* I find it at home, in a song by Violeta Parra on the tapes we listened to long before we understood—at least I didn't understand a thing:

> *Gracias a la vida que me ha dado tanto.*
> *Me ha dado la risa y me ha dado el llanto.*
> *Así yo distingo dicha de quebranto,*
> *los dos materiales que forman mi canto,*
> *y el canto de ustedes que es el mismo canto*
> *y el canto de todos, que es mi propio canto.*

> *I want to thank life for giving and giving.*
> *It's given me laughter and it's given me weeping.*
> *That's how I tell sorrow from joy,*
> *the raw materials my songs employ,*
> *and the songs of all of you that are the same song*
> *and the songs of all people, which are my own singing.*

But it takes a good while before I manage to find that tape. In the library an incorrect quotation is buzzing in my head and I'm standing there trying to place it, at the same time as I'm leafing through *I Have Seen Someone* and reading further in it. All the poems deal with this grief.

I borrow the book, sit down with it and copy out one poem after another. The simple form, the pared-down language! You don't need to rhyme, you don't have to be grand. *I mourn for you* can be written just like that. *I miss you, I want you here, or want to be with you where you are*—it can be enough to say that in a poem.

I even find the following; even this is printed in black and white:

> *Dearest, you whom I buried on Wednesday,*
> *don't worry about the man I met on Friday,*
> *don't worry about my new vacation plans*
> *my looking around for a new life*
> *all the talk, all the efforts*
> *they're just grief the whole lot*
> *just grief.*

The best thing that happened this summer and at the same time the worst was that I was with Stefan—so close and warm. But it wasn't right toward Cilla; somehow it wronged her memory. I felt guilty about being happy. If I forgot her for a while, I almost felt like punishing myself afterwards. Yes, punishment, that's what I got, all right—later, when Stefan dumped me. Serves you right! my conscience has said to me ever since.

But now, now that I've read the words in this poem, I understand something else. *They're just grief the whole lot*, even though they looked like joy and forgetfulness and a betrayal of Cilla. And Stefan probably dumped me simply because he couldn't stand it when the grief floated up and showed itself in the midst of our joy.

Didn't I cry out for Cilla—perhaps just when things were

the sweetest for Stefan and me? Yes I did, and it disturbed him, I could tell, though I didn't think about it then.

Of course he dumped me—I was hysterical. He couldn't put up with me, since I was up one minute and down the next. No one can put up with me, I notice that at school now. How is anyone supposed to, when I've gotten so terribly heavy. And all people, you and I and whoever, are shallow until they've been hit by something that teaches them to reflect. Maybe that's as it should be; I suppose it's all right for them to be like that. Maybe it's not so strange that people who float on the surface can't put up with someone who's been stricken to the core. They're probably afraid that I'll suddenly sink below that surface and want something from them, want something they don't have up there, want a seriousness that they can't offer and that they don't understand can actually be a part of joy. They can't manage it; they don't dare to risk it: they think they'll drown if they go below the surface.

But it's not a full life, just staying on the surface. The whole deep ocean contains so much more than the surface where the waves splash and roll. The depths are where everything big is hidden—wonderful to discover, and frightening only for people who don't dare to dive in.

■ ■ ■

On TV there was a film about twin sisters. And suddenly as I sat there watching, the thought crashed over me, cutting sharp as glass, as if for the first time: I'll never be able to hug you again, Cilla!

Never again will we warm up for the evening's rehearsal with our mirror game. Never again will it be you I see reflecting my movements.

I'll never be able to sneak out of an unwanted phone call by saying that Tina's not home.

Never again will we laugh together at something funny that we've seen.

We'll never lie next to each other again and talk through the whole night.

We're never going to quarrel again either, Cilla, no more of that either!


It wasn't the first time I'd thought that way, not at all, but it hurt just as much as the first time! I was pretty happy for a while there, almost as if you were with me. But now it hurt just as much all over again—no, worse. Because it hurts to think like that, of course, but it's much worse when the thought sinks, sinks once and for all and lets go of the lifeline of hope. That's how it was now. When the grip loosened and the line came up empty, an aching certainty remained, forlorn in the darkness: never again means never again. *Jamais plus!*


And if it's never going to stop hurting, it's never going to stop! I don't want to go on living with this pain, don't want it to leave me either, because then it'll just be worse when it comes back. I want to remember you in life, Cilla, and I want to forget that you're dead. But if I forget it for a little while, it hurts so much, so much when I remember again.

Help me, Cilla! Take me under your wing! Give me peace!

*Under the Cloud*

*I'm afraid of death and of dying,*
*afraid of the journey through the dark, cold tunnel.*

I'm afraid of seeing that light,
of trying to reach it but not being able to.

I close my eyes and try to forget that I'm dead,
but I'm there just the same, in the tunnel,
alone with my tears and my terror.

I'm so afraid!
Where is that god they all talk about?
Please! Someone! Help me! . . .
I walk and walk, but the light is still far, far off.
Then I hear the voice, my sister's voice,
so reassuring:
"Don't be afraid, I am with you."

I look around and there she stands, beside me
in the white nightgown she wore when she was buried,
her dark hair, her face, her eyes,
her smile, she still has her wonderful smile
and her Bob Marley necklace around her neck.
And her hands aren't blue and broken
    like when she died.
Now they're beautiful, so beautiful.

The next moment I'm in her embrace
and hug her,
laughing, dancing, crying.

I'm not afraid anymore,
for I'm here under the cloud
together with my twin sister.
For ever and ever.

*17*

ear up his photo! Forget his name! Tina has barely thought this thought and reached the tough conclusion—*Stefan is history!*—when a letter arrives from the county library saying that the fall get-together we talked about this summer is finally happening, now we'll all get to see one another again, everyone's welcome, and we can figure out if the camp had any lasting value.

Tina has a stomachache for a whole week before the meeting, but she goes to it, yes, she goes to it! She nods and smiles to faces on the left and faces on the right, because everyone knows, of course: here comes Tina, and it's not us she's looking for. Then a lane opens up across the floor, a lane that she need only walk along, walk and walk until it ends. And there, at the end, sits Stefan, who's pretending to read a newspaper. He pretends until her shadow falls on the print, then looks up and pretends to be surprised, pretends to smile—yes, that's probably supposed to be a smile, that grimace, and this is supposed to be Stefan's face, though the suntan is missing, there's no question it's Stefan looking up and saying hi.

Hi, Tina answers.

To think you can say hi when your heart is turning one somersault after another and your stomach is cramping up and your soul is trembling.

There's a chair next to him, waiting. Tina sits down in it. Now she's here. He's not going to duck out of this—right: she won't let him duck out of it.

Tina observes Stefan, looks at his face until he turns away, embarrassed. Then she looks at his ear and his hair.

Did your pen run dry? she asks into his ear.

What?

I've written a whole lot of letters. You haven't answered. So I'm wondering: did your pen run dry?

She expects, she almost hopes, that he'll say he never got her letters, that she must have had the wrong address. Then she'll say he's lying. She had the right address; she checked it after the third letter. But he doesn't say that. He says nothing.

I've been so low, she tells him. You could have answered.

Stefan doesn't defend himself, doesn't explain.

Did you read the letters? Or did you just throw them out?

No, Stefan says—he has to say something now. I read them.

But you thought they weren't worth answering? Or what?

Stefan opens his mouth several times, closes it just as many times, takes a breath as if to start talking, but nothing comes out.

Tell it like it is! Tina urges him. A girl who's dumb enough to write fourteen letters without waiting for an answer is a girl that Stefan Juhle just has to dump.

Tina purposely mispronounces the name: Stefan Yule. Be goddamned if I remember your name!

It wasn't *that*, Stefan finally manages to answer.

What was it, then?

You live so far away. I didn't dare to get attached to you.

What kind of crap is that? Tina wonders.

Well, your feelings, Stefan continues. They're too much for me!

Tina turns this statement over for a while. Comes to the same conclusion, no matter how she looks at it: Then this summer was just a sham!

A sham? Stefan echoes. Not the way I see it. What happened was for real. It was summer. Right—can't you understand that! A summer love.

When does it count? asks Tina.

What do you mean?

When does love count? Not in the summer, evidently. So when?

Stefan has no answer. And it doesn't matter. This whole encounter doesn't matter. To hell with the summer camp; that whole chapter is closed, can be erased. And Stefan—wipe him out. Almost any excuse would have been okay, any reason he might have come up with. But not what he'd said . . . what a fucking drag to discover you've been in love with a bastard!

Tina leaves the meeting.

■ ■ ■

In Studio Three, Synnöve tries something new. Well, in other groups it's not at all new, but here it is, since Synnöve has always made the members do everything themselves: all the way from the first concept and the first rough draft, everything's been hatched and developed by the group. Now they're going to tackle Dickens's *A Christmas Carol*, adapted for the stage by Synnöve's husband and directed by her.

How's that for newfangled!

Yes, says Synnöve. Now we've finished playing at self-reliance for a while. It's not a challenge anymore. You've got to learn the submissive sort of theater too, learn to surrender yourselves to a role defined by others and stay within a given framework. In fact, that's the most usual way of working in the theater. Besides, stage versions of A Christmas Carol are among the best-known plays there are. It's a challenge to tackle a story that everyone already has an idea of, tackle the familiar and yet come up with something new.

"Challenge" is Synnöve's watchword these days. Everything is a challenge. Or there's no challenge, in which case whatever it is gets dropped.

Fragments of the play slip into the group's warm-up exercises; other fragments they rehearse and develop. They hold meetings and have discussions and ponder who'll get which roles.

The play has quite a few male roles, and the drama club consists almost entirely of girls. Tina is assigned the part of Bob Cratchit. That's a really good role for you, Synnöve says. You need something to sink your teeth into.

At first Tina isn't at all enthusiastic about the part—the wimpy bookkeeper who would let his half-dozen children starve sooner than ask for a raise of one pence. Cratchit's temperament is very distant from her own, but gradually she comes to see her assignment as a *challenge* and takes it on with fierce determination.

Sandra gets a considerably more appealing task. She's to be the Fool. Continually onstage, she's the one who has to pilot the play through the dizzying gyrations of dream and the shifts back and forth in time that build up the narrative. It's a wonderful part, a *challenge* that Tina would gladly have accepted, but she can't bring herself to envy her friend, especially since she knows Sandra will do a fine job. She does a fine job with all the roles she gets.

Synnöve's only worry, she reveals at a meeting, is that the group lacks an actor suitable for the lead role: Mr. Ebenezer Scrooge, that terrible skinflint, the bogeyman of all poor children's nightmares, the one who must be overcome by the truth about his past and, in a credible way, be transformed, until in the last scene he is goodness personified. This challenging role requires an actor the drama club does not have.

Sandra, Lotta, and Tina leave the meeting together. Are you thinking the same thing I am? Sandra asks.

Probably, Lotta says.

Probably not, is Tina's answer, because her thoughts are already far from the play and have turned to the book she put aside the evening before.

Come on, Tina! Sandra says. You can save this stupid Christmas story.

Bob Cratchit isn't the world's savior, Tina points out.

Oh, gimme a break! Lotta moans. Who's talking about Cratchit?

What're you guys talking about then?

Do you know a certain Fredde Lindgren? Sandy asks pointedly. A boy in our class?

Naturally Tina won't answer such a dumb question, so Lotta takes over: A good actor, though he isn't a member of Studio Three. Got any clue who that might be?

Yeah, he's good, Tina finally agrees. He could manage Scrooge for sure, she thinks aloud, then announces it with certainty: I'm sure he could do it.

Well then, Sandra says. Then you'll talk to him, won't you.

Tina looks from Sandra to Lotta and back again. They're in

complete agreement; they glow with understanding. What's the point? Tina has to ask.

Nothing, Lotta says. Just that he can't refuse if you're the one who asks him.

Oh!

He can say no to us, Sandra chimes in. But not to you.

Nobody thinks there's something between me and Fredde, do they?

Well, as for who he's hooked on, Tina Dubois is surely the only one who hasn't noticed, Lotta answers.

Oh, gimme a break! Tina moans.

Trust Aunt Sandra, says Sandra. Go offer the guy the best role he's ever had, and you'll see how he snaps at it. Give him a kiss into the bargain, and you won't need to talk so much.


Fredde blushes like mad when Tina manages to get him alone. But once she's explained her errand, he forgets his discomfort and considers her question. And now he can even admit that he's already thought about joining that drama club of theirs. His success last spring kindled a flame, but after that he couldn't make up his mind. Didn't dare to, sort of, he says, and glances quickly at Tina's face—does she understand what he means?

Maybe she does understand him; in any case there's no mistaking the flame. There's a light around him when he gets going and talks, something that goes out when he casts that cautious glance at Tina. She senses that the atmosphere is getting too emotional, that there's a risk Fredde will start explaining why he didn't dare. So she tries kidding around, teases him by saying the character is so unsympathetic that the part would surely suit him.

I know, is all he says, so calmly that Tina shifts gears.

Can you come to our meeting this Wednesday? she asks.

He nods, and on Wednesday he's there. When Synnöve sees him, she doesn't need to ask any questions. She remembers his performance in *Let U = Unexploited* and realizes at once that Ebenezer Scrooge has arrived.

Much hard work remains to be done to get the play into shape. That work goes the way theatrical work usually does—and grows even more hectic because Synnöve wants them to be ready for a premiere on the day after Christmas. Tina enjoys entering into a role again; for long stretches of time she forgets the afflictions that weigh her down. Then she can grow really light-hearted and break out in laughter that makes her friends remember the Tina they'd gotten to know on the other side of the accident. It's as if the wounds of your own life heal better if you get to bleed from pretended injuries. Something to sink your teeth into, Synnöve had said. Maybe she had some secret motives for the assignment she'd given Tina—a Tina who'd remained silent far too long.

In breaks and after rehearsals, Fredde struggles hard to get Tina to notice him. Tina doesn't ignore him completely, but she doesn't want to seem too interested either, especially since Lotta and Sandra, wearing knowing expressions, are observing this additional little play. If it heats up for real, we'll expect an invitation, Lotta says. After all, we were the ones who . . .

Oh, would you get *out*! Tina snorts.

But nothing does any good. When someone really wants something, the moment of truth arrives sooner or later. Fredde makes sure he gets a chance to take a walk alone with Tina, so they can talk beyond the range of knowing looks. Are you still almost engaged? he begins.

Tina, who was expecting the question, had planned on answering that it was nothing for him to worry about, but now she can't bring it off. No, she says. It ended.

Tough luck! Fredde says in a commiserating tone. He doesn't go on and say, I know how it is, but that addition hangs unmistakably in the air.

Tina is so touched by his brief and sympathetic "Tough luck" that, departing from all plans and goals, she tells him it was a terrific shock when her fiancé, or almost-fiancé, just split. You don't get over something like that right away.

Nah, it's hard, Fredde agrees. Though of course you have to. Gradually, I mean.

I don't know . . . Tina hesitates. Do you really have to get over everything? *Can* a person get over everything? Can't you care so deeply about something that it's not possible to get over losing it?

Fredde seems to mull over the questions. It's pretty obvious that Tina is talking about something other than her almost-fiancé now, something bigger that she's lost. Her wound is still so fresh that everyone remembers she has it. Fredde, too, remembers, of course. *Everything* can't be gotten over, I'm sure, he says now. I didn't mean it could, either. But a guy who takes off—that's gotta be peanuts compared to the things a person can never get over. A jerk like that can't be any reason to go into a nunnery.

That's where the conversation ends, because Tina has to catch the bus. It takes her the whole trip home to overcome her astonishment. Who is Fredde, really? A person who talks like that is clearly someone completely different from the Fredde she remembers.

She is more than willing to be drawn into the next conversation, or the continuation of the interrupted one. If that's how things are now, Fredde says without explaining what he's driving at, but Tina understands anyway. If that's how things are, then maybe we could go together?

What do you mean by go together? asks Tina, and it's the first time she's ever asked to have the notion clarified; until now it's always worked well enough without definitions.

Fredde can't be precise about it, or doesn't want to. Everyone knows what going together means.

I don't think that . . . Tina says, when his silence has lasted so long that something has to be said. I mean . . . when a person's had someone . . . been engaged, almost . . . then a person sort of . . . I mean . . .

Fredde waits for an explanation, but Tina can't bring herself to deliver a conclusion she realizes will hurt him. A boy who's asking for a chance surely can't bear to hear that once you've tasted Love, you can't imagine playing with little boys anymore. Compared to Stefan, Fredde is a child. Presumably he senses this, but there's a difference between sensing something and having it thrown in your face. And if he does sense it, then he's doubly brave to dare to ask.

I guess it's like this, Tina finally says. When I think about it, I can feel that I haven't gotten over the shock after all. Like, I can't manage yet to . . .

That little word yet has scarcely slipped out between her lips when she realizes that it contains a half promise, a whole promise, a binding promise of a future for whoever has the patience to wait. And Fredde, who is hoping so ardently and listening so anxiously to her words and interpreting the slightest shift in her intonation—Fredde has surely heard the promise and immediately made up his mind to reach that future.

Ah well, he sighs. So that's how it is. Though we don't need to be enemies on that account, do we?

At that, Tina just has to reach out her hand to stroke the disappointed little boy on the back of the neck. But he doesn't know this as he stands there next to her, hoping the bus will be a few minutes more in coming. Nor will he ever know it, because she checks herself halfway and lets her hand drop. She smiles instead, from the heart, and there is light in her voice and her eyes as she answers that surely one can do without enemies.

That was exactly the right thing for Tina to do! With a glance at her face, Fredde gathers up and stores away that light.

Alone on the bus afterwards, she's forced once again to ponder what sort of person he is, really. What is it that drives him toward her, even though she's done nothing but reject him? And how can he, nice as he is, be so perfectly loathsome in the role of Scrooge, just as Sandra and Lotta anticipated, just as Synnöve wants him to be, just as *A Christmas Carol* needs if it isn't to be mawkish—yes, how do you manage that, Fredde Lindgren?

# 18

$\mathcal{E}$ternity does come to an end after all, it seems, since the fall term gradually crawls toward a finish. The grades Tina receives are a procession of wretched Fs, interrupted by the occasional D. To hell with school! To hell with teachers who think they've got something to say, think what they say is important. To hell with everyone who thinks that Cilla doesn't exist anymore. To hell with whoever thinks it's high time Tina got her act together. To hell with anyone who can't see that she *has* gotten her act together. In school that sort of act doesn't count. It has nothing to do with what they talk about there. It has no effect on grades. To hell with grades!

But that's not so easy to repeat when Albert is looking at the report card, muttering that he's never believed his daughter was stupid.

Tina can't figure out how to take his remark.

*A la bonne heure*, he says—all in good time. Right now we can forget it. Right now we're going to celebrate Christmas.

To hell with Christmas! There have been brief periods this fall when Tina could imagine that her grief for Cilla had faded slightly. Christmas arrives with the message that this isn't the case at all.

The big problem with Christmas, as she's known for a long time now, is that the old traditions can't be changed the tiniest bit. On the contrary: Jan-Olof has discussed with Monika how Cilla's death was tragic enough on its own; the sorrow can't be allowed to expand and make everyone abandon everyone else and stop seeing one another. Therefore, the family should celebrate Christmas at Rosengården as usual. This had scarcely been decided on when Jonny bailed out of all the festivities. No one knows where he went off to, but he was away for all of Christmas.

Christmas—to hell with it! There can't be anything sillier in the whole world than our Swedish singing and dancing rituals around the Christmas tree. How could Monika let herself be talked into it? How could Albert go along with this spectacle? There's never been a worse Christmas for Tina, and she can't believe there could ever be a worse one in the future, either. To be sure, she gets out of entertaining the relatives with some little piece of theater in front of the Christmas tree, gets out of making them sentimental with her rendition of some pretty music, but she doesn't get out of being there, doesn't get out of Christmas presents, doesn't get out of the long hours . . . above all she doesn't get out of being a single, a one and only, at every moment and in every place where everyone remembers that there were two of them last Christmas and the Christmas before that and all the other Christmases here at Rosengården.

Justine doesn't come; she wasn't even interested enough to

send her regrets when she got the invitation. So there should be at least one thing to be happy about, an absence to enjoy—and to save this Christmas, what would really be needed is for someone at Rosengården to be happy. But Justine's demonstrative indifference makes Albert bitter, and bitterness doesn't contribute much to the Christmas atmosphere.

As early as last summer, it had become clear that new times were at hand for Justine. When Monika and Albert arrived in Brou, they were barely acknowledged with so much as a *Bonjour*. Justine had found a man to share her life with, so now her old life must be cleared away. The man was Albert's age, so delight at Justine's happiness was muted, to put it mildly. Monika and Albert changed their plans and returned home as soon as they could. When Tina later returned from the Literature Camp, they congratulated her on having been spared their experience. Tina, who had the memory of Stefan's hands burning all over her skin, wasn't especially interested or surprised. Typical Justine, she muttered. Embarrassing when old broads hook up with guys young enough to be their sons. Monika explained in private that Tina had to try to show Albert some consideration. To lose your mother that way—you can understand that it stings.

Consideration! I'll *say* it stings to lose someone, no matter how it happens, Tina wants to answer, but she stifles her accusation, because an accusation is what it would have been.

At any rate, Justine hasn't come, hasn't sent regrets either, so her new love has lasted at least until now. And along with her, all of Albert's relatives stay away. This decision on their part is also something he frets about, but it's his problem, solely his problem. Monika's relatives show up as usual, her brother and sister with their spouses and children.

Among them is Tina's young cousin Mattias, five years old, who was always so happy and cheerful before and is now so serious and wide-eyed and observes Tina wherever she goes. He's not at all the way a five-year-old child should be. His sister Jannica has turned three and become a person now, a little person but not at all the way a three-year-old child should be.

They are Jan-Olof and Marika's two oldest children; there are two more—year-old Veronica and newborn Pontus—two little, little ones, who, thank heavens, can't remember anything that could make them accusingly serious in the midst of the grownups' attempts at make-believe mirth.

Mattias and Jannica are painting; each one is making a Christmas picture, or maybe they're making one picture together, since Mattias doesn't seem to have gotten very far with his. Jannica paints a dark-blue sky full of big yellow stars that blur into the blue.

Cilla's up there too, she says, and points at her painting.

I don't think you can remember Cilla, Mattias says.

She's always so nice to me, Jannica declares dreamily.

Tina's the one who's nice to *me*, Mattias says.

It's a shame she's dead, Jannica muses, as she plants another yellow fleck of star in her sky.

I'm sad too, Mattias points out.

For Tina, who overhears them, it sounds as if they're sorry about *her* death too. When she's shaken off the chilling sensation, she discovers to her surprise that this little conversation has lightened her heart for the first time this Christmas. There was something so matter-of-fact about her little cousins' comments. No muted voices, no guilt or shame veiling the words. They haven't yet had anything explained to smithereens. They know on their own how things are. And

*they're just grief the whole lot*
*just grief.*

Someone is dead; now she's in heaven because she's nice. Someone else is also nice. That's all there is to it.

Well, there's a little bit more. Two children who are grieving. Right across the gap in age that separates Tina from her cousins, she's recognized the burden of sorrow they're carrying. There's enough grief for everyone—isn't that what Georg had said? It's just that it's much too easy to minimize the load that others bear. Tina feels tormented by the way uncomprehending grownups can't believe that someone her age can suffer a grief like the one they themselves know. Now she feels almost ashamed at her own surprise that grief can dwell in children as young as Mattias and Jannica. How this discovery could have lightened her heart is more than she can fathom, but it has: for a brief interval she feels almost joy at sharing something so fine with her cousins.

■ ■ ■

A brief interval of joy—exactly. As for the rest of Christmas, to hell with it! She gives her relatives tickets to the premiere, which will take place as planned on the day after Christmas. Oh, what fun! they say, almost in unison. A *Christmas Carol!* Which part do you have?

Bob Cratchit, Tina says, completely indifferent to what they'll think.

At the premiere, Fredde's Ebenezer Scrooge serves up a rage that no one has seen the likes of during rehearsals. For Tina, who as Bob Cratchit has to bear the brunt of his persecution, the fear he arouses is all too keen after just a few minutes and makes her sink deep into the helpless nervous wreck that Bob

Cratchit really is. Fredde disappears, and Tina with him; Scrooge remains, spewing his hate-filled, stunted soul over Cratchit, taunting and humiliating the lowly slave. Cratchit has nothing to counter with: what can a poor devil do against this madman? When Scrooge has finally boxed Cratchit's ears and whacked him out onto the street with his cane, all Cratchit can do is stagger home to a doomed family and explain that all hope is gone.

After this, Tina can rest while the spirits lead Scrooge around through his past and insight gradually dawns in him. She needs to rest to recover from her surprise at having been flogged by Fredde. Those were certainly no stage smacks he gave her. What the audience thought was terribly well acted was in fact the real McCoy: battery right on stage. If that rage was acted, Fredde is a greater actor than anyone suspects.

What possessed him? Why did he behave like that? If he's thinking of beating me up in the rest of the performances, too, then count me out!

Then comes the final scene: insight has gotten the better of Scrooge and transformed him. He includes the whole world in his great, newfound friendliness. Oh, Mr. Cratchit, I must make amends to you. A raise of five shillings, ten shillings—tell me yourself what amount you consider suitable.

Instead of having Cratchit rejoice at the offer, as the script calls for, Tina pays Fredde back for his improvisation. Make amends! Good God, what are you thinking of, Mr. Scrooge! We're talking about a whole life, Mr. Scrooge. A whole life of humiliation for me and my family, Mr. Scrooge. That's something you can never ever make amends for with your filthy money.

Cratchit's unforgiving response draws Dickens's familiar narrative toward a completely new ending. Tina has the pleasure of seeing Fredde reel as he searches for a way out. The audience finds his faltering silence natural. But they nonetheless want a happy ending to the play. Go ahead, get out of that one, Fredde! You don't beat up Tina with impunity.

Mr. Cratchit! Scrooge begs and sinks to his knees, embraces the bookkeeper's legs, gets up and embraces the rest of him, whispers and mutters how wretched he is so his regret can be heard in the last row of seats, asks for pardon here on earth, from Cratchit, otherwise the goodwill of heaven is meaningless—to make amends, of course that's impossible, what's done can never be undone and thus can never be made good completely, I know that, Mr. Cratchit, but your pardon, I implore you, it is my only request, surely you are above envy and revenge, surely you have compassion for a miserable sinner, I beg . . .

He goes on like this, begs and beseeches until a stone would be moved to tears. What would Bob Cratchit be if he didn't grant forgiveness at last; what would Tina be if she didn't finally soften in Fredde's embrace? She's not made of stone. She forgives him and accepts a substantial raise.

After the curtain, the applause, and the flowers—much applause and many bouquets—there's a small late-night party to celebrate the premiere. Ham salad and bread to eat, and talk about how great the whole thing went. Synnöve takes Tina and Fredde by the ears, laughingly scolds them, or in other words praises them, for their mutiny in the final scene. About the beating at the beginning she has nothing to say.

A little music has been provided, and a corner to dance in, for anyone who wants to. They're short of boys, of course, but the girls in the group are used to dancing with each other. Everyone seems to take it for granted that Fredde will dance with Tina.

What the hell came over you? Tina asks her partner.

Wasn't that great? he asks with exaggerated surprise. Wasn't it a *challenge*? Didn't it come alive? Didn't Synnöve say we should play out real life on the stage?

Do you intend to continue playing out quite that much life, if I may ask?

Everything for art! Fredde vows.

Shit, I'm black-and-blue all over, I'm sure of it!

I don't believe that for a minute, Fredde says. Lift your top so I can see!

That'd suit you fine, wouldn't it!

She presses closer to him as they dance, so he can't pull up her top—which he's trying to do, or pretending to try. Funny, she can't be angry with him. He's revealed something during this performance; she doesn't know exactly what, but she likes it. On the other hand, she can't go along with getting beaten on four more nights. Taken by surprise, a person can accept a few blows one time. If you beg for more, you're perverted.

At that moment Fredde says that he doesn't really know why he got that way. Or I guess I know, but it won't happen again, that I'm sure of. I'm not completely perverted, after all. Tomorrow I'll hug you the whole time instead. Like in the final scene tonight—that felt good. I guess that would surprise Synnöve again.

If you start improvising some gay drama tomorrow, then you're going to get stopped short, Tina promises. Try to get back to the approach you used in the dress rehearsal.

*19*

hey call this time a turning point, but afterwards everything's just the same as before. Happy New Year! the whole world shouts, but Tina is afraid. All around that world, need and oppression hold sway and wars rage, but cheerful people, who can party just the same, are whooping it up everywhere. God doesn't exist, but in churches the clergy are consoling the grief-stricken with his name. Cilla's been dead for eight months, but her family and friends give no sign of this. *Happy New Year* means pretending that the bad old year is forgotten.

Tina is sure that Mattias and Jannica—two children who haven't yet learned forgetfulness and indifference—are the only ones, of all the people around her, who feel pain at the memory of Cilla. She heard Mattias say that Cilla was stupid to die.

She ran right out into the road, Jannica said from inside her playing. She didn't look first.

That was a dumb thing to do, Mattias said. If not for that she could have been here playing with us.

Tina is here, Jannica consoled him, pointing at Tina.

Later they left Rosengården, traveled away, beyond reach, but Tina senses that these children will always, always make her want to play. She'll never run away from them, never run right out into the road. Yes, that was a dumb thing for Cilla to do!

It is New Year's Eve. Tina is sitting over her diary and trying to collect herself so she can write something. A resolution, perhaps—that's the custom, after all. Or a few sentences summing up the past year. Good God, the past year!

*I hope you can see and hear what I'm thinking and writing to you, Cilla. Otherwise it would be so meaningless. I don't mean the thoughts themselves and what I write—I don't give a shit about them. But that you can hear me, that's what's important. That you're alive, because otherwise everything would be so meaningless. If death __was__ death, then life would be meaningless. But I know you're alive. "Death" really means that you're living someplace else.*

But this wasn't what Tina wanted to write—not really. She raises her eyes from the diary to the mirror, takes a deep breath and gathers her strength, waits for the right moment to whisper: Cilla, I'm so scared!

Cilla doesn't answer.

Yes, Tina is scared. Scared of several different monsters. Which in the end are maybe just one, the whole lot of them.

Scared that the night will again bring her nightmares once she's fallen asleep. She can cope with the day's thoughts, but against the nightmares she is defenseless.

Scared it will turn out that Cilla was just a dream. That her whole life as a twin was something Tina dreamt. She was alone the whole time and didn't wake up until the second of May.

Scared it will turn out instead that the life she's living right now is a dream. Suddenly Cilla will wake Tina up and remind her of what she'd said one time when she'd dreamt about romance and blond boys: *All dreams are really wishful thinking.* You said that yourself, Tina. So why are you dreaming this?

Scared of forgetting Cilla. Sometimes she gets so unclear that Tina has to peek at the mirror to remember what she looked like. In the drama club we were supposed to tell about a childhood memory. When it was my turn, I couldn't think of a thing! I'd forgotten everything! I panicked, couldn't remember anything. Later, when I came home and told Monika about it, she said: But don't you remember this . . . and that . . . and the other thing . . . Sure, then I remembered, of course. But the point is, it was possible to forget! Maybe I'll forget everything, all of a sudden, that's what I'm scared of.

Scared of getting stuck when I make believe that Cilla isn't dead. I pretend so intently that in the end I don't know what's true. I have to pretend once in a while, otherwise it's so terribly painful. But it's dangerous, I think; what if you suddenly can't get out of the fantasy. There's a risk of that, I know. Just a few days ago I had a lot more books than usual to lug home. You'll never manage to carry all that, Lotta said when she saw the pile. I'll get Cilla to help me, I said. Before I even heard what I'd said, Lotta was hugging me. Oh, Lotta, I'm so scared, but when you do that I calm down! Thanks for being in the world,

Lotta, thanks! No matter what you do: thanks for just existing! Scared of going crazy from grief. I think of Cilla so much and the thoughts just race around and around in my skull until I go nuts—I'm scared of that. Luckily, it's easy for me to talk, if only I have someone to talk to. With Lotta and Sandra I have two someones I can talk to about everything. They're such good listeners. Lotta is security personified; she's really my best friend. And Sandra, too, makes me feel safe. But she also has her own horror weighing on her, because she went along with freezing out Cilla. She let Cilla down—and never got to clear it up with her.

I'm scared that Cilla will hurt me because she's dead while I get to live. The Cilla I know isn't like that, but maybe my nightmares know her better?

That's exactly what we talk about, Sandra and I. Sandra says she can't believe Cilla wants to take revenge on me for her death. Haven't you said yourself that life over there, where Cilla lives now, is more beautiful than life here? You're the one still walking around on the ugly side. So what does she have to get revenge for?

And I tell Sandra that I think Cilla has forgiven everything and understood that the pressure from all the others was too great for Sandra to resist. We believe in each other, so to speak, and aren't so scared anymore when we've talked for a couple of hours.


But her greatest fear Tina prefers not to speak about at all, even though she knows that it helps to talk things through. The other fears she can talk about, no problem. She shares them with Lotta and Sandra, friends who lighten her burdens, and she tells Georg Jansson about them. He, too, is a good listener and can answer in such a way that she can sometimes believe him.

Even if you forget absolutely everything else, you will never forget Cilla. It's impossible, completely impossible.

The feeling that reality, both the present and the past, is a dream—that's an entirely normal chemical reaction, the chemistry of grief, something that switches on automatically in people to protect them against what would otherwise be overwhelming.

And we've talked about the nightmares. They're fueled by your guilty conscience, which pops up with all your own unjust charges, disguised as Cilla's accusations. Haven't you explained things to Tina yet, the way I asked you to? If you do that, you'll see that you'll sleep peacefully.

Naturally you have to pretend that Cilla is alive now, for exactly the reason you give: because otherwise it would be so terribly painful. It's not dangerous, not dangerous at all; it's a comfort, and you need it. When you don't need it anymore, you won't fantasize anymore either, it's that simple.

Yes, he can interpret the text so she believes him sometimes, believes him time after time, so that with a small rock of firm belief from each time she has gradually accumulated enough to build a little platform, climb up onto it, and get a bit closer to the light.

But her greatest fear she simply does not talk about, though perhaps she should. It's about those times when she discovers that Cilla is inside her, times when she feels with Cilla's feelings and thinks Cilla's thoughts, times when she really doesn't know who she is, Cilla or Tina.

She can't help noticing that she's become much more like Cilla now than she was just a year ago. It's not this change itself that troubles her—actually it feels quite nice, almost like honoring Cilla. No, it's when the indistinguishable likeness goes one step further, when thought, innermost thought, consciousness, and everything that constitutes one's own self suddenly doesn't know: am I Cilla or Tina? That's what she's scared of, or its extension—that the answer will expand into a transformed certainty: I am Cilla.

Tina is scared that she'll end up wandering through life being Cilla while everyone calls her Tina.

That transformation feels so whisperingly close sometimes that it's impossible for her to talk to anyone about the terror it evokes. Yet she *should* say something. Send out constant distress signals, so that if these fall silent one day, someone will understand that now it's happened. Understand and perhaps come to the rescue. If Tina is worth saving . . .

What's even harder to bear is the thought that this terrifying transformation is so confusingly similar to the explanation of life and death and the meaning of it all that Tina so fervently hopes is true. If we are all parts of a single whole, if all people in their cosmic depths are the same spirit and matter, then there shouldn't be any distinction between Cilla and Tina: you are in me and I in you, and there is no boundary between us. That's how it is, and knowing this is my greatest joy. But if I'm so scared, it can't be true that I *know* it. If I'm scared, it can't even be true that I *believe* it!

■ ■ ■

Then Bahir comes and asks: Have you decided?

He comes at exactly the right moment. It's wintry January now, but his question lights the lamp of memory and casts its glow on one of the fall's absolute high points, namely his saying to Tina that she wasn't in the least like Cilla. The comparison obviously wasn't in Tina's favor—at that time he hated Tina for the difference—but when you're feeling bewildered and threatened by the chance of a mix-up, such a message is a relief, a testimonial: you are the person you are and cannot be swapped with anyone else in the world.

I've practiced, says Tina. I'd like to try, for Cilla's sake I want to try, though I don't know what you want me to do, and I don't think I can do it, I'm not that good, I'm just telling you, please don't be so disappointed because I can't do it that you hate me, I can't stand being hated by you, not even for not being like Cilla.

Bahir, who came with steady step to ask his terse question, stands still now, grows unsteady, reels under the pressure of her torrent of words, reels and looks for support, lifts his hand in a warding-off motion, which he changes into one of his magical gestures, the one of almost touching, almost, but not quite, of leaving his hand hanging there, as if he wants to make two fingers feel the Bob Marley necklace but discovers that it isn't hanging at his fingertips—Tina's neck has no jewelry. And in the silence after she has uttered two different forms of the verb *hate*, he breathes with audible strain, while behind him Ola shifts from one foot to the other and looks away, yes, turns his back somehow, though there's no question he's standing so he can see and hear them, above all so he can hear their conversation.

I don't hate you, says Bahir, when the silence has filled the space it had to fill. If you really want to try, then I'm satisfied with that and will never hate you for it. A person can't succeed or fail without at least trying.

Ola pulls out a piece of paper and gives it to Tina: This is the address of our studio. It's top secret, just so you know. Bring your fiddle, we'll take care of the rest.

When? Tina feels that she's on the verge of going into a spin in the whirlwind around the two musicians. They want something from her, just that is cause enough for dizziness, but she manages to stay upright by clinging to practical details. When, then?

They agree on the following Tuesday evening, so at seven o'clock on Tuesday, Tina arrives with her violin at their secret studio, feeling nervous and small: these are two pretty famous men she's visiting, if you want to look at it that way, but looked at another way, she's visiting two young guys whose purposes she isn't entirely clear about. One of them was in love with Cilla; the other is sexier and above all more alive than any lover in the movies. She herself is fourteen years old and hasn't told anyone at home where she's gone this evening. The address was top secret, after all.

Bahir shows her around the equipment. Says the name of each piece, gives her samples of how they sound, spouts figures about frequencies and watts, performance and decibels. That stuff is Greek to me, Tina confesses.

Ola gives a laugh at her admission and delivers a synthetic drumroll. From this, various other sounds spring forth, all of which presumably have their own designations, for those who understand such things, but for Tina they're just a lot of beautiful sounds until they arrange themselves and flow into a channel she recognizes as the introduction to *Cilla Suite*: "Her Eyes Are Blue."

But Tina is soon reminded that she hasn't come here just to enjoy the music. Up to that point we're satisfied, Bahir explains during a short break, awakening her from the images she's seeing. But now here it comes, listen closely.

Listen closely, mm-hm, he isn't satisfied with the strings, Tina's understood that much, but what's wrong with them?

Can you get hold of that melody? Bahir asks, and hums it, while Ola plays the passage a second time.

Don't you have a score? Tina ventures to wonder while she feels along her fingerboard for the notes.

Ola laughs. Derisively? No, just laughs. A child has spoken in the studio. A score she's asked for! It's funny, the way children's questions often are.

Scores are wrought-iron bars for the music, Bahir explains Ola's laugh. You don't play this kind of music from notes. Look at these staves, he says, and holds up a sheet of staff paper. Tina sees it: iron bars—exactly!

But what does it start in? Tina asks. Is it in G? You may not have a score, but the notes themselves still have names.

It's all the same to me, Bahir says. G or Q or whatever you want. Ola, bring that up!

Strange people! They're on their way to the very pinnacle of the music business but don't know anything about notes. Is knowledge of the formal foundations really a barrier for the creative imagination? Can't it be a support, a framework to attach the free-floating visions to?

Ola, bring that up! Bahir has said, and Ola turns dials on his huge console and the strings play alone, the lead part and all other sounds are gone. Hold on to that! Bahir says now, and Ola keeps the first note going until Tina finds it on the violin. It's an intermediate pitch, a spot on the string where she has never placed her ring finger since she learned to play on key, nor any other finger either, but now it's the ring finger, somewhere between E and F—well, why not a Q, that's as good as anything else that doesn't exist.

When Ola lets the sound proceed, Tina keeps up for a couple of notes but soon has to give up. Glissando! she sighs.

A what? Bahir asks.

No person can play like that machine, Tina explains. The notes slide around without any fixed key. It sounds terrific together with everything else—why do you want to get rid of it?

Bahir makes a sign to Ola, who turns off the machinery and leans back into the shadows. Now he's not here anymore—they can speak freely!

We can't begin by giving up, Bahir says.

I'm not giving up. It's just that I can feel that I can't manage it. And I don't see the point of doing it. The music's super as it is—haven't you already had enough confirmation of that? Everyone likes this piece the way it is. I'm not giving up.

Here's how it is. Bahir holds up an index finger that means, In the first place: You're not supposed to play like the string machine. No person can do that, you're right, and I don't want any person to play like a machine; I want *you* to play like a person, as only people can. In the second place (says his middle finger), I've already told you that we, who are the ones who've played this suite until we know it now—we've heard that it *doesn't* sound super and that it's *wrong* to have the synthesized strings here. A solo violin, a genuine string, that's the thing we want to have instead. In the third place (his ring finger, right on cue), no matter how many people say the piece is as it should be, that's no confirmation. A million flies gorging on horseshit are no proof it's delicious. In the fourth place, you'll manage this if you want to. You can do anything you want to, anything— this too! And I plan on helping you, but the resolve has to be your own. In the fifth place: as to what the point is . . . it's for Cilla's sake, and that's enough.

With his fifth argument, Bahir has extended all his fingers. He holds his hand out to Tina with the palm upward, as if he's handing over an invisible gift, or as if he's begging for one—no, he isn't begging, his gesture declares that he's ready to receive and to share at the same time. His inviting her to give him something is his gift. And it's for Cilla's sake; that's enough.

Tina raises her bow and fills the studio with a Q.

*20*

*I*n the fall and winter it seemed to Tina that everyone was turning away, when they themselves perhaps believed they were talking to her. This spring people are talking to her and *with* her, she discovers. They say things that go straight into her and start growing there. Words are messengers from one person to another. If they come from the depths of the sender, they carry secret meanings larger than the words themselves. If they reach the depths of the recipient, they yield up their secrets. At the deepest levels, we have everything in common. Words help us discover this kinship. With words the writer stirs the reader across expanses of time and space. If the deep connection already exists, that stirring happens simply because one person has the gift of eloquence and another person is willing to listen. Perhaps it's a greater miracle when something that seems like a casual chat between people who at the outset are strangers is transformed, by some invisible turn, into a conversation between people who now feel a close connection—a connection at those deepest levels. The miracle is to discover the kinship, discover the depths.

That's how people talk this spring: miraculously. Not all of them, of course, but some of them. Where do they come from? Where have they learned this language? What did they say before? Tina wonders, until she discovers that the explanation does not lie with them. It's she who has learned to listen.

She listens to Cilla. She has finally opened the secret diary and read what Cilla didn't dare to talk about. I've already related most of what I found there; in some ways everything I've told so far deals with that.

It's a shame that Cilla could be so tight-lipped; that was her great flaw. If I'd known how she took things to heart, I would have stopped teasing her after the very first time. And I would have taken it back! Anything can be taken back if only you're sincere. But she didn't let on. Reading that did something so terribly painful to me that I can't find a way to describe it. I was so ashamed I could barely keep reading, but now I've gotten through it. What a relief it was in the midst of the whole thing to find that she'd forgiven me! *Tina is such a child. I absolutely don't mean anything nasty by that, because children are so* pure, *so* innocent—*that's how I mean it. It's the best thing a person can be: childlike!*

She could forgive, she could afford to see something fine in my childish silliness, because she suddenly knew that I was wrong—when she fell in love with Bahir! Beloved sister! I can hardly grasp that it's you, thirteen years old, who wrote so beautifully of love! And he never even suspected!

Fredde is one person she listens to. After finding him mentioned with a certain degree of respect in Cilla's diary, she listens for an echo of Cilla in his words. And when Fredde notices that Tina is listening, he slowly changes the topic of the conversation and leads it little by little to a confession that he was hopelessly in love with Cilla but never dared to tell her. I was shit compared to her, he informs Tina. And if she'd said anything like that to me, I would have died. No, I kept my distance. Avoided her. I knew I'd give myself away otherwise; I was scared to death when she stepped up and grabbed me at the rehearsals for Project U. Everything can be hidden—until you look each other in the eyes. Then the game is up.

Looks like you were wrong there, Tina says. Cilla didn't think you were shit.

Yeah, well, she said something much nicer to me then, but love . . . no way! She looked me in the eyes. I couldn't get away, and I thought: Now she can see it. But the project was all she had in her head back then. She didn't see me. She filled me with her resolve, but she didn't see me. And I knew: I'll never reach that high! So I wanted to go hang myself, to jump in the lake. But I didn't do it. Then we suspended the project. And then she died. And then we restarted the project. And I saw you. The way I remember it, you two together were so happy. But alone she was so serious and you were so unnaturally bubbly. Now you were sad, so terribly sad. And you were fantastic in that part in Project U! For me, you took Cilla's place. Do you know what I mean? Later, during the summer, I thought about how with Cilla I'd never dared to say anything until it was too late, and that I couldn't let it be the same with Tina. So when school began, I asked . . . well, you know.

It was good that you said no. At the time, when you said it, I didn't think it was so great, I felt like hanging myself again. But in the course of the fall, I realized that it wasn't you I'd asked, but Cilla. Do you see what I mean? And when you asked if I would join the cast and play Scrooge, you were still Cilla.

And later when you discovered that I was Tina, I got the thrashing of a lifetime for it, Tina puts in.

Exactly, nods Fredde. And your damned fiancé got a licking at the same time.

That's okay, Tina says. That's completely okay. He was a bastard.

Now I know that you're Tina. And we're together, though I haven't asked again. It's that simple now.

That's probably because I don't seem as high up to you as Cilla did, Tina suggests. That makes it simpler. But honestly, you know: I care for you, but I'm not in love with you.

I know, Fredde says.

He glances away, and Tina knows that she shouldn't look into his eyes right now.

■ ■ ■

Bahir is another person she listens to. Note by note and with limitless patience, he helps her through *Cilla Suite, Cilla Sweet*. One evening her listening leads her to understand what's wrong with the synthesized strings. It happens when Bahir says something about the purity of the solo part and calls the sound of the synthetic strings "dreggy." That reminds Tina of the solo voice that summer, the one that sang O, *never was the sea so shining in-* side her, all the way to *your first kiss*; reminds her precisely of the purity of the solo voice, a purity that lifted the song high, so high, much higher than when the repeat came, the whole song again, with accompaniment. No matter with what melting sweetness the instruments followed the voice, they weighed and pulled it down. Dregs—exactly.

Only when Tina has understood Bahir's aims does she succeed in capturing the melody and bringing her playing close to what he wants. Suddenly she has all of "Her Eyes Are Blue" in her fingers. To get it exactly right, she's had to tune the violin up to that unknown step between E and F. Evy, with her perfect pitch, jumps out of her skin one day at a lesson, when Tina has forgotten to retune. What's happened to the violin!

Tina tells her what she's been doing every Tuesday night. To her surprise, Evy is overjoyed. But that's wonderful, Tina! Don't retune for anything in the world! Do you really mean you're collaborating with Ola and Bahir! My God what a talented pupil I've got!

But Tina, who knows how hard it is for her to achieve what Bahir wants, doesn't feel all that talented. Now that "Her Eyes Are Blue" flows smoothly, she has a new problem, or an old phenomenon that has returned and become a problem. She ventures to tell Bahir about the flute that takes up its melody as soon as she's played a few notes. It's all well and good during the lessons Evy gives her, but in *Cilla Suite* a flute clashes badly with the music.

Mm-hm, Bahir nods. I can imagine. There's no room for a flute part here.

Just the same, flute is what Cilla played, Tina points out. If this music is Cilla, the way you once said it was, then it should really have a place for flute, too.

Definitely, Bahir agrees. That's probably what she's saying when she joins in.

Only then does Tina notice that Bahir automatically accepts that she really hears a flute when she plays the violin. And Ola, at his console, expresses no doubts either. You guys believe me! she bursts out.

Yeah, what else? Bahir asks. It's obvious you're in touch with Cilla. That's why I brought you in on this!

For me it's not so obvious. Sometimes it's almost scary.

Scary—come on! Bahir rejects the notion. Be grateful for it; it's a gift, after all. It's really only through art that a person can have that sort of contact across the boundary, though usually it takes more than just picking up a violin and playing it. Listen to any music that's got something to it. Look at any painting that's got some depth. Read any book where the author understood what matters. All real art crosses the boundaries that the philistines have drawn. Cilla lives, you know that as well as I do. But you're in touch with her; I'm not.

Ola sends "Her Eyes Are Blue" sweeping through the studio. Could this work? he asks, slides a lever—and a flute part breaks free of the flow. Tina has the hang of the melody and quickly finds the right place with her violin. Soon Cilla joins her and there are two flutes playing.

It's not exactly right, Tina declares. But it's better this way than before.

But synthesized flute, Bahir sighs. That's just as bad as the strings. Hell—what a drag that you're the only one who can hear the right flute.

■  ■  ■

Ola is someone else she listens to. He doesn't talk very often, and when he does it's usually in short, choppy sentences. But one evening, when Bahir can't make it to practice and Ola gives Tina a lift home, he stops the car at the turnoff and looks out across Death Road. So this is where it happened?

Tina nods. The effort needed to control herself makes it difficult to talk: Ola is so sexy that trying to seem unaffected by it is painful. If he made the slightest pass at Tina, she would fall for him like a ton of bricks. But so far he hasn't once shown the slightest interest of that sort. Now they sit silently a while and look at the spot where the accident happened. Then Ola speaks:

There are a lot of things I regret. Things I've done, I mean. Though there's not much point in regretting anything. But what I regret the most is that demonstration when we hugged the trees, you know.

Don't talk about it! Tina whispers.

I have to, goddammit! If we hadn't been so damned good at hugging, we would have had a highway here.

I don't believe that. Maybe in five, six years. But not now. And the environment—

The environment! Ola bursts out. Here's where Cilla died. If we hadn't been so damned good at tree hugging, it wouldn't have happened. If we hadn't been so damned good at hugging, there would have been a stop to the accidents on this stretch of road. The whole damned road is a death trap. And look at those brown pines all along Death Road! Smell the stench here! The environment isn't one bit better off than if we'd had a highway. All that environment talk is just bullshit.

Can't you just shut up! Tina screams—screams so her voice cracks, but it's too late, he's already said it. And what he's said is the truth. And it's something Tina doesn't want to hear, doesn't want to think about.

Rail at the authorities because they don't do anything about the traffic! Grumble because the police don't patrol the roads! Jeer at the signs the Traffic Department puts up instead of taking strong measures against the drivers! The same people who rail and grumble and jeer then come out and hug trees when there's a plan to put a highway through their wild mushroom patch. The same people who are shocked when the police carry off the tree huggers drive like lunatics on the wretched old road. Hidden crossings and curves, oncoming traffic without dividers, bus stops just over hills—and people call defending those kinds of death traps "protecting our precious environment." But since Cilla died, not a single one of the area's environmentalists has found the way up to Rosengården to ask for a signature on a petition against the highway that might stop the ravages on Death Road. Before, they were running up here like crazy, and sometimes they got a few signatures, too.

That's what the truth Ola is getting at looks like, and if things were simple, I'd probably know where I stood. If black were always black and its opposite always white, I would know what's right and what's wrong. The environment suffers just as much no matter what sort of road runs through here, so if human lives can be saved, my choice should be simple. But you can't save human lives by rebuilding roads. The only thing that will help, that will save both the environment and people's lives, is for each individual driver to shape up. Each person is a part of the whole, each little person bears a part of the general responsibility, and that part can't be shifted to "the others." "The others" are steered by completely different forces, forces that want the road built no matter what the cost, forces that don't care about the environment *or* our lives but will gladly use those pretty words as lures to trick the protesters and split the opposition.

The real purposes of those forces are so deeply repugnant that black goes gray goes white goes gray goes black, and I don't know anymore what's right or wrong, and instead scream at Ola to shut up. And he does, because he doesn't know either.

As individual people, we're too small, but a great responsibility rests on us nonetheless, completely on us.

Is that why? Tina asks after a long, long silence in the car. Is it because of that regret that you've played *Cilla Suite* for almost a year now.

Nah, I'm doing it for Bahir, Ola says.

You're doing it for Bahir?

If you could understand what he felt for Cilla, and if you could understand how much I owe him, then you wouldn't ask.

What he felt for Cilla I've certainly understood, Tina affirms. As for the rest, I don't know anything about it.

Everything I am, I've become thanks to Bahir, Ola tells her, and starts the car again. He took me and lifted me out of all the stupid crap I was stuck in and taught me what life's all about. Bahir is great. I'll play *Cilla Suite* until he wants me to do something else.

Tina thinks about what Ola's said, chews it over until they swing up into the yard at home. I understand things better now, she says. Not because I know what you were stuck in—but you aren't stuck there anymore, that much I can see. Bahir is great; you're the second one to say that. Now I really believe it.

Who else has said it? Ola wonders as she climbs out of the car.

Cilla, Tina says—a revelation from the secret diary.

■　■　■

Georg Jansson is yet another person she listens to. The distrust she felt toward him in the fall has long since vanished. Time after time he's proven that he's there for her—and wants it that way. He doesn't spend their meetings pumping her for thoughts and feelings, only to show in the end how interesting he himself is.

That image of how psychologists work is one that Tina has gotten from things Albert has said. Carina, the school psychologist, confirmed the image to a certain degree, but Georg is completely different. Thanks to him, I'm free of my nightmares; thanks to him, I know for sure that Cilla has forgiven me everything, that she isn't seeking me out to take revenge for anything, that whatever hurt we caused each other doesn't mean a thing anymore compared to the real love between us.

I miss you, Cilla, I miss you, I miss you, I miss you so badly that I could still fill page after page with nothing but my missing. I miss you at night, in the long nights, I miss you in the daytime, I miss you in the morning when I rush to the bus and know that you're running a half step behind me. But when I look carefully, so carefully before I cross Death Road, where the bus is waiting on the other side, then I remember why I'm so careful and also remember: you aren't there. Oh Cilla, I miss you so!

And you know: the other evening they played "Puerto Rico Salsa" on the radio. I've heard it only once before, when we danced to it, remember? The last Christmas when you were alive. As soon as the music came on tonight, I was there with you again. I had to turn it off, I just couldn't bear it! I will always have you in my blood, Cilla! But I'm not scared anymore, I know where I am, and I know that you're living near me, that you love me as I am and watch over me wherever I go. If I were to be suddenly run over too, I know you'd be there to receive me, but I don't long for it to happen anymore, because I know you're still with me, and that brightens my life.

And even though I've been able to feel this way thanks to Georg Jansson, it doesn't feel important to keep going to him.

■

Therefore, after some hesitation about exactly how to say it, one day Tina tells him: I don't think I'll be coming anymore.

I don't think so either, Georg answers at once, almost interrupting her.

I don't mean there's anything wrong with you, Tina explains. It's just that . . .

. . . that it isn't necessary anymore, Georg fills in. I can see that.

Everything's going much better now, Tina continues. She feels she should explain herself. My friends at school aren't such a pain anymore—you know, the way they couldn't bring themselves to talk to me. And it looks like the teachers have finally understood that I needed to go at half speed for a while.

Yes, they have, Georg nods. All the more so because you've gotten your act together.

Gotten my act together? Tina ponders. I don't know. I think a lot more now, think further, sort of. I care more about other people—I *see* them. Before there was no depth in anything I did. Maybe that's why Cilla had to die? So that I would see more.

As I've said before, Georg objects, I don't think there was any purpose behind Cilla's death. But it's certainly had that effect on you. Made you deeper.

It's almost embarrassing to talk about yourself that way: about your depth and whether you have any or not. Tina returns to the subject of not needing to come to Georg anymore. Because when it's working out okay in school, everything's much easier, because school's a pretty big piece of it all, you know.

If I were to guess, I'd say that you're in love, Georg says. In a serious way this time. And that this love is mutual.

Tina has to reflect before she answers. Is she in love? A year ago she wouldn't have needed to hesitate before answering. There was always someone she was in love with. For lack of anything better to do, you could always fall in love with some boy or other. So to speak. But somewhere along the way, Tina has changed. The world looks different from her point of view now, even though it's still full of boys: fine and cute ones, handsome and sexy ones, and then a few sulky types who are almost invisible but sometimes show a side of themselves that makes them interesting nonetheless. That's how the world looks: Tina loves them all—but isn't in love with any one of them. And in that she finds the answer she decides to give to Georg. Yes and no, she says.

Was it Tina who said that? Georg asks. "Yes and no." Yes, I'm not in love. No, I'm in love. Well—forgive me. That's none of my business. I'm just happy on your account. I see that you're doing well.

It's "Yes" because I love all people, Tina explains. And "No" because I'm not in love with anyone in particular.

Well, in that case the love is mutual, Georg nods. *Everybody loves a lover!* he quotes in English. Go, Tina. Go make people happy with that light you have around you.

## 21

*G*o make people happy! What an unheard-of commandment! As if Tina had a message for all humanity. But that's not how she feels. On the contrary: she's the one who's listening.

Maja Sjövall and Anna-Karin are two people she listens to simultaneously. It's April, and the path to this conversation has been long and winding. No—there hasn't really been a path, so it can't be called winding, but somewhere at the outset there was an obstacle: Maja and Anna-Karin were the two classmates that Cilla liked the least, and the feeling was mutual. It was Maja who started freezing out Cilla, and it was Anna-Karin who kept the temperature low.

What these two had to go through after Cilla died is a question Tina didn't devote any thought to at all, and she might never have done so, either, if this conversation in April hadn't taken place. And the conversation might never have taken place if Tina hadn't woken up in the night with the accident suddenly in the room with intense clarity. The feelings that she couldn't let out when the accident happened tear at her now, as the car tires screech, the essay snows down, and the stench of burnt rubber stings her nose. Cilla's been hurled far away. Martin is staring, staring.

She's been spared such attacks all spring, she's just taken leave of Georg Jansson and declared herself healthy and free of them, and now she's sitting up rigid in bed and screaming, screaming, screaming with reawakened terror and despair.

Albert hears her and comes in, puts his arms around her, holds her close, and slowly rocks her. You're home, Tina. You're in your bed. *Là là, doucement! Ma fillette*, did it happen again now?

It was so real, Tina groans. There's no distance between then and now, here and there.

Albert sits with her until she falls asleep again. *Doucement, là là, doucement!* Yes, Tina does manage to fall asleep, but in the morning the night's experience stays in her head and distorts reality: Cilla has just died.

So it's unbearable to go to school. Tina leaves Rosengården in the morning, pretends everything's normal, takes the bus, but doesn't go to school. Drifts around in town, sits in Studio Three's meeting rooms for a while and tries to read a script, but can't bear to do that either. Out again. That's when she runs into Maja Sjövall and Anna-Karin. They have two free hours in a row and are out enjoying the sunshine.

Aren't you sick today? Maja asks.

Depends on how you look at it.

What does that mean? Anna-Karin asks.

Cilla died last night, Tina says. She was run over. For me it was a close call, but Cilla got run over. Ever since then I've thought about how terrifically lucky I was, and it makes me so damned happy I just can't stand going to school.

Silence falls for a bit over three girls on a sidewalk. Two of them thinking about what they've just heard, the third regretting a little what she's said. No way those two makeup mannequins can have a clue what goes on inside of Tina! They're brain-dead! Cilla says. Cilla said—it's been a year.

I see, Maja says finally.

And Anna-Karin stretches out her hand and touches Tina's arm gingerly. Yes, Tina is real: Anna-Karin can feel the slight pressure under her fingers. Do you remember outside the hospital, when we ran into each other there? You told me Cilla was your sister, do you remember?

Tina shakes her head.

I thought you were totally weird when you said, "Cilla, my sister—we're twins." Later I found out Cilla had died. Then I didn't think you were so strange. And now you're strange again. What am I going to find out tomorrow to explain why you're talking like this?

They start walking, slowly.

It's not so strange, Tina says. It happened again last night. The accident, I mean. For me it isn't strange at all, it's almost the opposite, as if you get used to it, though, well, you never do, but it's happened so many times I've lost count already. If you think it's strange, then you don't understand what it is to be there, to see it and hear it when your sister gets killed.

What Tina says is an accusation; it remains hanging in the air. Anna-Karin breathes deeply and makes a start several times before she's ready to answer. Well, in that case, she finally gets out. That explains a lot. So I don't need to wait till tomorrow.

If it happened again last night, then you aren't strange at all. Christ it must be tough!

Now it's Maja's turn: I really admire you, Tina. You're so strong!

That's some tribute to get from someone you don't admire at all! Why? Tina has to ask. I don't see that there's anything to admire me for.

Yes there is: you're so strong, like I said. Ever since Cilla died, you've been strong. And then you have dreams like that and manage to go on living anyway.

I'm not strong, Tina protests. I'm a coward, a super-coward. I've tried the whole time to run away from everything. I'd like to cry right now, but I don't dare to. Not when you two would see it. You're strong if you dare to show your feelings.

We could go in here, Anna-Karin suggests outside the café. We can sit down in there, in a corner, and all cry together.

That takes more strength than I've got, Maja declares.


What have you two got to cry about? Tina asks when they've sat down.

Then she finds out. It isn't easy when an enemy dies, an enemy whose sister is alive, a sister whose identical likeness keeps the memory of the dead girl constantly fresh. It isn't easy when there's a minute of silence for an enemy, a minute whose silence grows terrifying. It isn't easy when there's a school psychologist who keeps asking and asking and trying to dig up what you'd rather forget. It isn't easy when there's a play put on in memory of the deceased; it isn't easy to become friends with the one who's died. All in all, neither Maja nor Anna-Karin has ever experienced anything worse than this past year. A hundred times they've set out to beg Cilla's forgiveness; just as many times they've been stopped by the realization that the person they would come to in reality was Tina. And she's been so sad and beyond reach the whole time. Now chance or some other power has arranged things so they've come to her nonetheless and been able to deliver their burdensome words. Now everything's been said, now they're crying in front of Tina, who sits there astonished and is crying herself.

Yes, she is astonished, bewildered at having discovered there was something behind those faces plastered with makeup, when she'd always believed there was nothing there but pure vacuum. This is a miraculous moment; reality has turned the slightest fraction of a degree and revealed a new facet of its wondrously cut and polished stone. The light falls on two superficial girls and disappears into depths they've carried within themselves all along.

But why? Tina asks. I've wondered that so many times. Why did you do that to my sister? Why were you mean to her?

Why? Maja looks to Anna-Karin for an answer. Anna-Karin looks to Maja. Why?

She was very stuck-up, actually . . . Maja mumbles. She despised us, sort of . . . yeah, that's it.

Maja doesn't want to say any more, maybe she doesn't really know. Anna-Karin gropes further. Lands way back in a time that Tina doesn't know anything about, in the sixth grade, when Anna-Karin and Maja were the most popular girls in the class. Without even trying—that's just how it always turned out. But then in the seventh grade, you two arrived . . .

Tina begins to glimpse an answer. Then in the seventh grade, we arrived. And we didn't do anything that Maja wanted, and we laughed at what Anna-Karin said. We didn't even care what their names were, in the beginning. Suddenly Cilla was the one who wrote the best poems in the class; her ideas shaped the fall revue; she was the one who got the class going. And the boys liked her. Not so they were in love with her, but they liked her; she was charming and lively, and they preferred her to girls like Maja and Anna-Karin. Falling in love was my department. And the girls couldn't get to me, I was too easygoing and cheerful. But Cilla had a seriousness that she readily fell into, and that made her vulnerable. That's where the envious ones could attack her.

I actually liked Cilla, Anna-Karin claims.

It's possible to believe her. It's possible to believe that she and Maja don't really know the answer to Why? anymore, have never really known, never seen themselves clearly enough to think it through, have just felt regret and more regret, when it was too late. Regret is always too late.

That's how it is, but a person can still be sincere in regret and in asking for forgiveness. It's possible to believe Maja and Anna-Karin now; it's possible to believe their tears; it's possible to believe that they won a great victory over themselves when they didn't pull away, but finally let this conversation take place.

Look! Tina cries, and points out the window.

They look toward the window, toward the sun-drenched rectangle in the café's dark wall. Yes, it's sunny outside; sharp images of people pass by, some of them talking without the sound reaching into the café. But what's Tina pointing at?

They don't see what she sees: that they're sitting in the murky dining saloon of a ship that, without any disturbing vibrations or sounds, is gliding through the world. That the strongly lit scenes outside the window are nothing but etchings, pictures of things that have happened in some other time, at some other place, pictures that by chance have turned up just as their ship is passing by. That this is what reality is. That everything exists everywhere and at all times. That whoever is open to it can catch some glimpses of this everywhere-and-always reality, can see through chinks in space and through a window of the ship he's traveling in.

■ ■ ■

Albert is a person she listens to. They called home from school and asked about her. Then it came out that she'd played hooky again. The world has really changed: this time no one was horrified. Instead Georg Jansson asked Albert to come in for a little talk. Of course, Tina has no idea how that conversation went.

But Albert comes home, takes Tina's elbow, and goes out with her for a turn in the garden. The green leaves have begun to come sneaking out, a shivering paradise has begun to prepare itself for the fact that May will soon be here.

I haven't given you much support through all this, Albert says.

Pappa! Tina wants to object, but Albert presses her arm a little more firmly, in a way that means she should be quiet.

I've nagged you about shaping up, when I should have stood close by you and dried your tears.

At that Tina starts crying softly. What Albert is saying is true, and she has hated him for his nagging about getting her act together. But now that he's talking about it, she's far past all hatred, and his words sound so tragic that she can only respond by crying.

He sees that she's crying, stops, takes out a handkerchief, and . . . yes, just as he said: stands close to her and dries her tears.

I want to tell you that all of that, the nagging and the hardness toward you, they were just grief the whole lot, just grief. They were my way of grieving.

I know, Tina says into his handkerchief. I know, Pappa, you don't need to explain.

No, I guess I don't need to, but I'd like to talk with you about it now anyway, *ma chère fillette*.

Tina nods her agreement.

I don't think there's a person in the whole world who has as much to regret as I do, Albert says, and now he's crying too. I've been thinking about how I behaved toward you and Cilla, and I can't, I just can't understand how a pappa can be so terribly mean to two girls who haven't done anything wrong.

You're being too hard on yourself, Tina says. That's not how you look to me or to Cilla, either.

It would be nice if I could see myself in some other way. But that's what my hell has looked like this past year. If at least my regret could have made me kind! But instead I've done nothing but carp at you the whole time.

It's just grief, the whole lot, Tina repeats his words, which are a line in a poem she's known for a long time now.

Everything that's happened to us in this family, Albert continues after taking in Tina's response, everything that's affected us, all the hurts, all our little conflicts, they're all trivial compared to this with Cilla.

Of course! Tina agrees. Obviously. And that's why what you call your terrible meanness is also trivial.

Albert is astounded. What it's taken him a year of brooding to realize, is obvious to Tina, his fourteen-year-old daughter.

It's something you learn from a thing like this, Albert says to Tina and the garden and anyone who can hear it. It's something you learn when a thing like this happens: you learn what's really important.

Yes, Tina says softly, carefully, because she can hear that Albert wants to describe how they look, the important things.

We humans have each other, just each other. Some people understand this straight off and live a good life together. Others, people like me, don't realize it until something like this happens. If I'm to find any meaning in Cilla's death, then it has to be that it taught this to us who remained: all we have is each other. And now I cherish those close to me as never before.

■ ■ ■

Monika is another person she listens to. At the dinner table on Walpurgis Night, Albert puts down his fork and knife and says: We're sensible people, aren't we?

Tina and Monika exchange glances. How can one respond to such a gambit?

We have to talk this through, Albert continues, and turns toward Monika. The day after tomorrow is your birthday.

Yes, so . . .

We've avoided deciding what to do about it. We need to decide now.

Is that so complicated? Monika asks.

Maybe it isn't. But in any case I want to hear each person's honest opinion about what we should do. We're sensible people.

Yeah sure, Monika says a bit impatiently. Well, I won't mind if you two don't feel like saying hip! hip! hurrah! and aren't full of cheerful congratulations on *that* day.

But surely we can't devote your birthday to grieving?

You said yourself that each person should decide independently. If you two want to grieve, then . . .

Nobody *wants* to grieve, Tina mutters.

Well, I'm not so—Monika starts, but interrupts herself and looks out the window.

Come on, say what you were going to say, Albert urges. *Dit carrément!*—Speak frankly!

Sometimes I wonder if it isn't precisely *wanting to* that you both go in for, Monika declares, without shifting her glance indoors from the garden.

Tina and Albert look at each other, look at Monika, look at each other again.

What are you trying to say? Alberts asks. You'll have to excuse us, but neither of us understands where that was coming from.

I don't know myself, really . . . Monika gropes for words. Working through the grief . . . This is going to sound so . . . I don't know . . . it's very serious, after all, it really is, and it's what you've both been doing: working through and working through . . . but I think . . .

At that she breaks off. They wait for the rest. When it doesn't come, Albert asks: What do you think?

This is going to sound so terribly hard-hearted! Monika says. I can hear myself how hard it sounds. I don't mean to accuse anyone of anything.

Say what you mean now, Albert urges her. It looks like it needs to get said.

I think . . . Monika starts over. Or rather, I heard it on the radio, and I think it's right, that working through grief means a person has his own unresolved problems.

Must have been some psychologist who came up with that, Albert mutters.

What kind of unresolved problems? Tina asks.

All sorts, is Monika's vague reply.

And that's what we've been doing, instead of being cheerful and positive—is that what you mean? Albert has sharpened his tone.

Listen to that, Monika comes back. Just tap on the cover the slightest bit and the crab starts scratching and scrabbling inside.

If you two are thinking of quarreling, then I'm going out, Tina informs them. I have to leave soon to play music anyway. So just go right ahead!

But what are you driving at, really? Albert asks, his tone somewhat calmer. That we're grieving—is that so offensive? And what's all this about "unresolved problems"?

It was a program about the grief when someone dies, Monika explains. There's nothing offensive about grieving—on the contrary. But what they emphasized was that there's a difference between grieving and working through grief. Little children, who aren't carrying around a whole load of unresolved problems yet—they just grieve. And once they've grieved, they can move on. But adults have to work on their grief, and that's the same as working on their own problems. And if they never get clear about those problems, then working on the grief never ends.

Oh, that one! Tina recognizes the argument. That's what Elisabeth Kübler-Ross says, isn't it. Or something close—

—Well, then, Monika cuts her off. In that case it deserves some attention, I suppose.

You'll have to excuse a simple man from the deep valleys of computerland, who's neither seen nor heard the latest dialogue in the theater of psychology. Just how does this connect to your birthday, which is what I asked about?

In that I won't be offended if neither of you feels up to a birthday party. I can understand that. You have your problems.

Our unresolved problems, you mean?

Your unresolved problems.

And you've resolved your problems, I take it.

I haven't resolved them, because I don't have any, Monika declares.

A long silence follows this answer. There's only one possible conclusion to this conversation, Tina thinks. Albert is heading toward an explosion. When he gets there, I'm splitting. Then Monika will go into the kitchen. Albert will go out and do a little digging. And on Thursday we'll sit here hating one another and chewing on birthday cake, and after five minutes we'll start talking about unresolved problems.

It's fine with me if that's the kind of birthday Monika wants. Thinking she doesn't have and hasn't had any problems is self-deception, a lie that helps her survive. Not just in the beginning, but for most of this whole year, I've had to force myself to play Cilla's role to cheer up Monika, had to be Cilla for Mamma, had to pretend I was more like the daughter she lost than the one she's got left. If I was scared of getting stuck in the role, scared that Cilla would stay inside me and take over, then what gave me some help in escaping that fear was precisely my distaste for playacting for Monika. So the help was mutual, and Monika can have her lie all to herself now, and I'm not going to jump up from the table and expose her by yelling: Look who's talking, you who . . . No, I'll wait for Albert's rage; an outburst is only natural after so much nonsense from Monika.

Then Monika says: Cilla knew she was going to die. Children know these things, and Cilla died before she lost touch with her inner child. She knew. She gave me a final salutation, the best one I could have hoped for when there was so little time. That smile—you have no idea what it's meant to me. It said that there was nothing between us that needed clearing up. I grieved for Cilla, but I didn't need to *work* on the grief. I cried, God knows how much I cried, while you were going about working on . . . Well, I don't know what it was, you didn't share it with me, but it wasn't tears, it was work, and I don't want to deny it was grief, but besides the grief there were a lot of problems, more problems than you could cope with, and that's why it's kept going. But when I'd cried myself out, I could move on, because Cilla gave me that going-away present as a birthday gift: her smile. *Thanks, Mamma!* she said. Does either of you understand what she was thanking me for?

Of course, Albert says softly. I'm sure you're right.

And Tina is crying. This certainly isn't the first time she's heard Monika talk about Cilla's final salutation. But it's the first time the story has sounded like this, the first time Monika's told the whole thing, the first time she's given her interpretation—that Cilla saw death approaching and thanked Mamma for the life they'd shared.

It's a beautiful interpretation, and I cry because I do that these days when something beautiful overwhelms me. Yet I don't believe that's exactly how things are; I think Monika's telling herself lies that help her survive. I have a different interpretation that I put more faith in, but Monika can hold on to hers; it makes her strong, while mine helps me.

If it's true that the body is a temporary garment, clothing our part of the greater whole that contains everything—our whole life, everyone's life, yes, everything all together; if it's true that we are all parts of a great collective spiritual whole; if it's true that, although our minds don't consciously know it, we are in contact with that whole and thereby—a dizzying thought—also with one another, with everyone, with everything, then it's entirely possible that the whole prepares itself a little just before our small part is about to throw off its garment, makes preparations that can be felt as some sort of spiritual vibration. Perhaps it's vibrations of this kind that can release an impulse in the person who's going to die soon: to put her affairs in order, to write a letter, or to be suddenly kind to someone.

In hindsight, it looks as if Cilla had a premonition of what was going to happen: the thank-you and the smile she gave Monika, the warm words she gave me on the way to the bus stop. But I resist the idea that one can have such premonitions. If you had one, then you wouldn't be likely to run right out into the road afterwards, because humans treasure this life in its fragile shell. No, those actions show that a person has been touched by vibrations from the preparations of the whole. The whole, in its all-embracing wisdom, doesn't fend off what we call death, because it isn't death; in reality it's the part's fusion with the whole, something that doesn't need to be fended off once the preparations have begun, because the fusion is perfection, you attain a higher state of being, a better and more beautiful life than you have when you live in your earthly garment.

## 22

ina the listener—finally she listens to Jonny too. He comes on Monika's birthday. Tina has invited him. I want Jonny to come, she said, when Albert asked them to speak up about what they'd like to see happen on Thursday.

Presumably he would have come anyway, but now someone not only wanted him here but had said so. It's almost as if Jonny isn't part of us anymore.

Have you forgotten us? she asks him when he turns up.

He gives her a brotherly pat on the head, hugs Monika and wishes her a happy birthday, thrusts his hands down into his pockets and walks around the room stiffly, a stranger viewing the furnishings. When he goes upstairs, Tina follows him. She lives up there. That's a reason to keep an eye on him.

But he's standing in the doorway of his own room, which is just as it was when he moved out. Tina positions herself behind him so there's no way he can go by her without pushing her aside. But he doesn't do that; instead he says to the desk in his room: No, I haven't forgotten any of you. It's just that . . .

Tina waits and waits behind Jonny. When will her brother understand that it's possible to talk to her now? Now they're alone up here; it's the perfect time for a talk. But Jonny is silent. When he fails to find the rest of his sentence, Tina says: I've missed you sometimes. But you were never here. Never.

It was absolutely impossible to live here, Jonny says. I was forced to leave. I didn't know that anyone missed me . . .

But Jonny! Tina says, and puts her hand on his back. Why doesn't he turn around! Maybe he's fighting back tears? His voice sounds so strained.

Well, I'm telling you how it felt to me. If I've come to understand anything, it's that I have to say how I feel. Here everyone went around grieving, but no one, not a one, understood that I was grieving too. I cared for Cilla too, for God's sake!

Has anyone ever denied that?

And I cared and still care for you, Jonny continues, without paying attention to her interjection. I really do, though maybe you don't think that counts for much. And you were completely wrecked by grief, it hurt so much to see it, because it was like losing both of you. And Albert was like a stone, and Mamma, well . . . Who was I going to talk to? Who was going to console me? I needed a hell of a lot of consolation, damn it! Where was I to turn? It doesn't matter—I just couldn't stay here. That's how it is. And since then the thought of coming by has been damned off-putting. Cilla's still here, after all. If I turn around, she'll be standing right behind you.

Tina turns her head and checks. Maybe!

Has anyone consoled you in your little place in town, then? she asks. Grieving can't have gone very well there, either.

Jonny sits down on the edge of the bed, just inside the door. From there he can turn his head and glance at Tina now and then. Tina's waiting for him to utter their magic incantation, the one that will tell her he's home and remembers some of the good things, too. But the incantation doesn't come. I've had a hell of a job, he says instead.

Are you talking about the drafting office?

No. I'm talking about Martin.

Tina has almost forgotten Martin. Almost. A hell of a job?

That's exactly right, Jonny snaps. Up here you all see your own grief and nothing else. I don't think you can conceive of what it's been like for Martin. Hell is pleasant in comparison. He can think of only one thing all the time: that he's killed a person. He does it over again every night. I've stayed at his place, so I know. Every night he does it all over again, Tina!

Tina nods.

I've talked with him day and night. This Christmas I watched over him constantly, all the time—he was totally down, there was no telling what he might do. I can safely say that by now we've talked about absolutely everything. And I've taught him to cry and scream like a baby, because I think that's the only thing that helps. I've tried it myself, if you want to know, and it's a relief. And he's done it—cried and screamed. And he's been in therapy and he runs six miles every day and he . . . God knows what else. But it doesn't help. When we're going into town from his place, we have to take a different road. His nerves are totally shot. And he's terrified of running into any of you, especially you, Tina.

Tina wants to object but realizes there's no point. It's not Jonny who needs to be persuaded, but Martin, and he isn't here. I'm sure he'll never come here again, Jonny says. I don't know what kind of miracle it would take to get him here.

Poor Martin! Tina says.

Jonny nods and sighs: Hell is a picnic in comparison! After all, it's not just anyone he ran over and killed, either.

It's his best friend's sister, Tina says.

Best friend's sister? repeats Jonny. Hardly *that*.

What, then?

He had a crush on you two, maybe you recall that, Jonny reminds her. Not just a little, either. I teased him a lot about it, back when it was possible to kid around with Martin. He'd better make up his mind, I said. But he didn't think it was so important. He really didn't see any difference between you. But when you talked about things, then he knew who was who, because you talked differently, after all.

Yes, he liked Cilla, Tina admits, and discovers at the same time that she no longer feels the old sting of jealousy.

And you too. Or rather: he didn't know which of you . . . And then that happened. And he didn't know which of you he'd run over. He's told me that: how he ran into someone from the family at the hospital and found out that one of you was dead.

Yes, Tina nods. He ran into me. I was the one who told him.

I've wormed that out of him, Jonny mutters.

I hadn't even taken it in yet myself that Cilla was dead, and then I'm the one who has to tell him.

What a hellish meeting! Jonny sighs. Now when he dreams at night, he still doesn't know which of you he's running over. Then he wakes up screaming. Damned shame he didn't get to scream then, when it happened.

Monika's the only one who got to do that, Tina says. And how she screamed! If you can believe what she says now, it helps to be able to scream whenever you need to.

I think what Martin is most scared of now is meeting you again, meeting you while he has the night's dreams in his head, meeting you and not knowing if it's you or Cilla. Does that sound strange?

Tina understands that fear perfectly; to her it doesn't sound strange at all. He can just come here and find out how things are, she says. He can check it out until he really understands that I'm me and I'm alive. Can't you tell him that? Can't you tell him that we're not mad at him here at Rosengården? That he's welcome here. That I still like him. That Cilla has told me that what happened was her own fault; it was our fault. We ran across the road without looking. I was lucky, Cilla was unlucky. That's it. We don't accuse him of anything. We don't think that Martin is to blame at all. We're the ones who did the wrong thing. Can't you tell him that?

I've said that already, more or less. Not exactly the way you said it now. I'll try it, it sounds convincing: Cilla has told Tina that . . . He'll believe that. I haven't tried that: Cilla says that . . .

It's *true*, Tina corrects him. Don't you believe me?

Jonny gives her a quick look, sees Cilla right behind her. Of course I do, he says.

You have to believe it yourself, Tina declares. Otherwise you won't be able to say it to Martin in the right way. You can always hear when someone's lying.

Jonny gets up and walks over to Tina. Puts his hand on her shoulder, on her collarbone, and utters the magic incantation, the one she longs for: You are my sister.

Tina puts her own hand in place and utters her part: You are my brother.

They have each other. That's all she wanted to know. You have to cherish what you've got.

■ ■ ■

Jan-Olof arrives with Mattias and Jannica. Marika's stayed home with the babies because they have colds. It was Monika who invited her brother to the birthday, with the whole family if possible, but this is fine too. It's more fun to bake a cake if you can get some people to come over and eat it.

Tina takes a child in each hand and goes for a walk around the garden with them. Dudde wags his tail and zigzags along behind them.

This is really *overrated*, Mattias says, and sighs happily.

Do you think so?!

Yes! He bends over and strokes the tender blades of grass. So soft! he says. He lifts a branch in the raspberry patch. What small leaves! he says. He takes in the whole garden and rejoices again: O-ver-ra-ted!

Jannica joins in with equal delight: O-ver-ra-ted!

Tina spins them around in the air; they hold on tight and shriek. Dudde barks at all this life where it's usually so still. He won't calm down until she puts down the children. You're both overrated children, you two!

At that they give her a thank-you hug. You're top-rated too, Mattias says softly in her ear. I'd like to live here. With you.

But who'd take care of Jannica then?

Dudde can do that.


Now everyone who wants to is going to walk to the churchyard. That's Albert's wish for today. A little time at the grave, so the birthday won't be spoiled by people twisting and turning because there's something they don't dare to talk about.

Everyone wants to go. They walk through the woods, since it's warm and the ground has dried out enough to walk on.

It's almost as warm today as the second of May last year, Jan-Olof claims.

No way! No one agrees with him. They all remember that it was hot then, muggy, suffocating. Today it's pleasantly warm.

They arrange some flowers on the grave. Tina contemplates how strange it is that Cilla's lying down there. It isn't really possible to imagine it anymore. She's much more with me at Rosengården. She's everywhere, but not right here in the ground. So much has changed in just one year. Cilla, who wanted to know if we would cry at her grave—she, too, has changed. Now she's glad that we're free to be happy, coming to look at her grave today. She really is, I know it, because—

Look! cries Jannica. There's Cilla!

She points at a blue butterfly with cheerfully fluttering wings that is sailing above the grave.

Hurrah, overrated! Mattias whoops and tries to catch it, but Jan-Olof holds him back.

The butterfly and the children brighten the time at the grave. When they leave, the butterfly follows them a short distance beyond the gates.

I believe it really *is* Cilla, Monika says. It's so happy!

Of course it's Cilla! Tina joins in. What else would a blue butterfly be doing here on exactly this day?


At home there's a surprise waiting for them. Tina spots a movement at the corner of the house. *Cilla's come home!*

No, but when the family rounds the corner, they hear: *Welcome, lovely May* . . . rising over the garden on the wings of clear voices. It's Tina's class that offers this greeting . . . *partner in our play* . . .

This is Cilla's day, after all, Sandra explains afterwards, as if anything needed explaining. We thought . . .

Of course, Monika says. What a shame we didn't know. We've just been down at the grave. It would have been fine to have a song there.

Happy birthday! Lotta says and hands Monika a small package.

Monika hugs her and Sandra and a few others who are standing nearby. You're all so sweet, every last one of you.

That response tells me that Monika has learned something important. A year ago she would have been awkward and made a fuss, *You shouldn't have* . . . and so on. Now she accepted the present and was glad, plain and simple.

And the present is a small framed photo of Cilla and me from when we were in a school revue in the fall term of seventh grade. I recognize the scene right away; but I had no idea there was a photo of it. It's a fine picture: we're both laughing our heads off and it's totally impossible to tell who's who. No wonder they had problems keeping track of us when we suddenly arrived in the upper grades!

Monika conjures up buns and cookies for everyone, but most of the boys and some of the girls leave almost immediately. Fredde stays behind. He makes a tour and looks around; it's the first time he's been here. He's quick to figure out that my room is upstairs, and when I turn my back he sneaks up the stairs to have a look. I don't have anything out that shouldn't be seen, so I pretend I haven't noticed. I've got my hands full just talking to the girls. Maja Sjövall in the house—I wonder what Cilla has to say about that!

Congrats, by the way, she says to me, and a few others join in and say the same.

Congrats on what?

Congrats on wha-a-a-t! Sussy mocks. And here's us, thinking Tina's a pal who tells us everything. Like hell she does!

There was something fishy going on, Mag says. I could sense it.

Can't someone please tell me? I ask.

She almost seems like she doesn't know a thing, Sandra says, and looks closely at me. But Tina's a really good actress, so who knows . . .

Would you *explain*, damn it! I yell, but they just laugh.

Is there a CD player in the place? Maja asks.

I point to Albert's stereo. Unless we go upstairs. But there's more room down here.

Hey, what's going on? says Albert, when Maja starts messing with his expensive equipment.

You'd better go help that poor girl, Lotta answers. Maja is an idiot with technology—she could destroy your set and blow the place up in the bargain.

Now they're all talking on top of one another and maneuvering and positioning themselves so I can't see what CD Maja is getting out. Albert helps her, preventing short circuits and any other damage. Lotta teases him mercilessly, makes fun of his caution—he's adorable, your pappa, she used to say. And right now he is, in fact—highly adorable. It suits him to be surrounded by a crowd of happy girls!

SILENCE! Maja roars, with immediate effect.

Tam, tammm . . . Two drumbeats are all I need to hear, yes, one is enough, but the second one comes so fast—two beats and I know: "Her Eyes Are Blue." And I have a feeling, have a feeling, my hands start sweating and my whole back is itching, but there's still a little while to wait before it's time, and then comes the violin, my violin, I'm on the disc! And now that I hear the music from the outside for the first time, I can hear how *fine* it sounds; at last I hear what they accomplished by taking out the synthesized strings.

My name is on the cover! In type as big as theirs: *Ola and Bahir, with Tina Dubois.* And a photo, too, of me playing. Ola must have snapped it sometime or other in the studio. The picture catches me off guard, I think it's Cilla I'm looking at. That's her seriousness, her intense gaze in the picture, the eyes that would suddenly see something different from what we saw, something only she could see. When I grasp that it's me, that my eyes, too, can look like that, then I suddenly realize—have a flash that makes it clear—what everyone always says, that we're so alike, so incredibly alike. And also realize that deep down I've never understood or accepted it until now!

I wonder if they've thought: a picture of Cilla, sort of, under the title *Cilla Suite*. But at the same time, I decide No! It just turned out that way. There are no ulterior motives. Bahir said that he had to make this disc because otherwise he couldn't do anything else. That's the motive. First create, then perfect, all in order to survive and be able to go further. Bahir is great; now he's going to go further. That and that alone was the point of my work.

But even so! I can afford to be happy on my own account right now. Ola and Bahir haven't said a word, but our work this spring has yielded a disc! My God!

Look at Tina! Lotta says. I can almost believe she really *didn't* know anything!

They all give me big hugs, congratulate me again, calm down

a little and listen, but are more interested in hearing about what it was like to play with the rock stars.

Could I ask one question? Albert interrupts. When he gets silence, he asks: Exactly which of all those noises did you supply?

The girls all boo at my father and tell him to go tuck himself in like a good little boy, he'll understand when he grows up. But Albert just laughs, and Jan-Olof backs me up and tells him that the music is superb.

Are you going along on their tour this summer? Sussy asks.

I don't know, I say, because in fact I don't. They haven't said anything. Besides, I have no idea what I'm doing this summer. I suppose it might be fun.

Get out! Sussy pants. Tina's *nuts*, just listen to her: "I suppose it might be fun," she says—about a tour with Ola and Bahir. Don't you realize what that means!

But I just can't get myself to say that I feel like I'm going to burst, I'm so happy, can't reveal that I'd say *Yes* in a snap if Ola or Bahir asked, *Yes* without thinking for a second about whether it would be difficult or impossible or dangerous, just an immediate: *Yes, I'll come!* I would, too. Which I don't reveal now, though, but instead wrap myself in great composure, pat Sussy on the shoulder a few times, and explain: That's all just worldly distraction. I'll have to wait and see.

Sussy doesn't really know what to think, but Lotta, who knows me better, gives me a hug, laughs, and agrees: We'll all wait and see. With confidence.


It occurs to me that Fredde hasn't shown himself for quite a while, so I run upstairs to see what he's up to. He's lying on my bed and looking at the pictures and poems on the walls.

It's not very nice manners for guys to go and lie down in girls' beds, I inform him.

I had such a lousy upbringing, he declares in a light tone, but he looks a bit embarrassed when he sits up. The music sounds better from up here, is his next declaration.

There's better company down there, I tell him.

Right now I have the best company a person could have here today.

I stick my tongue out at him as thanks for the compliment, then reach out my hand to pull him up from the bed. He grabs hold but doesn't get up, pulls me toward him instead and gives me a kiss before I know what's happening. By the time I've realized, I've lost my balance and am lying on top of him, and still haven't understood what's going on. I'm so completely confused that I don't jump up and leave, but lie there where I find myself, on top of Fredde, and he says: Stick out that tongue again and I'll ravish you!—after which he kisses me once more.

He's a beginner at it, if truth be told, but it's nice anyway, he's nice anyway, and I respond, he deserves it. I put my tongue out again, or in—it depends on whose point of view you see it from. Ravishment? Oh really, *à la bonne heure!*—all in good time! It looks like today's the day for absolutely everything to happen!

I come to my senses, or whatever you want to call it, and struggle up from the bed, point out to Fredde that someone could come by at any moment, so it would be best if . . . yes, that's right, I have to go down now anyway, and you can come down in a little while.

But when I look in the mirror, I realize I need to visit the bathroom to straighten my clothes and comb my hair—Fredde has done a good job of rearranging things. To think that he dared—finally!

And all this to the sound of *Cilla Suite!* I think as I go downstairs. No one has missed me, and no one seems to give it a thought when Fredde comes down a little later. At exactly that moment, Ola hits the three well-known chords. Fredde drops down onto the third step. Everyone falls silent at Rosengården as "Memorial Cilla" builds in the room. I don't play any violin part in that; "Memorial Cilla" was perfect all along.

It's natural for the party to break up after that. Only Sandra and Lotta stay behind. They're going to sleep over, we've decided.

To think you knew that it was Monika's birthday! I say when we're alone.

Listen to her! Sandra says and sends me her biggest smile— good God how pretty she is when she smiles!

And Lotta explains: Don't you know that every time you talk about the accident you start by saying it was on your mamma's birthday?

I've never really thought about it. That I say that, I mean.

You're far out! Sandra laughs. Overrated, as the little guy kept saying all evening.

If anyone is far out, it's Sandra, especially when she laughs!

If anything is far out, it's having friends. If anything is wonderful, it's being able to laugh with them. I know that at times I've accused people of superficiality. But no matter how great the treasures were that I found in the depths, it was still greater to be able to rise up in the end and breathe above the surface, to breathe air so clear that a smile could be seen and a laugh could reach me even from far away. Not until I had almost drowned among the heavy shadows at the bottom could I perceive the joy in the sparkling play of light across the ripples on the surface.